"I've come for the job," Nic said.

Ochessa hesitated only a moment. "I don't need any more ranch hands."

"Not *a* job, *the* job." Nic retrieved the bounty poster from inside his shirt, leaned forward, and held it up in front of her face.

Of course. Naturally he would be offering a gun for hire, not a strong back for bending.

Re-folding the paper, he tucked it away in his back pocket. Several similar fliers were poking out of his saddlebag. He must have collected all the ones she tacked up in town.

"It doesn't say anything about expenses," he continued.

"That's because I don't intend to pay any."

"That should narrow down the applicants considerably." His gaze settled on her lips. "Or are you planning to offer incentive of a more personal nature?"

"Listen, Breedlove. Don't get your hopes up—or anything else. Whoever I hire can live and eat at the ranch for free. And they can stay at Will's cabin if the search takes them back to Kansas."

He seemed disappointed. She didn't care, or at least she shouldn't care. What this man thought held no consequence for her. Being a drifter, he would most likely ride out of her life as quickly and unexpectedly as he'd galloped into it.

"Well..." Nic urged the mule one step closer.

"Well, what?"

"Do I get the job or not?"

Cowboys, Cattle, and Cutthroats

by

Gini Rifkin

Cowboys, Cattle, and Cutthroats

Cover Art by *Debbie Taylor*

The Wild Rose Press, Inc.
PO Box 708
Adams Basin, NY 14410-0708
Visit us at www.thewildrosepress.com

Publishing History
First Cactus Rose Edition, 2018
Print ISBN 978-1-5092-2288-9
Digital ISBN 978-1-5092-2289-6

Published in the United States of America

Dedication

In memory of the real Ochessa Starr.
Dedicated to my sister, Kathy, for three huge reasons
and countless small ones.
And to all the High Plains Cowgirls.

Special thank you to The Wild Rose Press
and the amazing Amanda Barnett.

Glossary

Because language varies, historically and geographically, my wonderful editor suggested a glossary might be helpful. I love learning new words and terms and hope you do too.
Gini

Draw, Arroyo, Wash—topographical terms indicating a gully

Punching paper—Shooting at paper targets

John B—slang for Stetson hats made by John Batterson Stetson

"Willing to swim the river for her"—indicates a man brave enough (or in love enough) to swim a river to save his woman

Split the wind—to leave quickly, usually on horseback. Whistle pig—slang for a groundhog, or woodchuck type animal

"As he payed out line"—To pay out a rope or cable by letting it go slack.

Light a shuck—to depart in haste for another location, especially in the dead of night. It is derived from the use of corn shucks as convenient torches for lighting the way home.

Chapter One
Kansas, late spring 1879

Nic Breedlove made it a practice to ignore heroic impulses. Then again, there were some situations a man couldn't ride away from and still call himself a man.

Silently, he watched the figures dressed in black hightail it over the far ridge. The desire to follow burned hot. No matter. He'd found them once, he could find them again. Changing course, he urged his mount toward the cabin. Smoke spiraled up from the small structure.

Damn, they'd set the place on fire.

Bent low in the saddle, Nic road at a gallop, hurtling down the narrow wash—trees and rocks a muted blur. At the front door, he reined in hard, and his mount skidded to a halt. Leaping from the saddle, he grabbed a wooden bucket, filled it at the watering trough, and dowsed the flames licking their way up the outside of the west wall.

Luck prevailed. Wallace County had received a good bit of spring rain, and the damp Kansas sod inspired smoke rather than fire. He glanced around. Where was the homesteader who laid claim to the shack? He knew the men riding out didn't hang their hats here.

Tossing the bucket aside, he prowled around to the front of the cabin. The yard was scraggly but clean, and

1

the house small but sturdy. At his touch, the door swung inward. He stepped across the threshold and peered around the dim interior.

The calico curtains had been torn from the windows, the table overturned, and the chairs smashed to kindling. The pillow and bed ticking, as if slashed by a grizzly bear, spewed feathery innards across the old bed frame and onto the floor.

A strangled moan rose from the far corner. Nic shoved a small chest of drawers aside and crouched down beside the injured man. For some reason, he'd thought to find an old-timer with weathered skin and a gray beard. The person before him was young, probably in his early twenties. His sandy colored hair matched his sparse chin whiskers. The spark of life barely flickered in light brown eyes—wide with pain.

Nic's gaze slid lower, and he clenched his jaw. The sodbuster had been gut shot. Grabbing a curtain, he wadded it up, and pressed the soft fabric to the belly wound. He glanced around for another cloth but didn't see one within arm's reach.

The young man stared up at him and smiled weakly. "I'm as good as dead mister," he gritted between clenched teeth. "But I thank you for trying to help."

"What's your name?" Nic asked, in an effort to keep the fellow's thoughts away from his condition. As encouragement, he offered up his own.

"I'm Will," came the replied. "Will Starr."

"And the men I saw riding off. They did this to you?"

Will's cheeks flushed, and his eyes momentarily brightened as if anger overshadowed agony. "They're dark horsemen," he explained, "and as black-hearted as the clothes they wear."

The young man's declaration didn't tell Nic anything new. The stories and reputation of the outlaws dressed in black preceded them. The yarns were gruesome, blood-curdling tales. And their leader had spent years perfecting his cruelty.

Will snagged the front of Nic's shirt with one hand—his fingers twisting the fabric. "You could help stop them," he said, as if privy to his thoughts.

"What are you talking about?" Nic gently freed himself from the young man's grip.

The boy shuddered and slumped back against the floor. His eyelids drooped, and he made a sound in his throat. His face turned white as a goose's backside, and his hands went cold as a high mountain stream. It looked like Will was about to meet his Maker.

Nic's upper lip curled, and his shoulders grew taut. He wanted to crush something with his bare hands. What a lonely way for a man to die—out in the middle of the prairie with only a chance stranger in attendance.

"You got kin to be notified?"

Will worked his mouth, trying to speak. "Never mind that." He ground out the words between groans of pain, his eyes still closed. "You have to take the box to Denver."

Nic studied the room. He didn't see any box. Maybe the outlaws had taken it. They had obviously been searching for something. He opened his mouth to reply then froze.

Someone was coming up the draw. Listening intently, he counted the hoof beats. Two, maybe three, horses approached.

Will's eyes fluttered open, and he seemed to rally. "They're still a ways off," he mumbled. "The sound echoes funny through the arroyo."

Nic rose and stepped to the window. "There're two of them. One looks to be a boy, the other an Indian."

Watching the strangers as they meandered closer, he tried to quell the familiar feeling that trouble was heading his way. Trouble he didn't need.

"Take the box and go," Will said, "before it's too late."

He turned his back to the window. "You're in no condition to fend for yourself, kid."

"Whether you stay or not won't change what's gonna happen to me. I'll go easier knowing the box is safely on its way."

Nic shoved his hat back an inch or two and pondered the odd request. What could be so important about this box that it was the last thing on a dying man's mind?

Experience told Nic he didn't want to know. Yet, a penchant for intrigue demanded he find out.

****

Ochessa bit back a sob and threw the last shovelfull of dirt onto Will's grave. Odd the way the sky could be blindingly bright, yet her heart be bound in such darkness.

They had reached Will just in time to bear witness to his final ramblings, and to glimpse a man riding away, hell bent for leather, toward the road leading to Monotony. Will had struggled as he told them the man's name with his final breath.

Anger fueling her actions, she slammed the blade of the shovel deep into the ground. The handle stood straight-up, quivering as if in fear. Kneeling down, she rolled the large rocks they'd gathered into place.

Lame Bear pounded a handmade cross into the loose soil at the head of the mound of earth. Then the old Indian lit a twist of sweet grass and chanted in Lakota Sioux, the performance of such a ritual a rare happenstance. There were few people Lame Bear loved well enough to invoke his God on their behalf.

The gesture brought renewed tears to Ochessa. Scrambling to her feet, she forced her grief to a less accessible corner of her soul. In the twenty-two years she'd lived and breathed, she'd already learned there would be time later in the cold lonely hours of the night for weeping and mourning. Right now, with a sparse amount of daylight to burn, they needed to finish up and be on their way. It wouldn't do to let the trail grow cold.

The shock of losing her older brother, had her stepping along in a daze as she gathered up food from the larder, and the few mementos left intact. With Will's extra pair of boots tucked under her arm, she headed toward the corral. His horse was gone. She glanced at the chickens and pigs and turned them loose. Like her, they were on their own now, and they too must learn to survive on common sense and uncommon determination. Sadly, their future success seemed about as unlikely as Ochessa's own.

Pausing beside one of the rental horses hired from the livery in town, she transferred the goods in her arms to the saddlebags and contemplated the newly turned grave one last time.

Sorrow, stark and white, crystallized around her like a blanket of ice. It numbed her senses and froze her fears. How easy it would be to jump headfirst into the arms of despair. But fighting the seduction of oblivion, she prodded her anger back into life. The red hot emotion clawed through her body and raked through her mind, leaving raw loneliness to sting like bad whisky in the wounds left behind. She relied upon the pain and fury. Her rage gave her the will to live, and the means to endure another day. At least it had so far.

Jamming a stray lock of hair up under her worn felt hat, she tightened the faded red stampede strap under her chin and swung up into the saddle. It would be well dark by the time they reached the town.

As she waited for Lame Bear to mount up, a sense of abandonment added to the sorrow. The idea of leaving Will behind broke off another piece of her heart. But with no wagon, or even a horse handy, transporting him to the train station and home wasn't a choice.

They'd wrapped him in the torn sheets. And after banging together a coffin made from broken furniture and the cabin door, they had buried him deep. Covered with the rocks, he'd be safe enough for now. Come the fall, when the weather turned cool, and the ground remained unfrozen, they'd return for him. His final resting place should be beside their parents at the ranch in Colorado.

Forcing her gaze from the grim scene, she faced forward and clucked the horse into a walk. Lame Bear mounted up and cantered forward to ride at her side. Straight-backed and steely-eyed, did he see more than the road stretching out ahead? No doubt he still lingered under the dream-spell brought on by his chanting and praying and sweet smoke. Ochessa saw nothing but loneliness.

She'd traveled to Kansas to inform her brother of the death of their mother. Now Will was dead too, her last blood kin. Lord she was tired of keeping company at grave sides. Damn tired.

Chapter Two
Monotony, Kansas

In a few minutes, it would be midnight. The waxing moon hung in the sky like a shaved sliver of white gold, but Ochessa needed no illumination to guide her hands as she checked the load of her Colt Army revolver.

Before he died, Will had gritted out a wild and rambling tale about a packet of legal documents, and the puzzle box they'd played with as children. She'd given him her word of honor to find both. Then he'd named and described the man who had taken the ornate cube. This inspired another promise, one made to herself. She wouldn't rest until she saw Nic Breedlove turned over to the sheriff—to be tried and hanged.

Tracking the man to the Antlers Hotel in Monotony had been child's play. Most outlaws would have covered their trail, but not him, the cocky son of a buck. She'd left a note for Breedlove at the front desk, along with instructions for the clerk to make sure he got the message. Would he make an appearance, and meet her in the alley tonight? As bait, she'd mentioned a large reward for the puzzle box. Such an offer had to arouse his curiosity if nothing else.

Holstering her weapon, she crossed her arms over her chest, and tucked her hands into the folds of her coat in an effort to keep her fingers warm—and to stop them from trembling. She knew meeting this stranger, under these circumstances, bordered on crazy. But she hadn't been able to think of any other way to do what needed to be done.

Gunfire erupted from the saloon down the street, and she jumped. The unexpected sound set the town dogs to barking and her heart to pounding. Then raucous laughter sliced through the night once again, and she relaxed and listened as someone hammered out a new melody on the poorly tuned piano. Monotony was anything but monotonous.

Shifting her weight from one foot to the other, she scrunched and unscrunched her toes inside her boots. She should have worn thicker socks, but after leaving Will's cabin, seeking revenge had been her foremost concern, not personal comfort or sensible attire.

She still couldn't believe her brother was gone. Waiting in the dark, her thoughts turned toward home, sending misty childhood memories running and laughing through her mind. She'd only been five years old when Will taught her to ride her first pony, and barely nine when he'd shown her how to smoke her first cigar. And just a few years ago, when she'd fallen through the ice on Timpkin's pond, Will had pulled her out, saving her life.

He had been her big brother, and best friend. Even after he'd grown up, turned footloose, and taken off to make his own way in the world, he'd kept in touch with her. It had been a comfort to know he was out there, hopefully thinking of her. She'd always held onto the possibility he would one day surprise her by wandering back through the front door of the ranch house. Now he was gone forever, the lifeline between them severed for all eternity. She would never again be playfully annoyed by his brotherly teasing or be sheltered by his protective love.

She gritted her teeth. Someone had to pay for the anguish stabbing her like a physical pain, and in a few minutes the man she'd like to see make good on that debt should be at hand.

But what if he put up a fight? She shouldn't have insisted Lame Bear wait at the train station. Yet, if the two of them were caught, the law would be especially hard on Lame Bear, and though he may be willing to take the risk, she was not. Besides, she needed to do this on her own. Will was her kin, and it was her responsibility to set matters right. Everyone would expect her to exact retribution for Will's murder. She expected it of herself.

Even if it meant shooting Nic Breedlove?

As the truth of such an eventuality sank in, took hold, and held tight, her mind reeled. Not that she couldn't handle a gun—she was good, darn good. But tonight's outcome put her in the position where the end result could mean taking the life of another human being—or losing her own. Would Breedlove turn out to be a coldblooded killer? Did she care? Suddenly that thought didn't seem so unappealing. Her parents were dead, Will was dead, even the dang bull was dead. Why not join them? Why keep struggling to go on? Why care about what happened to the ranch?

These uncommon thoughts brought her up short. She loved her home and the surrounding land. Loved it like a child. All her life, Ochessa had watched it grow and change. Had nurtured it through drought and flood, through blistering heat and numbing cold. She couldn't abandon the ranch, even though at times it felt as if the land had abandoned her.

She closed her eyes to clear her mind, but saw Will's face contorted in pain, felt his suffering. She had to keep her promise to him, which was reason enough to stay alive—at least for now. They'd barely had time to say goodbye. He'd only been twenty-four years old. It wasn't fair. But then life rarely was.

At the sound of muffled footsteps approaching, her eyes flew open, and her head snapped up. Peering through the darkness she sucked in a sharp breath. It was Breedlove all right—tall, dark, and deadly. He wore his guns slung low on his hips, his Stetson cocked back on his head. He walked unhurried but looked as if he were all muscle and broad-shouldered power ready for action.

Something about his swagger caught her eye—he advanced so leisurely and sure of himself. If it was a bluff, it was a good one. And what's with the fancy clothes? He was all duded up. He hadn't appeared so appealing riding like blue blazes away from Will's cabin.

She eased her hand to the butt of her pistol and withdrew deeper into the shadows. Dressing like a riverboat gambler wasn't going to save his hide.

Remaining silent, she waited for him to come closer. Once she had the papers and puzzle box, once this man was behind bars, maybe then the vision of her brother dying in her arms would fade from her memory.

"Anybody there?" he called out.

"Over here, Breedlove." She guided him with the sound of her voice, although she had the eerie feeling he knew exactly where she stood.

"What's the idea of meeting like this?"

"I would have thought a man like you would be accustomed to late night rendezvous in questionable surroundings."

"I don't know what you're talking about." His voice sounding innocent enough.

"Where's the box?" she demanded.

He remained silent then reached for his gun.

Two shots rang out.

Ochessa hadn't even cleared leather. What the deuce was going on?

Behind her something heavy thudded to the ground.

Gun now in hand, she stepped from the shadows, and looked over her shoulder. A few paces up the alley, a man lay face down in the dirt. He didn't move or make a sound. She ran to his side, kicked the revolver away from his outstretched hand, and nudged him with the toe of her boot. Dressed all in black, he was dead or unconscious, she didn't know which, and didn't much care.

What about Breedlove?

She retraced her steps.

Great, he was gone.

A small dark patch marked the ground where Nic had stood. She retrieved a pinch of moist earth, raised it to her nose, and sniffed. It smelled like the corral after the young bulls were made into steers. Breedlove had been hit.

Brushing her soiled fingertips against the leather of her split-skirt, she glanced around. It would be a shame if he crawled off to lick his wounds and die in private.

Up ahead, a cat yowled, and a wooden crate

toppled sideways strewing garbage across the alleyway. She ran forward. Nic lurched out of the darkness, stumbled and slumped to the ground at her feet. He didn't move. He barely breathed.

She holstered her weapon, knelt down, and felt for a pulse in his neck. Not finding one, she heaved his body from his side onto his back. Laying wide his coat and vest, she grabbed hold of the fine linen shirt he wore and ripped, sending fancy pearl buttons flying off in all directions. With her cheek to his chest, she listened for the sound of a heartbeat.

Crisp dark hair shadowed his torso, tickling her cheek and nose, and for a moment, her mind only registered the fragrance of bayberry soap and leather. Then she noticed the fading warmth of his skin. Closing her eyes, she concentrated harder and heard the life sign, there but faint and irregular.

She sat up, glanced around, then ran her hands along his sides, trying to locate the bullet wound or the puzzle box, whichever came first. His body, lean and hard, offered not an ounce of fat to be found. What kind of life did he lead that left him looking hungry, yet on the edge of perfection? Boldly foraging higher up under his shirt, she glided her fingertips over his right shoulder then the left.

Nothing.

She pushed his dark hair back from his brow to get a good hard look at his face. Blood glistened and ran like a curl of red ribbon from his temple down his cheek. A head shot—and almost fatal. The laceration appeared fairly deep, though no bone looked shattered.

Instinctively, she tore off a section of his shirt, intending to use it to bind his wound. Then she hesitated and blew out a deep breath of irritation and indecision. Why should she help him, a no-account gunfighter who probably deserved his comeuppance?

She glanced down the alley. It also appeared he'd saved her from ambush, and if he died, she might never find the puzzle box. But if she took him to the sheriff in this condition, there would be too many questions, too many delays. She had a ticket for the late night train to Denver, and she intended to be onboard when the Kansas Pacific left the Monotony station.

Twisting the piece of soft linen in her fingers, her gaze slid from Nic's face to his bare torso and she studied the slow rise and fall of his chest. Why would he murder Will, and then risk his life to save her? It didn't make sense, and now she felt obliged to help him. Or at least she was bound to see he received a fair trial before his hanging.

With the annoying realization her plans had gone terribly awry, she folded the fabric into a long tail and secured it around his head. Still out cold, Nic didn't move or even moan.

Now what? If she wasn't going to leave him here in the hands of Fate, what was she going to do with him? Being hotheaded and headstrong had once again gotten her into trouble. Big trouble. She should have taken Lame Bear's advice and had Nic Breedlove arrested as soon as they reached Monotony.

As if conjured by her thoughts the old Indian materialized out of the dark. Not having heard his approach, she started, then sighed in relief.

"You been gone a long time." He hunkered down at her side. His voice remained calm, but his brow furrowed. "You need any help?"

Lame Bear was a master of understatement.

Of course she needed help. She always needed help. No matter how hard she tried to run her life or the ranch she couldn't seem to make ends meet or her dreams come true. She contemplated Lame Bear's weathered face. The show of strength and fearlessness in his eyes gentled her chaotic thoughts, and she took a moment to mull over her options.

It didn't take long, there weren't many.

"It's too late now to go to the sheriff." Using Nic's shirt she wiped a spot of blood off her hand. "But this man is somehow involved in Will's murder, and I'm not about to let him slip through our hands."

She rose to her feet and glared down at the stranger who was becoming a bigger and bigger encumbrance in her already too complicated life. "I don't think anyone heard the shots over the noise coming from the saloon. If they had, they'd be here by now. I say we smuggle him onto the train and take him to the ranch. Once he's conscious, and we get the box and documents, we can turn him over to the authorities in Denver."

Lame Bear remained silent, leaving her to guess if he favored the plan or not. Then by way of consent, he rose up beside her, and slid his hands under Breedlove's shoulders. Ochessa placed Nic's hat on his chest and grabbed his boots.

Keeping to the shadows and backstreets, they struggled in the direction of the railroad station, their progress slow. The man she hated was heavier than he looked.

Pain soon burned in the small of her back, and her arms felt like lead as she gritted her teeth and fought to keep a firm clasp on Nic's well-polished footwear.

Approaching the train from the far side, they paused to make sure they hadn't been followed. A shaft of lamplight from the boarding platform slipped between the cars illuminating Nic's face. Her gaze flickered over his body, lingering on his narrow hips then traveling back up to a ruggedly handsome face. Unconscious, he appeared vulnerable, almost innocent.

She cursed under her breath and let go of his feet.

Lame Bear lowered his end of the load to the ground. "He's not too bad looking for a white man," he offered, as if privy to her thoughts. "Is that why your bullet missed his heart?"

She tore her gaze from Nic's well-planed cheeks and pleasing lower lip. "I didn't shoot him. Somebody else did."

"I'm glad to hear it." Lame Bear gave her a smile, and a nod of his head.

"Why?" It seemed strange he would care one way or another how the man involved in Will's murder met his end.

Lame Bear's long gray braid slid forward as he leaned over to peer down at Nic. "When I prayed over young Will, I had a vision. In the dream I saw a different face. This is not the man who killed your brother."

"But you let me go to meet him, to have him arrested for murder—or worse."

Lame Bear straightened and met her gaze. "There was no stopping you."

She couldn't argue with him there.

"Besides," he added, "I thought your vision might have told you a different story."

Ochessa mulled this over. She didn't have visions,

just hopes and dreams, but more often than not, Lame Bear's phantasms proved correct. Again, a sick feeling welled in her chest, then spilled downward to churn in her stomach. If push came to shove, she had been ready to gun down this man. Or at least try, she thought with a shudder. She could never have out-drawn Breedlove. He had moved faster than a prairie fire and could easily have taken her. And now Lame Bear wanted her to believe he was not the man she sought.

Oh what difference did it make? She was alive, and he was injured, and it didn't change the fact that Will was dead. "If Breedlove didn't do it—"she grumbled, grabbing Nic's legs—"who did?"

"That is still a mystery to me." Lame Bear hefted his share of the load. "All I could see were images of darkness."

"A stranger dressed in black also showed up in the alley." *Talk about your image of darkness.* "He's the one who shot this yahoo." She nodded toward Nic who swung from side to side between them. "And we saw Breedlove riding from the cabin. Will lived long enough to tell us his name and that he'd taken the box and papers. What more do you need to know?"

"I need to know the truth. Will did not accuse this man of any wrong doing." Lame Bear stood taller as he stepped along, his expression hard as hickory. On rare occasions he showed this side of his countenance, and when he did Ochessa couldn't help but picture him in his younger years, a leader of his people, a man respected and sought-after for his wisdom of the past and his ability to know and accept the future.

"Retribution is like the white man's whiskey," Lame Bear cautioned, as they struggled onward. "It seems like a good idea at the time, but too much can make you crazy. Be patient. Seek justice instead of vengeance. That too will quench your thirst."

"Well I wish you'd told me about this darn vision of yours before we dragged this jackass halfway around the town and back? We could just as easily have left him on the doorstep of the town doctor."

"Maybe this man was sent to help us. Maybe that is why we should help him."

She clamped her mouth shut, knowing better than to argue with Lame Bear's mystical logic. But plain old gut instinct told her Nic Breedlove would turn out to be a whole lot more hindrance than help.

Chapter Three

Out of breath and unchallenged, Ochessa and Lame Bear finally reached the Pullman Sleeping Car. Having purchased her train ticket at the last moment, Ochessa had been given no option but to pay for the more expensive accommodations. The compartment, supposedly one of a kind and experimental, had a layer of dust frosting the interior. Apparently, the fancy little railcar with multiple compartments was not sought after by cowpokes, common folks, or even financiers.

At the time, the unavoidable expense had infuriated her. Now, as they deposited their unconscious traveling companion on the upper berth, it seemed a stroke of good fortune.

Stretching her aching back muscles, she forced her thoughts into order and retrieved the drawstring pouch from the pocket of her skirt. Loosening the cord, she emptied the contents into Lame Bear's extended palm.

"Here's the last of the money. Pay off Breedlove's hotel and livery charges and by hook or by crook, bring both his mount and his gear back here."

"What about his ticket?"

Lord she hadn't considered that. "I'll think of something," she reassured, although at present no bright idea came to mind.

Lame Bear grunted noncommittally, tickets meant nothing to him. The Supreme Court still fought over the ruling regarding race separation on trains, and in an attempt to save money and avoid the raising of societal hackles, Lame Bear had insisted on traveling in the stock car.

As he turned toward the door, Ochessa stepped forward and rested her fingertips on his sleeve. "Be careful. Don't put yourself in any danger."

The old man paused. "I think it is too late for that." With a twinkle of amusement gleaming in his eyes, he slipped into the corridor. A wisp of Lame Bear's enthusiasm almost seemed to take form and hover in the room.

As she closed the door, it dawned on her that although Lame Bear mourned the loss of Will, he rather enjoyed the other aspects of their calamity—the unpredictable adventurous parts. Of course this came as no surprise. For as far back as she could remember, there were intervals when Lame Bear would disappear from the ranch for months on end. He never fully explained those absences, stating only that he followed the cry of the wolf for a season. Back then, Lame Bear had been younger, and a part of him could not thrive in a house made of wood and stone, and he could not breathe amidst the dust of the corrals and the smoke of the branding iron.

He still lived alone in his tipi, and although he took to the hills less frequently, a restless spirit evidently still called to Lame Bear. He continued to seek new experiences, just as Will's siren had enchanted him away from the ranch and the family.

She took off her hat and set it aside and hung her holster and pistol on a wall peg. As old as Lame Bear was, you'd think he'd be content to settle down. Or perhaps the wanderlust never waned in a man. She prayed the current intrigue would satisfy his craving for adventure, because if Lame Bear left too, she didn't know what she would do.

Nic's moan cut through her thoughts. She turned up the wick on the wall-lamp and stepped closer to the berth. As she eased the blood soaked-cloth from his head, guilt rankled in the back of her mind. She had lured him to that alley, so indirectly the wounding of Mr. Breedlove had been her fault. On the other hand, he wasn't some innocent bystander in this affair. Even if Lame Bear turned out to be correct, and this man hadn't shot Will, it was plain as creek water Breedlove knew something about what had happened. She shouldn't waste any sympathy on him while they awaited proof as to whether or not Lame Bear's vision would come true.

Retrieving a towel from a small built-in cupboard, she poured water from the pitcher into a bowl, then examined and cleaned the laceration. Again, she marveled at how fortunate he was to be alive. Tying together small hanks of Nic's long hair, she approximated the edges of torn flesh. The bleeding slowed dramatically, but the injury was bound to leave a scar along his temple. It wouldn't be his first, she'd noticed others when searching for the bullet wound. He hadn't escaped life unscathed.

He probably deserved every mark, she reasoned, while rinsing and drying her hands. Then her attitude softened. Or maybe like her, life had run roughshod over Breedlove, leaving tracks of hardship he'd neither asked nor bargained for. Nic gave a sudden cry of distress, the sound more heartfelt than pain induced. What followed came out garbled and unintelligible, but the anguish behind his words was recognizable. She guessed his subconscious carried a scar or two as well.

She stepped closer to the raised bed and placed the back of one hand upon Nic's forehead then his cheek. No sign of fever, and his breathing seemed regular. He moaned again, this time with an almost childlike sound. She laid two fingers across his mouth to quiet him. His grimace relaxed into a cocksure smile, which seemed much more at home there, yet the expression didn't soften the angle of his jaw which spoke of stubborn pride and male arrogance.

The berth barely accommodated this lanky prime example of the male species, and for a searing instant she wondered what he'd looked like naked.

Where had that thought come from? She'd been spending too much time on the *lone prairee*. Breedlove had all the markings of a no-account drifter, a bounder. No doubt a man fast with a gun for getting into trouble, and good with a horse for getting out of it. And he needed a shave, she thought irritably. Although in truth, the shadowy stubble only added to his manly appeal.

Annoyed by the direction of her thoughts, she levered away from the berth and flopped down into a small corner chair to await Lame Bear's return.

Men were strange creatures she mused, unbraiding her willful clutch of hair. Between Lame Bear, her brother, and the ranch hands, she had some inkling as to the day to day logic men employed, but she still could not truly understand a man's philosophy of life.

What made them all want to leave home? What made them want to abandon the one thing she would give up her life to keep?

****

As the train left the station, Ochessa shoved Nic's pistol, saddle-packs, and hat in an empty storage bin beneath the berth. With no time to spare, Lame Bear had brought the articles to her after loading Breedlove's mount in the stock car. What a laugh. Turns out, the man rode a dang mule for crying out loud. Watching him hightailing it away from Will's cabin, the image of what he'd been riding had been clouded by dust and moving fast. She supposed it could have been a mule, a big one.

A search of his possessions had yielded the puzzle box, but they hadn't found the documents or enough money amongst his belongings to buy another ticket. She hated to think what might happen if she were caught with a stowaway onboard.

As the train sped through the night, she racked her brain for a plausible scheme, but an hour later, when the inevitable knock sounded at the door, she still hadn't come up with any bright ideas.

"Ticket please," a muffled voice called out.

In a panic, she stared at Nic then back at the door.

The knock sounded again.

"Just a moment," she called sweetly, stalling for time.

Heart racing, she unbuttoned and shed her calico blouse, then wiggled out of her leather skirt. Shoving Breedlove's inert form as far as possible to the other side of the mattress, she crawled up onto the berth, lay down beside him, and fluffed the counterpane over the both of them.

"You may come in now."

A stoop-shouldered, white-haired old man opened the door and peeked around the edge. "Ticket, please," he repeated, tastefully averting his gaze from her scantily clad form.

"Yes, of course. It's right there on the— Oh my—"

A strong calloused hand slid upward along the curve of her bottom, coming to rest on her hip. She went mute, afraid to move. Had Breedlove awakened, or had that been some kind of involuntary spasm?

"Ma'am?" The Conductor appeared confused as he cocked his head to one side and hazarded a glance in her direction.

"On the seat," she blurted, fluttering a hand in the general direction of the chair.

The old man turned to retrieve the ticket.

She jerked her hip backward in an attempt to unseat Nic's hand, but as the train lurched around a curve, his body shifted, slamming up against her from behind. His hand slid forward, ending up dangerously close to her cotton-clad crotch.

Stifling a gasp, she extricated Nic's hand from her lap. He didn't move nor make a sound, and his breathing continued deep and regular as if he slept soundly. Perhaps he really remained unconscious, his movements accidental. She reached behind her back, and wedged a hand up against his chest, trying to hold him at bay as she peered over the side of berth.

What was taking so long? The conductor studied her travel voucher as if it were the first one he'd ever laid eyes on.

Cresting a hill, the train picked up speed, and the rail car pitched to one side. Despite her effort, Nic rolled closer, leaving her teetering on the edge of the mattress, his dead weight trapping her hand between her backside and his—front-side.

With excruciating attention to detail, the old man punched her ticket, and set the stub aside.

Oh merciful heaven, please hurry.

"On behalf of the Kansas Pacific Railroad," the man proudly squawked, "we hope you enjoy the ride." Leaving quietly, he closed the door on his way out.

Exhaling a frantic breath, Ochessa attempted to wrench her hand free.

"If you latch onto anything down there you like," a deep voice growled in her ear, "feel free to try it on for size."

****

The woman beside Nic gave a squeal of alarm, pitched off the berth, and hit the floor with a thud and a curse. Her pantaloons were in a twist, outlining her shapely bottom, and the top few buttons on her camisole had come undone—demanding Nic's pain-riddled attention there as well.

In a glorious tangle of bare arms and legs, she glared up at him through a swirling haze of taffy-colored hair. Tawny and golden, she reminded Nic of a mountain lion, claws unsheathed, spitfire flashing in eyes the color of expensive brandy.

"Howdy, ma'am," he drawled.

Moving slowly so as not to jar his head, he freed himself from the counterpane.

"Who would have thought traveling in a sleeping car could be this entertaining. I do hope Mr. Pullman's idea catches on."

"Enjoy it while you can, mister."

In a remarkable flurry of white cotton and lace, the young woman scrambled up onto her boot-clad feet and reached for the gun and holster hanging on the wall peg.

Instinctively, Nic went for his own revolver. Coming up empty, he raised both hands in a show of surrender. "Seems you have me at a disadvantage." He added what he hoped was an irresistible smile.

With a show of nonchalance, fingers laced behind his head, he lounged back against the wall at one end of the bed. His wound throbbed unmercifully, although he'd be darned if he'd let this little minx know.

Inhaling deeply and slowly, he stifled a grimace of pain, and prodded his thoughts into order, trying to make sense of the situation. Her voice sounded like that of the woman in the back alley. Carefully shifting his gaze, he studied her face. She wore no makeup, but a healthy tan bronzed her cheeks, and thick dark lashes ringed her slightly tilted feline eyes. Something about her seemed familiar, but he didn't think he'd ever seen her before. He wasn't likely to forget a face like hers—even if he'd met her while blind drunk.

Tearing his attention away from her irate though provocative pose, he gave the train compartment a good look-see. For the last few hours, he'd been drifting in and out of consciousness. Once he'd overheard her talking to an old Indian about his mule and saddle. And before the conductor had shown up, he had a vague recollection of her brushing her hair and pacing about the small niche like a caged animal.

Despite these brief flashes of insight, not one thing to which he'd been privy helped him figure out who this female might be, or why she had gone to such lengths to kidnap him. Curious as to the reason she'd done it, and intending to find out, he swung his legs over the edge of the mattress and levered to a sitting position. The room tipped out of kilter. Nausea slogged through his stomach, and the prurient interest the girl had inspired, drained away even quicker than it had appeared.

At his unexpected movement, she broadened her stance, and tightened her grip on the revolver. If she expected him to launch himself off the upper berth at her, she needn't have worried. Just remaining upright required all his effort and concentration.

Again, he ran his hand over his empty holster then gingerly plowed his fingers through his hair, careful to avoid his wound. A man could sure feel naked without his pistol and...

"Hey, where's my hat?"

Mutely, she stared back at him over the barrel of the Colt.

Panic twisted in his guts. They hadn't gone and lost his hat, had they?

"Doggone it, woman," he groused, "that plainsman was broke-in near to perfection."

She didn't blink at his show of temper.

"It takes months of coaxing and encouragement to get a hat to feel that good." He scrutinized the sleeping car one more time. "Why it's more work and aggravation than courting a woman."

"It won't matter much what you're wearing on your head, if you have a rope around your neck."

"Now hold up there, missy. I'll admit I'm no saint, but I haven't committed any hanging offenses—least-wise not in this country."

"What do you call murder?"

"Murder? The hell you say. I've never killed anyone—except in self-defense."

Her eyes glowed like amber in sunlight. "I think you're a lying son of a buck, but you can explain everything to the sheriff when we reach Denver."

Until he had taken care of the box and papers, Nic didn't intend to speak to anyone, especially a law-dog. And he certainly didn't intend to be dictated to by a female. She did create quite a picture though, standing there in her boots and bare essentials, holding a forty-five on him. Her hand didn't shake, and she held the big Colt as if she'd handled a gun before. For some reason, that appealed to him.

His concentration slid from her sweet pussycat lips to the erratic rising and falling of her bosom. His erection returned with marked enthusiasm, and a fleeting fantasy of being forced at gunpoint to pleasure her raced through his thoughts.

He slid to the edge of the berth, and slowly lowered himself to stand before her. She stepped as far away as the compartment would allow. The pain shooting through his brainpan nearly rocked him off his feet, and for a minute there were two pussycat women staring back at him instead of one.

"Why did you lure me to that out of the way meeting and try to kill me?" he asked, fighting the urge to reach out and touch her.

"I didn't shoot you," she flung back, confirming his suspicions. "It was the man dressed in black. The one *you* shot."

So the man lurking in the alleyway had been one of the outlaws. He'd only seen a menacing figure creeping closer with a gun aimed at her back. The dark horsemen were a busy lot.

"You keep dangerous company," he accused,

watching for her reaction.

"What makes you think he was there with me? I'd say the man would be more at home in your circle of acquaintances. And for your information," she added, with a toss of her head, "if I'd shot at you, you'd be dead."

He couldn't help but admire her cocky self-assurance, but on the other hand her attitude had begun to rile him a bit, and he sure was tired of staring down the barrel of that gun.

"So what's stopping you now?" He nodded toward the revolver. "It's a little harder when you can see a man's eyes before you pull the trigger, isn't it?"

She swallowed hard, and her gaze widened ever so slightly.

A smile tugged at his mouth. She was bluffing. He hadn't kept body and soul together this long by not recognizing killer instinct, or the lack there of, in his opponents.

"Well?" He forced the issue.

"Stay back," she warned, fully cocking the hammer.

He ambled forward.

"I mean it."

Two more steps left the muzzle of the gun pressed up against his chest.

Her shoulders slumped, and she took a step back.

Meeting no resistance, he slid the gun from her hand, and eased the hammer down to halfcocked. Angling the barrel upward, he opened the loading gate, and freed the cartridges with the ejector rod. The bullets hit the floor like a clock striking five.

"Now, why don't you tell me what this is all

about?" He tossed the empty revolver onto the chair.

As if coming to her senses, she lurched to one side, trying to step around him.

He reached out, spun her around, and captured her face between his hands. "Talk," he ordered, staring down at her.

She clamped her mouth shut, her lips flattened into a stubborn line, the expression in her eyes hot with anger. Shifting his hands to her upper arms, he gave her a shake of encouragement.

Still no response.

A tear slid down her right cheek. That was the last thing he had expected. Left with only one sure way to mollify a woman in tears, he slanted his mouth down on hers, tasting her long and slow. For all her cool toughness, she felt soft and warm, and smelled fresh like a forest after a spring rain.

No longer in tears, she jerked her head back and gasped for breath. "Get your hands off of me," she gritted.

He walked her backward, gently pinning her up against the wall. "When you crawl half-naked into a man's bed, you might expect this type of reaction."

Her scantily clad breasts mounded soft and full against his chest, and he couldn't help nuzzling the crook of her neck. Something about this female excited a part of him long forgotten. She acted tough yet felt so incredibly vulnerable beneath his hands.

Spitting out a rather creative expletive, she grabbed at his hands and then punched his chest. He should release her, but he feared to let the feeling slip away. Afraid he might never find it again. It must be his head injury—he was dreaming or remembering a time long ago.

Coming to what was left of his senses, he drew back and captured the woman's wrists, wrestling her to immobility. She ceased her struggles, but didn't cower before him, and the hate in her eyes stung him more sharply than a slap across the face.

"Why did you stow me away on this train? Not that I mind the company."

"You shot my brother," she snarled, "and I aim to see that you pay for it, if it's the last thing I ever do."

"And just who might your brother be?"

She blinked several times as if more tears threatened, tears she intended would not fall.

"I doubt you were formally introduced. He was the man you shot and left to die alone in that cabin just outside Monotony."

A wave of understanding stampeded through him. That's why she looked familiar. Aware now of the family connection, the resemblance appeared unmistakable. He mulled over the startling discovery. Then an even more remarkable revelation became clear. The Indian on the train had been the same Indian he'd seen riding up the draw at the cabin. And the scrawny boy riding with the Indian hadn't been a boy at all, but this tawny, slim, cougar of a woman.

"What's your name?" he asked, wanting to verify the connection.

"Ochessa Starr."

"I didn't shoot your brother Will."

"Then who did?"

He considered telling her then decided against it. No use getting her involved any deeper. Anyone who tangled with the dark horsemen was asking for big trouble. The man they'd encountered in the back alley gave proof of that.

"I don't know." He lied, taking the easy way out.

She stared at him with those golden eyes—penetrating, knowing eyes—like a cat's. He wanted to squirm and look away, but respecting the value of a good bluff, he met her stare head on and held it.

They both glanced away at the same time. His gaze drifted downward over the smooth curve of her neck and white shoulder. In contrast, her tan arms indicated outdoor work. As he pondered that thought, the dainty camisole and what the linen barely covered, snagged and held his attention.

She noticed him looking, and a delicate blush infused her cheeks.

"Let me go." Her voice was now barely above a whisper.

He wanted to but couldn't move. Couldn't bear to break the strange unexpected spell of comfort and excitement merely holding her close brought to him. And he couldn't resist stealing one more kiss.

Nic brushed his lips gently across hers. Had she pressed closer? He released his grip on her wrists. She didn't push him away. He kissed her again, and a sound resembling a purr escaped her. She wrapped her arms around his neck, and his mind reeled.

The gauzy fabric beneath his fingers begged to be breached, and as he complied, she gave a little mewing sound and arched closer.

Nic had never made love to a woman on a train before. He'd traded passionate pleasantries with a sweet young thing on a sampan in the Yellow Sea, and felt the earth shake with an actress on a late night stage out of

Deadwood, but this beat those forms of transportation hands down.

As they held one another tight, the locomotive strained and groaned up hill. The swaying motion of the train served to intensify the rocking of their bodies against one another. He'd never reached the boiling point this fast in his life. He wanted to rip away what few clothes she wore and bury himself deep inside of her.

Did the girl feel it too? She plundered his mouth and twisted her fingers in his hair. Suddenly, he had the sensation the tables had turned and now she ravished him. Oddly unsettling, but a feeling to which he thought he might grow accustomed.

"What really happened to my brother?" She whispered the question in his ear.

He nestled her cheek, inhaling her scent. So that was her game, she was only pretending. How charming—and stupendously naive of her. Nic had been tempted by females who knew how to play a man's body like a fine tuned fiddle. This little gal was in over her head. But it would be unkind of him not to let her try.

"I told you. I don't know."

The train-whistle shrieked, covering up the hollow ring of his lie. It also obliterated any further possibility of conversation.

The floorboards throbbed with the pulsing of the engine, and a rumbling sensation gathered in the soles of Nic's feet and roared upward through his body. The mechanical beast crested the promontory, and on the far side of the steep grade, the train rocked and swayed as it raced downhill, gaining speed. His heart beat faster and faster, keeping pace with the wild clacking of metal wheels skimming over iron track.

Ochessa slipped her hands beneath his torn shirt—warm hands that hesitated only briefly as she stroked his chest and urged him on. Her breath streaked across his neck, hot, quick, and desperate. "Tell me, please."

A shiver convulsed down Nic's spine. He slid one hand across the front of her body, and the moan that slipped from between her parted lips suggested she had gone beyond feigned interest.

The engine rumbled onward, hurtling them through the ever brightening dawn. Just as he hoped the ride would never end, the train slowed dramatically then stuttered and jerked to a halt. He slammed up against Miss Starr, cracking his head on the wall behind her.

Drenched in renewed pain and the intrusion of the real world, he withdrew his hands from the heat of her body and glanced out the window. The station sign swinging in the morning breeze declared they were in Denver. Never in his life had he been so disappointed in reaching a destination.

His gaze slid back to his abductor's sweet face.

She stared up at him, her cheeks flushed, her pink lips slightly and seductively swollen. He wanted to eat her alive. Then the smile in her eyes altered into an angry glare, once again revealing her true feeling. She pushed against his chest and opened her mouth as if to speak.

Trying to head off another altercation, he swept her into his arms, and all but flung her onto the hinged upper berth. Knowing her Indian friend would be coming for her shortly, he shoved the canvas panel closed as gently as possible and gave the lock a twist.

Ignoring her muffled cries of outrage, he retrieved his pistol, hat, and saddlebags from the storage compartment. With a shake of his head, he chuckled at the names she called him. For a female she had a remarkably open-minded vocabulary.

Chapter Four

As Nic left the compartment, he spotted the old Indian coming his way. Making a quick turn, he mingled with the milling passengers heading in the opposite direction. At the platform between cars, he unhooked the guard chain, jumped down to the tracks, and hightailed it to the back of the train and the stock car—eyes squinting against the glare of sunlight.

Maybe he should have stayed and reasoned with the young woman. He didn't doubt her story about being Will's sister. But she seemed hankering for revenge, not the truth. And while it was indeed murder, and he didn't blame her for being outraged over the death of her kin, he wasn't responsible and didn't intend to take the blame.

Besides, in his present condition, thinking straight and reasoning with her wouldn't have been an easy task, especially while being pinned in place by the fire in her pussycat eyes.

He scrubbed his hand across his face. Bleary-headed and disoriented, he felt trapped in a bad dream. The kind that woke you with a start and left you afraid to go back to sleep. The kind that set your heart to pounding, and your skin to sweating. He gave a snort of sarcasm. Awake or asleep, dreams had never been kind to Nicodemus Breedlove. Leaving had been the smart thing to do.

Gaining the stock car, he located his mount. Sadie was the biggest, most unattractive mule he'd ever laid eyes on—but he couldn't love her more had she been a thoroughbred race horse. Her momma was a draft horse, her daddy a mammoth Jack, and she had turned out the curious result of both. Big and powerful, she could outlast any horse on the trail, and her knack for foraging when feed became scarce came in mighty handy. He'd won her in a poker game, and since that time they'd been through a cross country adventure together.

"Howdy girl," he crooned, giving her a scratch behind the ears.

A blue roan, she had tall white stockings, and a dappling of white spots on her rump, and her interesting appearance truly gave one pause. But despite lacking visual perfection, he'd named her, Sadie, after the prettiest woman he'd ever known.

"Did the ride have a peculiar effect on you too?" He slipped on her bridal and saddled her up.

Like most occasions, she seemed to be taking things in stride. Although she did give a wide-eyed snort at the blood-stained shirt he wrestled off over his head. Tossing it aside, he tugged a new one from the panniers secured behind the saddle and shrugged into the clean cotton.

After an approving nod at his enhanced appearance, the big mule calmly followed him down the ramp from the dim stock car to the street. Again, the brilliant daylight seared a path through his eyes to the back of his head. He squinted and clenched his jaw. Then the warmth accompanying the glare penetrated his mood, and his optimism rose a notch. He just needed a hot bath, and a hot time at the gaming tables, and he'd soon be his old self again, or maybe he'd be somebody new.

As he moseyed on, the memory of feline eyes and faked kisses aroused his senses. A willing woman to warm his bed for a day or two wouldn't hurt either. He ran a finger around the inside of his shirt collar, but the fit of his trousers was what needed adjusting.

He stabled Sadie at a respectable livery, then crossed 14th Street at Larimer and headed toward the Tremont Paradise Hotel. His head hurt like the devil again, and he slumped in relief as the cool dark atmosphere of the hotel lobby washed over him like a welcoming balm.

Within the fortress of wood paneling, a battalion of palm trees and ferns stood guard over the rich decor. Aubusson rugs muffled footfalls and voices, and a small more private enclave on his right had been outfitted with bamboo furniture and slatted wooden blinds. A fat-bladed ceiling fan turned lazily overhead, and memories of an edge-water eatery in Madagascar scratched at the back of his mind. What a wild deuce of a place that had been—a haven or a hellhole, depending on your point of view, where a man could lose himself for a day or a lifetime. He shifted his attention and squinted back at the sun drenched streets of Colorado. It was the rainy season in Madagascar.

Nic signed the register, procured a key, and went straight to his room. Nudging the door shut with his foot, he dropped his saddlebags on the bed and removed his hat.

He studied his headgear from all angles then stuck his finger through the hole made by the bullet that had grazed his head—another grievance against the dark horsemen. Flicking a bit of lint from the wide brim, he carefully set it aside. Finding his Stetson crammed into the storage bin of the train had been one of the most pitiful sights he'd encountered of late. When it came to a man's hat, women were sure sparse on sympathy and understanding. At least that fightin' filly had been.

His pulse quickened as he recalled the sensations stirred by the feel of Miss Starr's slender form trapped between the hard need of his body and the hard wall of the train compartment. The whole remarkable interlude had been so unexpected, so overwhelming. She hadn't succumbed or surrendered to him, and whether it had been for show or not, she countered his bold advances head on, answering his passion with a healthy abandon most conventional women were afraid to admit to.

For one unsettling moment, he wondered if it had truly happened. Maybe he'd been unconscious the whole time, and it was all just a randy hallucination brought on by his injury. Speaking of which. He stepped to the chiffonier, and studied his face in the mirror, carefully tracing the edges of his wound with his fingertips. Turning away from his haggard reflection, he leaned back against the tall chest of drawers, resting his elbows on top of the dresser.

Why had Miss Starr cleaned him up and stopped the bleeding when she fostered suspicions he was a murderer? Apparently her thirst for revenge came coupled with a chivalric code of honor. A tough combination for anyone to live with, and setting herself up for a big fall. He should know. He'd traveled that road a time or two. It didn't pay. Now he only worried about himself, his mule, and his hat. And of late, finding a way to stop the devil.

Besides, what Miss Starr's motives or philosophy might be were of no concern to him. He had his own plans, with no intention of changing them. He would deliver the kid's box as promised, collect an appropriate reward, and then take care of his personal business.

After that, who knew? Maybe he'd light a shuck out of Denver and head for South Dakota. Since the demise of Wild Bill, the demand in Deadwood for trusted men who were good with guns kept growing. He'd passed through the town during his younger wandering days. What could be simpler?

Levering away from the bureau, he paced the confines of the hotel room. His blood roared in his ears, and excitement pumped through his veins, intoxicating him quicker than liquor. He lived for adventure and knew how to handle it. He should. He'd left home at age fourteen and bargained and bluffed his way through life for as long as he could remember. Then he realized it wasn't the thought of the reward or going to Deadwood that quickened his pulse, it was the woman.

Exhaling long and slow, he wondered where Ochessa lived. Or perhaps the less he knew about her the better. He needed money, not entanglements, and surely that's what she would prove to be. Sooner or later all women transformed into clinging vines. Then their soft slender arms turned to tentacles of iron, shackling a man in place, squeezing the breath from his lungs.

Besides, when women were involved, things always got messy. Females could inspire the most logical of men to foolish acts, and the most foolhardy of men to heroic deeds, and that's when mistakes were made and accidents happened. That's why he limited his activities to selected mercenary ventures, and the occasional bounty hunt. No commitments to women and no overhead. Of course, he had to admit, it had been a long time since a female had made him feel that good that fast.

Pausing beside the bed, he dragged the saddle packs closer, liberated a pint bottle, and uncorked it. "Here's to cat-eyed women and dog-eared luck." He downed a burning mouthful of rye whisky. The mean-spirited brew scorched a path to his stomach while it cleared his thoughts and eased the pain in his head.

He hazarded another swallow and shuddered.

When financially solvent, Nic drank nothing but the finest liquor. Yet being a pragmatic man of fluctuating means, he took what he could get and enjoyed himself just the same. Life was too short for lamenting, or for waiting around for the good times to show up on their own.

Capping and setting the bottle aside, he thought about Will Starr and wondered what dreams and ambitions the kid had set his sights on. What plans for happiness had been laid to rest with his silent lips and unseeing eyes? They hadn't had much time for talk before Nic had taken his leave, but Will had seemed a decent fellow, somehow embroiled in a deadly situation. Thoughts of the kid led to thoughts of the documents and the box, and he stared at the saddlebags.

Originally, he had expected to find a big clumsy trunk hidden on Will's property. Some old sea chest padlocked and draped in chains. But the kid had died protecting a small puzzle box wrapped in red velvet and stowed, along with several documents, behind bricks in the fireplace wall. The intricately carved box, inlaid with precious metals, tempted the eye and fascinated the mind. And although no bigger than his fist, so uncommonly strong. He hadn't been unable to force it open to discern what rattled about inside of it like a pea in a pod.

Nor had Will divulged the secret to unlocking the box, or what the papers meant, only that he should deliver the box to a Mr. Jonathan Thacker of the Wells Fargo Company in Denver. And Nic fully intended to honor that last request—as soon as he found out what was hidden inside. Will was dead because of the box— he might be in danger as well. It seemed prudent to know what he carried around, and it would make coming up with a fair and equitable courier charge for Mr. Thacker a whole lot simpler. After all, regardless of the heartrending circumstances, a man had to turn a profit when and where he could.

He slipped his hand inside the saddle pack to retrieve the cube. As the soft whisper of velvet met his touch, he breathed a sigh of relief. Liberating the small bundle, he unwrapped it, and stared in disbelief. Clouds blotted out the sun, and the hotel room dimmed.

She'd stolen the box—and replaced it with a bar of soap bearing the Pullman Railcar insignia. With a growl, he tossed it aside. Then he raised his right foot, braced it against the frame of the bed, and jerked up his pant leg. Shoving his fingers down inside the top of his boot he felt the rough edges of folded paper.

The smile returned to his face. At least she hadn't found the documents.

****

The sheriff, having been shot by an unknown

assailant, remained laid up with a bullet wound, and the deputy who stood before her was a duly elected fool. Ochessa opened her mouth to tell him so, when Lame Bear clamped his hand down on her shoulder.

She snapped her mouth shut. Lame Bear was correct. Too angry to argue intelligibly, it wouldn't help to antagonize her only hope for justice. But Deputy Rawlins' attitude mystified her. He seemed strongly disinclined to get involved, stating since the incident had occurred in Kansas it was outside his jurisdiction. But with Nic Breedlove being in Colorado, he could at least try to track the man down for questioning.

"If we had the bullet," the deputy droned on, "we could do some of those fancy ballistic tests like in that Minnesota State court case the sheriff heard about. But so far all we've got is your word against this drifter's. I believe you when you say this man had something to do with the death of your brother, but without a witness, it's just your word against his. And your story about back alleys and dark horsemen, well that's even harder to prove. It won't hold water with the circuit judge. He ain't one to waste time on anything other than an open and shut case."

She groaned inwardly. Why even bother? By now, Breedlove would no doubt be long gone. Once off the train he'd probably headed straight out of the county. She couldn't even pin a charge of robbery on him since she had recovered the Chinese puzzle box from his saddle pack.

The lawman opened his mouth to speak, but she couldn't stomach any more of his pathetic excuses. This conversation was over.

"Thanks for nothing."

He held his silence, appearing smugly victorious.

Hands clenched at her sides, she stepped from the office onto the dusty streets of Denver.

Allowing Breedlove to escape from the train had fouled up everything. What had she been thinking? Dusting off her rarely used feminine wiles to wield as a weapon to gain information had failed miserably—humiliation flared at the memory. The bawdy interlude had betrayed *her* emotions rather than *his* motivations. And she had almost enjoyed his outrageous advances. Worse yet, her body had responded with a mind of its own. As addlebrained as she'd acted, you'd think *her* head had been grazed by a bullet.

She should have shown more self-control. Criminy Dutch, so what if Nic was tall and ruggedly handsome? Half the men who worked for her were just as appealing. Maybe it was the way he looked at her—his eyes shining bright with adventures already lived, and those yet to be realized. Or the way his mouth curved so easily into a lazy sarcastic smile.

Shoving her hands into the pockets of her leather skirt, and with Lame Bear at her side, she set off down the street. Fanciful female thinking and emotional nonsense had no place in her life, at least not now. When Ochessa was just a little girl, with her father alive and running the ranch, those attributes had served her well. He'd found her attempts at charm and guile adorable, always indulging her whims and demands without a second thought. Then she'd turned ten years old, and he died.

For the next twelve years, she tried to live up to her mother's expectations, which meant hiding her feminine feelings as she learned to be a no-nonsense-woman who could do anything she put her mind to. On that score, her mother had been correct. If she intended to survive, she needed to be strong-minded and clearheaded. She needed to think like a man. And today that held especially true.

There were pressing matters to attend to, and like it or not, for the moment Nic Breedlove was off the hook. But as soon as she had the ranch up and running again, he would be her number one mission. She'd hire an army if that's what it took to track him down and find out what he knew about Will's death. But she didn't have the strength or money to wage two battles at once and could only concentrate on one calamity at a time. Nic would have to wait. She already regretted having wasted the better part of the morning reporting him to the authorities.

"As usual, I should have listened to you, Lame Bear, and not bothered going to talk to the deputy."

"It's a hard job always being right." Lame Bear gave an exaggerated sigh.

His dry humor brought a halfhearted smile to her lips.

"I was not always so smart," he reassured, "we all trade youth for brains. Not a fair arrangement, but what are you going to do?"

Reining in her anger and frustration, she marveled at Lame Bear's ability to cope and keep pace with the world. "Life is becoming too complicated and full of newfangled notions," she griped, as they crossed the wide avenue. "Ballistic tests and open and shut cases. What happened to the day when a man was as good as his word, and a handshake was as binding as a three page lawyer's contract?"

Sadness haunted Lame Bear's expression. "Those times are gone with the great herds of buffalo. You must grow, or you will perish. Do not take it personal. Change does not recognize merit or need. It is just what it is."

She knew he was correct, but it didn't stop the bitterness that burned in the back of her mind—curling the edges of her darkest thoughts. Lately, most of the changes she'd experienced had been forced upon her with cold indifference and brutal finality. Just how much growing and changing was one individual expected to undergo?

"Look to the future," he encouraged, "have hope."

Ochessa wished she could, but she had no faith in tomorrows. Lame Bear was getting on in years, and the ranch seemed on the verge of slipping through her fingers. As far as she could see, the future held only the promise of heartache and broken dreams. She'd forgotten what it felt like to be hopeful.

At the corner, they turned south and headed down the street past Mattie Silks' and the Old Elephant Corral. At least one thing had worked in her favor. She'd gotten the puzzle box away from Mr. Breedlove. She knew the secret of opening the cube, and what she'd found inside belonged to her now.

Part of her wished she could have seen the expression on Nic's face when he discovered the box missing, replaced with a big old chunk of soap. Another part of her knew it was wiser and safer not to ever see him again—and not merely because of the stolen kisses and desperate touching. There was something pleasingly unsettling about that man. Being around Nic made her giddy, like when she drank too much coffee, or when she rode the range for too many days with too little sleep. And that made her afraid. Not of him, but of how much she liked the feeling.

Yes, it was just as well and with Nic at least temporarily out of her life, she could deal with the business at hand.

Lame Bear still at her side, Ochessa paused outside Frontenac's, and peered over the set of swinging doors leading to the inner sanctum of the gambling hall and saloon. Whiskey fumes and cigar smoke haloed the men gathered around the bar as they wagered on the outcome of tomorrow's shooting match. A contest she intended to win.

The participants were required to sign up before noon today. The clock on the bar room wall read eleven thirty—she had barely made the cut off. Some of the wealthiest ranch owners in the country had turned out for the competition. It had been advertised in newspapers from coast to coast, and the winner would be well rewarded. First prize was a stud bull descended from the best Hereford stock in the United States, with a bloodline that could be traced all the way back to Kimroe.

The cherished Longhorn cattle were losing their foothold in the bovine hierarchy, and raising short horns had become more acceptable—acceptable, profitable, and practical. To keep her land, and gather together enough money for her new venture, she needed capital and assets she could turn into cold hard cash. She had to win the shoot, she needed this bull.

Each contestant must tender three hundred dollars, or a safe commodity of equal value. Another reason she had gone looking for Will, to see if he could pitch in on the entry fee. And in a way, he had come through for her. The solitary ruby she'd discovered inside of the Chinese box would more than cover her fee. And with that champion bull, she could rent him out as stud, or turn around and sell him to ensure the survival of the Rising Starr Ranch. Without the animal, she'd be forced to sell out—at a loss.

Desperation crushed the air from her chest, and she felt hot and cold at the same time. The usual feeling of terror she experienced whenever she thought about losing the ranch. The Rising Starr was the only home she had ever known, and this was her last chance to keep alive the legacy left by her parents. It would also be the last chance to transform that legacy into her version of the future. Too bad she'd have to cross paths with Eustace in order to succeed.

Eustace, the man sponsoring the contest, owned the spread next to the Rising Starr on the near side of the South Platte. A rivalry between the two ranches seemed to have existed since the first beef cow dropped the first prairie pie in Colorado territory. And for some reason, over the years, the competition had grown from half-hearted to dead serious. As a child, she'd never been privy to all the particulars, and even to this day Ochessa didn't really know what had started the discord.

Lame Bear touched her arm to gain her attention. "I'll wait up the street."

She studied the wise eyes of the man she had come to love as a second father. "Okay. Watch your back, I won't be long."

Proud and unafraid, he moved on alone. What was it like to walk his path? When they left the seclusion of the ranch, the real world always took her by surprise.

Here a man was judged by who he knew and the whiteness of his skin. At the ranch a man was generally judged by what he knew, and how hard he worked. She liked her world better.

Following Lame Bear's example, she mustered her courage, squared her shoulders, and pushed through the swinging doors, entering the nebulous domain of male humor, male pride, and male bullshit.

The room grew noticeably quiet as she strolled along the length of the saloon. Ignoring the stares and whisper, she made sure to avoid the wet patches ringing the spittoons. Halting at the table where Eustace sat, she grabbed up a pen to enter her name on the roster.

He snatched the quill from her hand.

"I'd sooner shoot that bull and turn him into sirloins then see him go to the Rising Starr." He spoke loud enough for all those in the room to hear.

Murmurs of surprise rippled through the crowd.

Eustace wasn't going to let her compete. She hadn't even considered that eventuality. She should have. Now what? She sucked in a deep breath, to stave off the mind numbing shock.

"You talk like you think she could win," a nameless voice drawled.

The buzzing stopped, and dead silence took its place as a man wearing a flat brimmed hat low on his forehead stepped from the shadows.

Nic. He hadn't left town after all.

"She ain't got a chance in this world or Heaven's realm," Eustace sneered, "and I don't need no interference from an outsider."

Nic headed for the bar, and casually leaned against the wide expanse of mahogany. "Money's money. If you don't think she can win, seems to me you're losing an easy three hundred dollars."

Eustace took pause at that. No doubt the idea of fleecing her appealed to him. "That's assuming she's got the entry fee," he jeered. It was common knowledge she had fallen on hard times, owing credit all around town.

The crowd seemed to be holding its collective breath, waiting for her answer.

She slipped the ruby from her shirt pocket and held it out in the palm of her hand. "I think this should cover it."

Even in the dull atmosphere of the saloon, the gem gleamed with uncommon brilliance, and along with the other patrons, Eustace grunted in appreciation.

From the corner of her eye, she saw Nic straighten and come to attention.

Homer Watson, the freight agent and commodities broker, stepped forward to examine the stone. "That gem's worth a great deal more than three hundred dollars, young lady. It's one of the most perfect rubies I've ever seen."

Self-doubt screamed through her mind. Maybe she'd be better off to sell the jewel and pay off her creditors. But then, she'd be right back where she started with no capital for investment, and no new beginning. In another year she'd be in debt again. She had no choice. She needed that bull *and* the ruby.

"Only the winner gets back what he's staked for his entry fee," Eustace warned, as if reading her thoughts.

"Suits me."

Eustace plucked the jewel from her hand and replaced it with the pen. No chance to turn back now.

Employing a death grip on the quill to keep her hand from shaking, she signed the book and picked up her entry number.

"I'm going to enjoy watching you lose," Eustace goaded, tucking the jewel away in a metal chest already bulging with paper currency, silver coins, and little bags of gold dust.

"Don't get your hopes up. They don't call me Shooting Starr for nothing."

God above had she really just said that? Nobody called her Shooting Starr, but a good bluff never hurt. When you dealt with men, you had to be self-confident and show no fear. She'd learned that lesson fast enough trying to keep up with her brother and managing the ranch hands. You also had to know when to take your leave. She glanced around the room.

"Until the morning, gentlemen." Her gaze swept the room then she headed for the front entrance and Nic.

As she strode past the end of the bar, he caught her arm.

She stood stock still, her heart pounding in her chest, the memory of his kisses, his touch, and the raw passion he inspired ripping through her. She'd better be careful, or he would send her reeling back to that unknown world, the one she couldn't help but want to explore.

Fighting the urge, she grabbed at his hand, prying his fingers from her sleeve. Then she forced herself to meet his unwavering gaze. Why hadn't he left town? Did he simply enjoy tempting fate and living dangerously?

"Will you join me for dinner tomorrow night?"

Nic's question took her off guard.

"I did help to get you into the contest," he coaxed, when she remained silent.

"I don't need you to champion my causes. I can take care of myself."

"I daresay you probably can." The smile he gave Ochessa warmed his eyes and her belly.

She stared at his broad chest while considering his offer. It was one way to find out more about what had happened at Will's cabin. And one way to learn more about the man himself.

"Just dinner?" She didn't bother masking the suspicion in her voice.

He thought a moment, his gaze traveling the length of her body then back up to her face, coming to rest on her lips. "Just dinner—and a kiss freely given. As I recall you're rather good at kissing."

Her mouth flattened into an angry line. Leave it to this donkey's backside to publicly embarrass her. The barkeep guffawed, but quickly turned away when she aimed a venomous glare in his direction.

"I'd sooner kiss the bull."

Nic shrugged. "I reckon once he's yours, Miss Starr, you can do with him as you please."

Chapter Five

On the day of the shooting match, Nic shook his head, then continued circling the makeshift arena newly erected on the south side of town. A perfect ruby—a gem more blood red than this morning's sunrise. That's what had been inside the puzzle box.

He'd been careless. He'd forgotten the dusty trails of the American West could be as riddled with intrigue as the winding streets of Cairo, or the forbidding backroads of the Carpathians. Worse yet, he'd been sentimental, a dangerous condition at best, leaving him hoodwinked by a pretty face, and emotionally swayed by the heartfelt tale told by a dying young man. No one to blame other than himself he chided. He should have verified the box was in his saddlebag before he left the train.

He'd learned early on if he didn't look out for himself, no one else would, and even at the tender age of fourteen, he'd sealed his pact with Fate, swearing to always come out on top—no matter the cost. Since that time, a heap of fast-running water had gone under the bridge—and years of hard won experience over the dam. But for Miss Starr, he'd broken those rules and promises, and now she had the upper hand. She was on top, an interesting position in matters of the heart, but not in this instance.

He kicked at a stone and kept circling. Perhaps all

was not lost. The ruby had to be stolen. Could there be more? Or maybe the documents held the answer, maybe they were what the dark horsemen had been searching for at Will's cabin—the reason Will had been killed.

So far, the papers hadn't proven to be interesting or informative. He'd tried contacting this Jonathan Thacker fellow, hoping to get a handle on the situation, but the wispy-haired lad manning the front desk at the Wells Fargo office informed him Mr. Thacker got tied up in California tracking down a desperado who robbed a stage in Colorado Springs.

Thacker could be gone for days, and answers from that quarter would be long in coming, which left Ochessa and her ruby. Did she know where the gem came from, or what Will had been up to? Nic hoped to find out tonight at dinner. The thought of seeing her again, kindled desire. He squelched the feeling. Their meeting had to be purely business, with her merely a means to an end—a lucrative one.

What a risky move, staking the gem for a cow, or to be more precise, for a bull. He could understand investing money in a well-blooded horse. At least you could race it for a quick profit, but a bull? What kind of woman hazarded a small fortune on such a notion?

A woman with a purpose and the guts to see it through. He smiled. A woman like Ochessa Starr, or Chessy Cat as he'd come to think of her. She seemed rather exceptional. Being attracted to the unusual, he felt comfortable with the extraordinary, and he reluctantly admitted it was a point in her favor.

In a rare moment of fancy, he daydreamed about what he would purchase with that ruby—or the finder's fee. Logical things, like a decent suit and a new pair of boots, several nights at a high-stakes gaming table, a better saddle, a well-aged bottle of Scotch whiskey. And most importantly, two new Stetsons—one to replace the bullet riddled one he was forced to wear, and one for *just-in-case*.

Continuing to reconnoiter, Nic reached a small stand of cottonwoods. The irregular cluster of trees made a nice secluded niche, offering suitable concealment, as well as a panoramic view. The perfect vantage point for watching the contest, and for watching spectators, like the man dressed in black who'd been nosing around the arena earlier this morning.

After blasting through Monotony, the dark horsemen must have headed west, holing up somewhere close by. Good. It would save him the trouble of doubling back to find them a second time. But why were they here, and not headed for Mexico? And talk about ballsy, bold as brass they'd sent one of their own into town for a little personal observation. Tactically it made good sense, and according to information he'd gathered along the trail, the thieving bunch ran their operation with military precision. And he knew why.

They also seemed to have a penchant for turning up in close proximity to the ruby.

There were no specific descriptions of the gang members, only the fact they wore black, and since the ending of the war, you couldn't arrest a man because of the color of his clothing. Their leader was another story. The man should be arrested on general purposes, regardless of dress.

As a crowd gathered, Nic lounged against the raspy bark of the nearest tree and speculated about the outcome of today's competition. He hoped Miss Starr wouldn't be beaten too early on. It would put her in a choleric mood for their dinner engagement. Bracing one foot against an opposing tree trunk, he settled in to wait, and realized he hoped she would actually win the contest.

****

The elimination rounds had been going on for at least two hours. Ochessa cradled her rifle and tried not to fidget as she watched Wilbur Swenson step up to the firing line and shoot. He missed the target by a good inch. That left her and the Texan.

Although her palms were dry, she nervously wiped first one hand and then the other against her skirt. She should offer up a prayer of thanks to her mother for forcing her to spend all those hours punching paper. If the target shooting hadn't been wrought as a punishment, she would have.

Then she pictured her father, Jedidiah Starr, his tanned and weathered face creased by an easygoing smile. He always made her believe she could achieve whatever she set her mind to. But those were long ago times, and he wasn't here to help. It was all up to her, a condition severely taking its toll of late. Ochessa had become obsessed with the continuation of the ranch, as if somehow its survival and hers were linked. And maybe they were.

She shifted her stance, and again studied the crowd, trying to spot Nic in the churning sea of faces. Her mouth went dry, and she couldn't decide if she were more nervous about the contest or meeting Nic tonight for dinner. She had a wagon load of practice when it came to handling guns, not so much with men.

Chastising herself for worrying over Nic at a time like this, she forced her attention to the only person who should concern her at the moment—the man who stood between her and first prize. Focusing her thoughts, she watched her opponent as he prepared for his turn at the target.

Houston Bill Williams fiddled with his rifle sight, checked the direction of the wind, kicked a clod of dirt aside hindering his stance then tested the wind again.

If he didn't hurry up and shoot, she was going to scream.

Finally, after all that fussing, he fired, missing center by a hair's breath.

That should be enough.

She glanced over at Eustace. Although not a particularly warm day, he was sweating like block ice in August. That thought bolstered her spirits.

Ochessa took her place, nestling the familiar worn stock of the old Winchester up against her shoulder and cheek. Time seemed to stop as she squinted down the barrel at the target, and memories of a lifetime seemed to pass before her eyes. Her future would be decided in the next instant, the mere span of a heartbeat. Now she couldn't help but pray for guidance, forgiveness, good fortune, and anything that would encourage God to smile down upon her just this once. A comforting warmth drove the chill of uncertainty from her heart, and it felt as if her father stood at her side. It was now or never.

She inhaled, let her breath out halfway, held it, and squeezed the trigger.

The crowd cheered as she hit dead center. Bill Williams shook his head and clapped her on the back.

The rush of relief left her shaking. Her legs felt wobbly, and she feared she might lose what little food she'd eaten today. Gulping in a quick breath, she stood a little taller, and tried to act as if she hadn't expected less.

Lame Bear flashed a rare grin in her direction, and flanked by two of the burliest cowboys working the Rising Starr, he went to collect the bull.

She ambled toward Eustace, to reclaim her entry fee.

"That was fine shootin', Miss Starr," Charlie Peterson acknowledged in passing. Charlie ran the mercantile, and while she didn't doubt the sincerity of his good wishes, she knew he also figured he would now be collecting on the backlog of debts she owed him. No one would be more relieved than she when the bills were paid, and she could hold her head high and not beg for credit.

She paused before Eustace. "My ruby if you please."

Ochessa had been raised not to brag, letting her actions speak for themselves, but today she couldn't resist.

"You look a might pale." She held out her hand, and he deposited the gem in her palm. "You can come and visit the bull anytime you like."

The color rushed back into Eustace's cheeks, and he turned ruddier than a rutabaga. In truth, he looked headed for apoplexy, and she wished the feuding between them would stop.

"Come on, Eustace," she said, feeling magnanimous. "I won fair and square. Let's end the fighting. It's a new beginning for me. Let it be a new beginning for us as neighbors as well."

"Never." He slammed the cash box shut.

She shook her head at his irascible male pride, still wondering why the animosity had begun in the first place. By the time she recognized such trouble existed between her parents and Eustace, it was already well established. And after her father had passed away, her mother still refused to discuss the matter.

"It was dumb luck let you win, and bad luck saw my bull go to the likes of you."

Ochessa smiled, refusing to let anything or anyone spoil her thrill of victory. "Lame Bear," she called. We're naming the bull, Lucky."

****

At first Lucky Starr was a half-ton of uncompromising muscle and attitude. But like most males, after he settled in, and had been well fed and introduced to the cows, he showed the more agreeable side of his disposition.

Arms draped over the top rail of the fence, Ochessa studied the huge beast. Hard to believe he belonged to her. For a short horn, he was fiercely beautiful—like a rugged mountain peak or a raging thunderstorm. The bull turned his head and stared at her, then with a mighty humph, he trotted over to a willing cow to have at it. Ochessa forked more hay over the fence and pumped fresh water into the trough. So far there was no question about the bull earning his keep.

After a few moments of energetic rutting, Lucky bellowed with what appeared to be blissful satisfaction then he abandoned the cow and wandered off to catch the last rays of the setting sun.

Typical. Regardless of species, the male gender seemed content to quench their desires with cold detachment. Either that or the complete opposite seemed true, and they tried to tell you what to do and how to think as if they could lay claim to your brain as well as the space between your legs.

At least that's what she'd heard. Except for one short-lived, long-regretted entanglement, the rest of her knowledge on romantic relationships came from overheard snatches of bunkhouse humor and trail drive conversation.

At the sound of hooves on soft earth, she glanced up.

Lame Bear strode forward, her horse in tow. The fringed jacket she kept at the house lay across the saddle.

"Sure you don't want company on the way to town?"

She reached for and put on the jacket. "No. But thank you for the offer. I'd feel better knowing you were here at the ranch in case the bull or Eustace decides to start trouble tonight. I wouldn't put it past either one of them."

Lame Bear handed her the reins. "Be careful as you travel, and in town as well."

"I will," she said lightly, mounting up.

He grabbed the horse's bridle, preventing her from leaving. "See that you do."

Lame Bear's voice held an edge sharp as flint. She studied his face. His expression fit the seriousness of his tone. "A shadow hovers near the valley we call home."

His words struck an ominous chord, and the hair on the nape of Ochessa neck bristled. She could have gone a month of Sundays without hearing those words. "I'll be careful," she promised.

The old man relaxed his stance the tiniest bit and stepped aside to let her pass.

Ochessa cut across Rising Starr property, and headed toward town. It should take less than an hour to reach Denver. She tried to relax and enjoy the ride, but Lame Bear's portent drummed in her brain like a never-ending tattoo—keeping rhythm with the hoof beats of her horse. She patted her trusty rifle nestled in its leather sheath, then nervously glanced around. She had never been frightened out on the prairie before, but now she imagined a dark figure lurking behind every cottonwood tree and pile of stones.

She needed to calm down. Her nerves were coiled tighter than a whip snake. She reined the little mare into a slower pace. Earlier this afternoon, she had been looking forward to being alone on the ride in. She'd hardly had a moment to herself since they'd returned from Kansas. At first, she had welcomed the constant confusion. It kept her mind off Will and her mother. But tonight, she sought this brief solitude and isolation, hoping it would renew her vigor. She would need all the strength she could muster to get through dinner with Mr. Breedlove.

At the thought of Nic, a warm glow rushed through Ochessa. It made her feel restless—and reckless. A voice inside warned she shouldn't be doing this, warned she'd be safer jumping off a cliff rather than spending a few hours with a handsome stranger who confounded her good sense with a mere glance, and broke through her defenses with the slightest of touches.

Recollections of their interlude on the train fanned the warmth into a hot ember, banked and ready to flare up with a minimum of encouragement. Something undefinable about Nic set him apart from other men. She'd never reacted this way around any other male with whom she'd crossed paths. She didn't know if that was good or bad.

He hadn't run when he'd had the chance, and he'd spoken up for her at the shooting contest registration, but exactly what were his long range intensions? She doubted they were good, although she had to admit, his declaration of innocence regarding Will's murder had begun to sound more and more believable. But even if he hadn't killed her brother, he was still a dangerous man—a bad 'un. That's what her father used to call a man who lived for today, never looked back, and thought the rest of the world did the same.

She figured the reason her father knew so much about the subject stemmed from the fact that in his younger years he fit the mold himself—until he'd fallen in love with Ochessa's mother. Then he'd changed his ways. Most men never did. She'd better keep her guard up and her wits about her. Information was all she sought tonight, and a few hours of her time all she intended to invest.

The lights of the city came into view. The town seemed especially bright and noisy tonight. The shooting match had attracted many out-of-town contestants and spectators, now they milled about, and an all-night celebration appeared to be in full-swing.

Heading down the main street, she kept an eye out for Nic's mule. There she was. Her stomach tightened into a knot. He would pick the fanciest beanery in town. Muttering her displeasure, she reined in at the Blue Palace Hotel and Restaurant. An overpriced and overdecorated eatery, where the people frequenting the establishment had their noses so high in the air she wondered how they managed to eat at all. If Nic hoped to impress her, this wasn't the way.

She slid from the saddle, tied her horse to the hitching rail beside his mule, and tossed a coin to the raggedy boy who kept an eye on the patrons' horses.

Entering the vestibule, she crossed the lobby, ignoring the blatant stares flattening up against her like tumbleweeds along a fence line. To her right sat the restaurant. To her left the tavern area. Her gaze flickered from face to face seeking Nic's. There he was, at the bar, nursing a drink. He appeared decked-out just as splendidly as the night he'd been shot. How did he manage to still appear so intimidating in such finery?

He caught sight of her and raised a brow in surprise.

She hadn't taken the time to change her clothes. After all, Nic wasn't courting her or something ridiculous like that. They were merely sharing a meal, and hopefully an enlightening conversation.

Nic sauntered over and paused before her. "Glad you could make it." He flicked a piece of hay from the collar of her chambray shirt. "Didn't go to too much bother I hope."

The sarcasm in his voice did not escape her attention.

"Look, Breedlove, I can eat at home. I came here for only one reason, and you darn well know what it is."

He cocked his head, fixing her with a quizzical gaze as if he hadn't the slightest notion as to what she might be eluding.

"Information," she declared.

"How disappointing. Here I thought my good looks and overwhelming charm had turned the trick in convincing you to join me tonight."

She forced a heavy sigh to overlay the expletive she couldn't stop.

Unperturbed by her manner, or the curious glances they were receiving, Nic took her elbow and grandly escorted her to the restaurant area and a table bearing a reserved marker.

Solicitously, he held out her chair and waited for her to sit, then pushed it in. Folding his lanky frame into the seat across from her, he smiled and shook his head.

"What?"

"You have dirt on your cheek."

Oh great. She grabbed the linen napkin, and as discreetly as possible, wiped at her face.

"The other side," he directed, his widening smile confirming his apparent amusement at her discomfiture.

She was losing the upper hand in their meeting, if indeed she'd ever had it. Regardless of how much she wanted to talk to Nic and find out what he knew, she shouldn't have agreed to join him here. She should have met him during the day at the open-air market, or at the ranch—any place other than a fancy-ass restaurant. This place put her at a disadvantage, never a good position for negotiations or investigations.

Ochessa set the napkin aside. Why didn't Nic say something? He just kept staring at her. When she finally thought of something to say, the waiter appeared. He paused beside the table and glared down at her like she had just crawled out from under a rotting log.

"Madam's order if you please." He sounded as if his nose had been stuffed with cottonwood fluff.

"A plate of steamed vegetables." The very idea set her mouth to watering. "And fresh bread with lots of butter on the side. Oh, and jam, too."

She didn't miss the man's confusion but didn't renege on her choice of food. She refused to eat meat, believing something shouldn't have to die for her to live. Since her mother's death, she even insisted the occasional wild animal harrying the herd be live-trapped or driven off rather than shot. Her pain-in-the-butt peculiar ideas hadn't made her popular with the men. In fact a few had quit. She also knew the ones who stayed generally ignored these requests.

"Anything else, madam?" the waiter prompted, as if he could not fathom a meal without meat.

"A knife and fork to eat it with would be helpful."

The snooty little man cringed at her response.

Nic suppressed a sputtering cough. Then as if he hadn't eaten a decent meal in a long while, he ordered several entrees off the menu. "And, a bottle of *Pedro Domecq*, if the wine cellar permits."

"Very good sir." In a flagrant show of appreciation for Nic's good manners and culinary expertise, the waiter gave a little bow before leaving them alone.

"Let's get down to brass tacks, Breedlove."

"My first name is Nicodemus."

Of course. Not Dominic or Nicolas, as she had surmised, but Nicodemus. The perfect name for a *bad un*. She didn't repeat it back or offer the courtesy of letting him use her given name. Silently she studied his face, matching the unwavering stare he seemed to have mastered. Generally a good judge of character, Nic

65

confused her. His strong jaw and clear green eyes indicated qualities in direct opposition of her low opinion of him.

His contemplation intensified. Mixed emotions seemed to rush at her from all sides, the feeling colliding in the middle of her chest. She twisted her hands in her lap, suddenly wishing she'd taken the time to comb her hair, and to change into footwear not caked with dust and the familiar smell of the ranch. She even wished she'd worn a pretty dress rather than the leather skirt she unflaggingly wore.

The return of the waiter interrupted her lamenting. Two boys toting food-laden trays, followed in the man's wake. She eyed the mound of edibles. It seemed sinful and extravagant, yet somehow wickedly exciting. With unabashed enthusiasm, she grabbed the flatware set before her, and tore into the food. The waiter rolled his eyes, and quickly took his leave.

Nic poured two glasses of wine.

She preferred a shot of whiskey diluted in a cup of chamomile tea, but at the moment, a belt of anything with even half a kick sounded good. Accepting the cut-glass goblet he offered, she forced herself to sip slowly. It had to be the most incredible wine she had ever tasted. It slid down her throat like liquid silk, comforting her from the inside out. A sigh slipped from between her lips, and she allowed herself a moment of pure unguarded sensation.

Nic's demeanor seemed to soften as well. An unmistakable glow shown in his eyes, and he looked as if he were privy to an important secret—one she wished he would share with her. A strange hint of camaraderie abided in his features, making her want to trust and confide in him.

"Care for something more substantial than carrots?" He gestured toward the platters of roast pork and prime rib weighing down his side of the table.

"I don't eat meat."

"How curious. Are you allergic to it?"

"People aren't allergic to meat." Although for future reference she decided that excuse might come in handy.

At Nic's continuing silence and expression of expectation, she took a deep breath and launched into her usual recitation in defense of her eating choice.

"It isn't a new concept. Classical writers such as Plato and Plutarch abstained from eating meat. Even the mathematician Pythagoras advocated the idea."

"Those men are dead, and lived on the other side of the world," he pointed out.

"Well, the idea also took hold in Great Britain and Germany."

"Fascinating. And does anyone born in the last few centuries participate in this curious way of life?"

"Henry Thoreau, Percy Shelly, Charles Darwin." She threw the names at him like well-aimed punches. "Even Clara Barton, for Heaven sake. And," she continued, running now on a full head of steam, "in 1856, the Vegetarian and Octagon Settlement Company formed a likeminded group right here in the United States. They started a community in the Kansas Territory."

"Quite impressive," Nic admitted. "And how are these innovative folks in Kansas faring twenty years later?"

Cripes she hated when people brought that up.

"They were starved out the first year and went back East."

Nic burst out laughing.

"The point being," she contended, "they had the courage of their convictions, and although flying in the face of popular opinion, they tried to live their lives as they saw fit. It didn't hurt anybody else."

Nic's expression turned peculiar, reminiscent of an indulgent parent after a child's not too successful piano recital. Her argument sounded a bit lame even to her own ears. She took another sip of wine. "Of course, most of these groups also advocate temperance. A notion with which I completely disagree."

His smile returned, and he raised his glass in a toast. "Congratulations on winning the contest today."

The change of subject came as a welcome relief. "You were there?"

"Yes, of course. And you'd better watch your back." His expression turned sober. "One of the boys in black attended today's shoot as well. He seemed interested in watching you."

Her elation at discovering Nic had bothered to come to the shoot collided with her worry over these men of darkness. She'd heard folks in town talking about them. Calling them men without faces, whose fearful reputation preceded them, and whose evil lingered in their absence.

"Remarkable shooting, I might add." His compliment steered her thoughts back around full circle.

She toyed with the stem of her glassware, fighting the urge to consume more wine. She already felt as if she'd finished an entire bottle, leaving her wanting to explain to him how her life had depended on winning. Leaving her wanting to reveal to him her most dreaded fears, and her greatest triumphs. But why would he care?

"I had no choice but to be the best."

Nic relaxed back in his chair. "Do you always rise so admirably to the occasion?"

How did one answer a question like that without sounding either arrogant or foolish? "I try to."

His presence created such mixed emotions in Ochessa. Even when he'd held her firmly against his solid form on the train, an odd sort of comfort had warred with her anger and distress.

"How much do you know about the ruby?"

Not totally unexpected, the question still took her off guard. Then irritation battled her surprise. "It's red and its mine. That's all I need to know."

"It's stolen," he flatly informed her.

How could that be true? Will had been as honest as the day was long.

"Are you calling my brother a thief." The very idea had her half rising out of her seat in anger.

"I never said that."

She eased back onto the chair. Poor Will. How had he really met his end? She was about to ask but could find no room for words around the renewed sorrow stuck crossways in her throat. Swallowing hard, she tried again. "What really happened to him?"

An expression akin to sympathy flickered across Nic's face. Then a mask of indifference, which seemed to fit him much more comfortably, reappeared. "When I reached the cabin, your brother had already been shot. When we heard someone approaching, Will all but begged me to take the box and leave."

"And of course you did." Not knowing why, she dumped all her anger onto Nic.

"It's hard not to honor the last request of a dying man." Nic's statement made her feel guilty about her outburst. "Had he known you were coming up the draw, I'm sure he would have made his plans accordingly."

"But why would Will trust you?"

"He didn't have a lot of choices, and I guess I just have an honest face."

"No doubt a useful attribute."

"It doesn't hurt."

"What were you suppose to do with the box?"

"Take it to the Wells Fargo office here in Denver."

"Wells Fargo..." That bit of news gave her pause. "But why?"

"I'm not sure. Most likely Will worked for them."

Of course. This theory made sense. It would be just like him to do something adventurous with his life, such as fighting for law and order where none existed or was wanted. She knew there had to be some reason why her brother chose to live on a mockery of a farm out on the Kansas flatlands. He'd been fed-up with the ranch and their mother, but if he did work for Wells Fargo, why choose to live on the outskirts of Hades, a haven for cutthroats and murderers. Couldn't he have just as easily worked in Denver? She may never know, and only had Nic's word for what had happened.

"When you deliver the gem to Wells Fargo," Nic instructed, "ask for Jonathan Thacker."

Guess again cowboy. No way was that going to happen. "Will didn't say anything to me about the Wells Fargo agency, only that I should find a man named Nic

Breedlove, and the box he carried. The ruby belongs to me now, and I have other plans for the jewel."

Nic seemed amused at her response but didn't argue the point. That was in his favor. He appeared to be a man who knew when to leave well enough alone and keep his opinions to himself.

"What about the documents?" This time *she* threw the question out and watched for his reaction. "Will said you had those too."

"Did he?"

Dang, he was good. His expression didn't change one iota as he skirted her question.

Doubting any more information would be forthcoming, leaving seemed a good idea. She had no more questions for him and didn't intend to answer any he might have for her.

She stared down at her plate. Too bad she'd barely touched her food, which had been downright delicious. Indulging in another sip of wine to bolster her courage, she levered up from her chair. "I really must be going. Thank you for dinner. It's been—interesting."

Nic leaped to his feet, threw enough money on the table to cover the bill, and followed. "I'll walk you to your carriage." He fell in step at her side.

"I rode my horse, and I can find my own way."

Ignoring her rebuff, he ushered her out into the night.

Pausing on the boardwalk, he captured one of her hands and held her back. "You still owe me a kiss."

She snatched her hand away. "I don't owe you anything. You owe me. I saved you from bleeding to death."

"How do you figure that? I wouldn't have been

shot in the first place if you hadn't lured me to that back alley and then needed me to save your hide from the dark horseman crouching at your back."

"All right so we're even. It's not a contest."

"Then what is it, Ochessa, this thing between us?"

She knew exactly what he meant but refused to answer. Something definitely existed between them—something akin to the hum in the air just before a lightning strike.

He adjusted his worse-for-wear hat, settling it more firmly upon his head. The motion seemed one of habit, and she stared at his hand remembering his touch upon her body, and the way he had coaxed her beyond feigned interest headfirst into wholehearted participation.

"There's nothing between us."

Lightly gripping the lapels of her jacket, he walked backward, tugging her along and into a sheltered nook beside the restaurant.

Her gaze slammed into his. Even in the dim light of seclusion, his eyes shone brightly. They were deep, like bottomless pools, and she wanted to tumble headfirst into them, not caring she might drown in their depths.

Nic lowered his mouth to hers, and raw need kicked at her midsection and plunged downward.

Abruptly he pulled away. "Is that nothing?"

"Yes." She lied again, wanting more, and resenting him because of the way she felt.

He gave a snort of laughter and released his hold on her jacket.

Hands levered against his chest, she pushed away from him. Then turning, she ran as if her life depended upon it—and maybe it did. Collecting the reins of her mare, she vaulted into the saddle.

Nic followed and grabbed the bridle just as Lame Bear had done, but she didn't wait to see what he wanted. The leather strap jerked free of his grasp when she turned the horse toward the street and urged her into a run.

"Good bye, Mr. Breedlove," she called over her shoulder. "Have a nice life."

****

Nic watched Ochessa tear down the street.

Her hat slipped back, saved from complete loss by her stampede strap, and her tawny hair turned into streamers of gold as the moonlight shown down on her. Even after the rest of her image disappeared into the darkness, for a moment, he saw flashes of those unruly locks.

Waiting long enough to be sure no one followed her out of town, he finally turned away.

She did a good job of pretending to be a tough little gal. But he hadn't missed the trembling of her chin when she spoke of her brother. She hadn't broken down, though, hadn't given in to the grief he knew must be crushing in on her. Chessy Cat...the softest, sweetest, wildwood feline he'd ever had the pleasure with which to tangle.

With a shake of his head, he retraced his steps along the walkway. What an almighty fool. He sounded like a schoolboy. But if simply kissing her aroused him this much, what would it be like to lie next to her, to share her heat, to lose himself in the depths of her body? Probably an idea better left unexplored or even admitted to.

Ochessa appeared genuinely surprised to learn the

ruby was stolen. Yet it didn't seem to change her thoughts on whether or not to keep it. He really didn't blame her.

As the night had turned cold, he thought about her riding home alone in the dark. He should have gone with her. *Not his responsibility.* Hands in his pockets, shoulders hunched, he picked up his pace, striding past the shop displays and side-stepping a pair of drunken cowboys—weaving their way along from one saloon to the next.

He should feel relieved. At least now she seemed to believe he had nothing to do with her brother's death. Instead he felt guilty for not admitting to having Will's map and documents. Of course her *finders keepers, losers weepers* philosophy about the ruby worked both ways. He didn't owe her anything, and now he was out the price of the wine and fancy meal he'd just paid for.

Nic chuckled remembering the heaping plate of vegetables she'd ordered. His Chessy Cat was a curious kitten—in more ways than one.

Reaching the entrance to the small restaurant/hotel where he was staying, he entered and headed for his room.

Although rather short, the meeting had turned out pretty much as expected.

So why did he have this unsettling, drop-dead feeling of loneliness?

Chapter Six

Nic pushed his empty breakfast plate aside. Had it only been two days since his rendezvous with Chessy Cat? It seemed longer.

The matronly waitress came over and offered him a third cup of robust coffee. He smiled but shook his head. Unaccustomed to staying long in one place already had him feeling like a race horse shut in a box stall, no need for more of the dark brew to jangle his nerves and step his pulse up even higher.

Gaining his feet, he left money for his meal and the attentive waitress and headed back to his room. He took the boardinghouse stairs two at a time, slowed his pace at the landing, and headed down the hall, then hesitated. The door to number seven stood ajar. He patted the key in the pocket of his shirt. He'd locked up when he'd gone down to eat.

The bacon, eggs, and biscuits churned in his stomach. Gun drawn and hugging the wall, he inched forward, mentally pleading with the old floor boards to keep silent as he advanced. At the door, he paused to listen. Hearing no sound, he slipped inside.

His belongings had been scattered as if a whirlwind had been turned loose to play at will. Several dresser drawers stood open, and the sheets were dragged from the bed. Nic had a pretty good idea who the intruder might have been.

Nudging the door shut with his foot, he threw the bolt, and holstered his gun. The dark horsemen were getting restless too. No surprise, as he doubted patience was their strong suit. But how had they made a connection to him? He'd been careful.

The story regarding Ochessa's entry fee had gone around the town and back, so they knew she had the ruby. Maybe he and Chessy Cat had been seen together at dinner, indicating they were partners or at least acquaintances. Were they after the documents too? Searching his room would be the logical place for them to start—and much easier and safer than ransacking her ranch. But they'd come up empty, which led to the unsettling feeling Ochessa's place would be next.

Retrieving the map and documents from his boot, he unfolded the tattered parchments and spread them flat on the bureau top. He'd already committed every pen stroke, dirt smudge, and grease spot to memory, and the reassuring feel of the paper eased his mind.

At least now he understood why they were so important, and why Will instructed him to keep them safe. It wouldn't do for the information to fall into the wrong hands—hands capable of murder. Yet Will hadn't said to deliver the papers to Wells Fargo, only the cube. Maybe Ochessa's brother hadn't had time to indicate such before Nic was obliged to take his leave.

The map showed the layout of a narrow gauge rail line connecting Denver and a small town west of Golden. The proposed route wound up Clear Creek Canyon to Georgetown and a short distance beyond. Last evening, during a friendly game of poker, he'd made discreet inquiries about the history of the area. The information gleaned turned out to be interesting—

and incriminating.

Prior to the tracks being laid, hundreds of miners worked the area, their played-out dreams of gold replaced by the new promise of silver. Then to everyone's surprise, it turned out the land itself, not the minerals, commanded the most in worth. Rail tycoons, shipping commodities into the mountains while bringing millions of tons of ore out, coveted the property as a commercial venture with short-term goals and long-term profits.

Copies of recorded deeds and proof of ownership for property all along the rail line were included with the documents. A list of names related to bond issues and Federal land grants implicated unlawful seizure of that land from the original owners. The information was powerful, incriminating individuals from here to Washington D.C. A lot of money had been involved in these transactions, and Nic figured some of it had changed hands under the table. The men playing poker last night also mentioned there had been a rash of suspicious fires, resulting in several miners being burned out, and even a few being burned to death.

Nic set his hat aside and raked his hands through his hair. Will indicated the gem, the payroll, and the documents had all been stolen together in the stage robbery. Had that been due to extraordinary luck, or extraordinary planning?

He fingered the torn edge of one of the papers and glanced around his room. Things were getting complicated. Nefarious railroad dealings and scandalous high finance were best left to bankers and lawyers. Nic simply wanted the reward for the ruby and the payroll—if he could ever get his hands on either. A reward and chance at retribution. The best thing to do, for now, was to sit tight until Thacker returned.

Poor Will, recovering the gem and the papers had cost him his life, and now Ochessa could be in peril. The prize better be worth the danger and aggravation. Guess they'd see. Most of life's trickiest situations boiled down to a battle of nerves—a tactic at which he excelled.

He set the room in order, and then slammed the last dresser drawer shut. He should warn Ochessa about these men. Of course that would lead to explaining who was responsible for her brother's death, and naturally she would want them brought to justice. Nary a man this side of St. Louis had the *cojones* to challenge the band of outlaws who held the northern plains by the throat, but she would.

With any luck, she'd be safe enough with her Indian friend, and half a dozen ranch hands to watch over her. She wasn't the only one trying to eke out a living. He had his own worries and plans for the future. The reward money he sought would go a long way toward changing his life and securing his prospects.

On the other hand, Miss Starr turned out to be a hard woman to forget. Like the ruby, a rare find, and nearly as tough, she appeared to savor the world without hesitation as she charged headfirst into life. And for a female, she seemed straightforward and unencumbered by calculated wiles and simpering need.

Gathering the documents together, he sank down onto the edge of the bed. He couldn't deny he thought her a pretty gal—despite the shadows under her eyes. And while he bet she did her crying at night, did she cry alone? There must be plenty of men interested in her—

and her property.

It might be wishful thinking, but he wanted to believe she was as much of a loner as he was. Without meaning to, Nic hoped no other man tended to her needs. The idea fostered jealousy where none should be expected. Besides, he reasoned, Ochessa seemed an all or nothing kind of woman. If another man presently courted her, she wouldn't have openly trifled with him on the main street of Denver.

With a frown, he re-folded the papers and tucked them back inside the top of his boot. It was a moot point. The smart thing to do was to stay away from Miss Starr. He'd learned long ago that survival depended on the brains in his head, not the bulge in his pants.

But he sure had enjoyed kissing her outside the hotel restaurant, the act confirming one thing for certain—he liked making Chessy Cat purr. What would it be like to make her howl?

Grabbing his saddle pack, he left the room.

In the lobby, he swung by the front desk to speak with the clerk.

"I was to meet a friend for breakfast," Nic fabricated, "but he never showed up. Did you see any strangers around here this morning?"

"No sir." The cadaverously thin man shook his head. "Ain't nobody been through here other than our registered patrons. Oh, and the deputy." He leaned closer and lowered his voice. "He's got a lady friend stays here. Sometimes he visits her upstairs, if you get my drift."

"I see. And you're sure no one else came by."

"Yes sir. I have full view of front and back stairs

from here, and I haven't left my post all morning."

"Well thanks then. Guess my friend couldn't make it."

That information struck him as curious and unexpected.

On the boardwalk, Nic paused to squint up at the sky. One undaunted cloud saved the brilliant blue from startling perfection, and that bit of white fluff eased his mind. In the world he knew, perfection didn't exist.

Reaching Holladay Street, he entered the Wells Fargo Express office where he waited as patiently as possible for the clerk to painstakingly transcribe a detailed memo. The pale-cheeked lad sported a thatch of straw-colored hair the shade of winter wheat, and his posture spoke of serious intent.

"Any word yet from Mr. Thacker?" Nic asked, when the young fellow finished his task and recognized his presence.

"Yes sir." The lad retrieved a telegram from atop the stack neatly piled on the desk. "Here's your reply, sir."

~*~

On next train to Denver...stop...very interested in your information and willing to compensate for recovery of stolen property...stop...lay low until my arrival. J. Thacker

~*~

The missive had been sent this morning—from San Francisco. Thacker's train trip would take three or four days, meaning Nic had no choice but to stay a while longer in Denver. He supposed it could be worse. His luck at the gaming tables seemed to be holding strong, and the mention of compensation made the prospect of waiting bearable.

"Thanks, kid." He searched his pockets for a coin.

"Beg pardon, sir," the boy piped up, his tone dead serious with an expression to match. "Wells Fargo agents are not allowed to accept monetary compensation from any persons involved in an ongoing case, or a possible impending case. I do, however, appreciate the thought." Blind faith lit the lad's previously solemn face.

Nic smiled. He'd traded blind faith for his sanity and control of his own destiny, but he could still respect the characteristic in others. "I admire your veracity, and I hope it serves you well."

Hefting the saddlebags onto his shoulder, he left the building and ambled down the boardwalk. At the livery he paused, peering inside the dimly lit stable. As he crossed to the grain bin, his footsteps stirred the dust sending motes dancing through narrow shafts of sunlight. Grabbing a pan and a handful of feed, he sneaked the tidbit to his mule. Sadie huffed and whined in anticipation then contentedly munched the special offering.

"We're going to be here a while longer, girl. But if things work out, when this is over, I'll buy you your own hay farm and we'll retire there." Sadie snorted and canted her head giving him her best *I'll believe that when I see it* look. Setting the empty feed pan aside, he scratched along her jawline and under her chin. Her lip blissfully quivered and went slack.

"I mean it this time." But exactly where would that be, this coveted patch of land?

With a start, he realized he'd never given the idea

of settling down a lick of consideration. Even now, he didn't want to think about it, couldn't actually conceive of calling any one place his own. He trailed his fingers down Sadie's neck then shifted to grip the top rail of the stall door.

He saw the entire world as his home, with a welcome light always burning somewhere. A bare bones philosophy, he supposed, but enough for him. Or at least it had been. Lately his shiny solitary existence seemed a bit dull around the edges. He felt older than his twenty-seven years, and sometimes, an unfamiliar gloominess dogged his steps.

Pondering such deep thoughts set his head to throbbing, and he gingerly ran his fingertips over the still raw scar. Perhaps these rambling ideas were the aftereffect of his recent head injury. Yet, he couldn't help thinking that now that he'd returned to America— the country where his life had begun—he'd come full circle.

Ten years had passed since he went *searching for the meaning of life*. Yet he felt none the wiser for the miles he'd covered. He still questioned the absolute power of Fate, believing choice tempered Providence. If a man didn't chart his own course, he might as well ramble aimlessly through the world with no more thought or direction than a poor animal. So where did Ochessa fit in? Another fascinating question to ponder. Or maybe this headstrong woman was part of the answer, and not the question at all.

Unaccustomed to melancholy considerations, he gave Sadie a final pat, and sauntered around to the back of the livery in search of the blacksmith. The rhythmic pinging of metal on metal led him to the man he sought.

What a sight.

Ginger haired and ruddy-cheeked, the smithy dwarfed the water barrel beside which he stood and the anvil over which he labored. The size of the leather apron, covering his chest and thighs, would accommodate making knee-britches for three small boys, and with an expression serene as a child's, he hammered away like a demon.

When the man stopped to dowse the glowing hot metal, Nic drew closer and called out. "Good morning. That's a powerful swing you have."

The smithy glanced up, set his work aside, and wiped his brow with a big blue kerchief. "Mornin' to you, mister." A smile creased his wide innocent face. "The arm comes with the territory."

Rummaging through his saddle pack, Nic retrieved a leather scabbard and unsheathed the Kukri. Simply handling the knife sent a spark of remembered excitement sizzling through him.

"That's one fearsome knife ya got there, friend." Unmasked appreciation accompanied the smithy's remarked. "Where'd you come by such a weapon?"

"Nepal." For Nic, the single word conjured memories of brightly colored cloth, and the smell of freshly ground spices.

The smithy wrinkled his brow in thought. "Whereabouts might that be?"

"The other side of the world and then some."

He'd spent three years living in Nepal, long enough ago that it seemed like a dream. And although he stood in the blazing Colorado sun, an icy shiver passed through Nic as he recalled the intriguing marketplaces of Katmandu, and the forbidding silhouette of Everest.

"I don't generally do sharpening on Wednesdays," the big man informed him, hands on hips. "But for a knife like that, I'd make an exception."

"It's well honed." Nic lightly flicked the tip of his thumb across the edge. "I see to that myself. What I need is another blade to match this one. You interested?"

"Blade ain't been hammered I can't duplicate or go ya one better."

Nic appreciated a man who showed pride in his work, and the self-confidence to admit to it.

"What's your price?"

"Fifteen dollars."

Nic gave a low whistle. "That's a little steep."

"I got some Damascus I been savin' for something special. I reckon this would be the time to use it."

Nic eyed the glass carboy marked acid sitting nearby. The job would be labor intensive, the acid used in etching the steel. "In that case, you've got a deal."

He handed over the knife, and as the wooden handle—worn smooth from use—slid from his grasp, reluctance gnawed at him. He knew the feel of that blade in the dark of night, and in the blinding heat of battle. He'd wielded it when hacking his way through jungles thick enough to stop the forward progress of a gnat. And he'd used it to chop kindling to keep from freezing to death. Not simply a weapon, but a comrade in arms, insurance against the unexpected—reliable and dependable.

Other than Sadie, the knife was the only thing in his entire world he could count on. That's why he needed a spare, had become obsessed with procuring one—and that meant putting his trust and his knife in the hands of this man.

The Smithy admired the long curving blade, and the crescent-shaped notch near the shank. "I got a couple of jobs ahead of you. Two days be to your liking?"

Nic glanced at the jumble of odds and ends piled beside the forge and along the wall. At least two months' worth of work awaited this man's attention. Nic's project appeared to have sparked the craftsman's interest. That alone mollified his concern.

"I'll be around town for a short while." Nic handed over the scabbard. "Take your time."

The smithy scratched a symbol on a chip of wood, and gave the token to Nic. Then he nestled the knife back in the leather and placed it in a box bearing the same etched pattern. After shaking hands, the bear of a man returned to his anvil.

"If that's the size of their knives," he pondered, throwing wood on the fire and working the bellows, "What do they carry for side arms?"

Nic smiled at the man's remark as he retraced his steps through the livery.

Back on the street, he passed the barber shop, halting when a bright yellow flier tacked to the outside wall caught his attention. Clean, the edges smooth, the square of paper hadn't been up for more than a day or two. As he read the contents, his feeling of contentment faded, and a hot sick feeling squirmed in his belly.

~*~

Seeking the services of reliable Bounty Hunter for the capture of man or men responsible for the murder of Will Starr. See Ochessa Starr-Rising Starr ranch.

~*~

"Dad-blame it," Nic ground through clenched teeth. Ochessa wasn't merely asking for trouble, she was shouting it from the rooftops and offering to pay for it.

Don't get involved. *Lay low*—the warning in Thacker's telegram echoed in the back of his mind. Besides, if ever a woman could take care of herself, Ochessa could. He wanted to believe that, but this time she ventured out of her league, unknowingly about to tangle with men who lived by their own rules. Rules giving them free rein to kill at will and never look back.

He glanced up and down the street then tore the notice from the wall.

Chapter Seven

Ochessa stood on the covered porch of the stone ranch house, surveying her property with pride and hope. Being a worthy steward of this land had become the most important thing in her life. How she reveled in the comfort of her own home, her own bed, her own view from the outhouse.

Now, basking in the midday sun, the land shimmered with the burgeoning heat—promising another unusually warm day.

Savoring the mug of cool well water, she wished she had time for a siesta. But today she needed to make peace with past demons and future fears—she needed to face her troubles head on. Granted, there were sorrows she would never get over, but there were things she must get on with.

Balancing the cup atop the whitewashed railing, she descended the steps and wended her way through the buffalo grass toward the family cemetery. The marble headstones poked up through the dirt like teeth in the grinning mouth of the earth. A shiver took her by surprise, and despite her previous lofty thoughts, loneliness—cold as the graves toward which she headed, draped its arm across her shoulders.

She stepped around her grandparents' markers. They were carved with names heard in stories from her childhood, conjuring faces she only knew from photographs. It was difficult to miss someone you had never met. The others stones were different. They were sentinels guarding her tangible past, and her well-worn grief.

She laid her hand upon her mother's marker— *Olivia Langston Starr*—bright and new, the lettering was easy to read. And like her mother's personality, the stone felt cold, with chiseled edges sharp as flint.

"I did love you, Mother," she declared. "I should have told you more often. But you were always so occupied with running the ranch, or angry because Father was gone. Will and I missed him too you know. You were so stubborn and strict with the both of us. That's one of the reasons Will left home."

As she talked, she grazed her hand across the top of the stone, dislodging a twig and a thin layer of prairie dust. "But I guess Daddy getting killed in that stampede started it all. Will grew to hate this land and the cattle and everything that reminded him of how Father died. He wanted you to sell the ranch. Wanted us to move away and start over. But you were determined to keep Father's dream alive. No one blamed you for that, you loved him, wanted him to be proud of you. But in the process, you killed the dreams of your children. And now Will's dead too."

Tears burned her eyes, and she took a step back, her hands gripped tightly together. She felt guilty, and hadn't meant to say all those things, but the words and emotions just kept pouring out of her.

"I know things would have been different had Poppa lived. I remember when your smile could be gentle, with laughter reflected in your beautiful brown eyes. Back then, you inspired peace and happiness in the family, your warm embrace always available to drive away a little girl's childhood fears and unhappiness. But after Father left us, everything changed—you changed. A part of you died with him, and what was left was hard as hickory and uncompromising. Maybe you loved him too much."

She tried to imagine what it was like to love a man with that much passion? Would she ever know?

Ochessa had endured gut wrenching grief, but for the loss of a brother and her parents—not for a husband. Maybe that's why she never understood her mother's heartache. Losing a husband must be like losing your past and your future all in one brutal moment.

"You loved us as much as you could I guess." She gently traced her mother's name with her index finger. "It's just that sometimes, it wasn't enough. Perhaps your grief and the love you lost, was more than any woman could bear."

Tears spilled again from her eyes, and she hung her head and sobbed. The desperate little sound tumbled across the empty prairie leaving her feeling small and lonely.

Turning around, she leaned back against the headstone. "I'm sorry we were so often at odds, Mother. And I'm sorry if I disappointed you."

What would her mother think of her new plans for the ranch? Did it really matter? With Will gone too, all the decisions—old or new—were hers to make.

She stared at the sky, bright blue and never ending, and for a fleeting moment thoughts of the future replaced the sorrows of the past. What did it hold for her? The only life lesson her mother had taught her was how to be strong. No one had educated her about the softer side of life, the passionate part, the womanly part, the part a man looked for in a wife.

Turning around, she studied her father's marker. Worn away by weather and time, the edges were smoother, the lettering not so deep now. He had imparted to her the worth of the printed word, and she had learned that lesson quickly and well, devouring every book upon which she could lay her hands. She heaved a sigh. This had led to more sword-crossing with her mother. Unless a book pertained to ranching or cattle production, Olivia Langston Starr believed reading to be a waste of time.

Swiping the tears from her cheeks, Ochessa touched her fingertips to her father's stone. The moisture left a bright patch, darkening the stone to its once deep rich hue. Then it evaporated, gone in an instant, like so many things in life.

She stood between the two headstones, just as she had once stood between her parents, and she thought of Will. All alone and so far away. No matter how long she lived, no one could ever replace him in her heart, or in the world. No one would ever walk in his shoes. His shoes…

Turning, she sprinted to the house and retrieved the pair of boots she had brought back from Will's cabin in Kansas. Returning to the yard, she hurried to the woodpile, set the footwear on a stump, and with ax in hand, she wailed away at them. She had done the same for her father and mother. Destroying a loved one's footwear, a grim heartbreaking task, exemplified the finality of their death, but in some strange way it also offered healing. An act of kindness, it prevented anyone else from owning or distorting the footprints they had set upon the earth.

Each set of shoes or boots held its own story, a snippet of history from the life lived. She recalled the favorite pair belonging to her father, worn thin from use. Then there were his *special order* boots, shipped all the way from some fancy shop in New York City. He had worn them only once, to a Sunday social, complaining all the while he danced they were too tight, and he would never walk normal again. He'd also pointed out that pretty and expensive didn't always mean quality or suitability.

As bittersweet thoughts clamored around in her head, she slammed the ax down—now with anger, now with sorrow, blow after jarring blow. The job done, she set the ax aside and gathered the shredded leather, then she returned to the family plot to scatter the pieces among the headstones. Here they could mingle with the earth or become part of a nest for some creature seeking shelter. Either one a fitting tribute.

As she stared at the leather bits with tear-filled eyes, laughter and good-natured talk drifted over to her from the grub shack. Their noontime break being over, the ranch hands were heading back to their various jobs. Giving one last look at the markers delineating her life, Ochessa hurried toward the house and scrambled up the steps to the porch.

A smile sought a foothold upon her lips and failed. She tried harder, refusing to allow the men to see *the boss lady* sad and crying like a baby. It would ruin the image she worked so hard to portray.

Bone tired, the need for someone to lean upon overwhelmed her. Lame Bear tried to comfort her, but she needed more. She needed someone to hold her tight, someone to lie to her and tell her everything would be all right. Someone to fill the empty space in the bed, leaving her contented in the night, and eager to see what the day might bring.

Mental exhaustion weighed heavily too, and new doubts niggled at the back of her mind. What if she made wrong choices, ones that were irreversible? Good or bad they affected the ranch, and the people who worked for her.

So far, she'd gotten along on bluff and bluster, acting tough around the men, while ignoring the womenfolk in town who made fun of her because she dressed like a cattle wrangler and didn't care to join in their groups and games. The coming week would especially require personal stamina. For the first time, she would oversee the branding and castrating—no place for sissies. The knowledge she would never again be involved in such wretched undertakings, made the ordeal bearable.

During the evening, she continued to practice roping a bale of hay behind the barn. She would rather have spent her time learning to cook or sew or trying to remove the ever present dirt from beneath her fingernails. But garnering the respect of the men was based on what she could do, not how she looked or cooked.

Her no-nonsense mother had easily kept the cowhands in line. And they were generally peaceable around Lame Bear, although occasionally they resented taking orders from him. And last month when the payout came up a bit short, she'd instructed the foreman to promise the men a bonus if they toughed it out over the next few months. It hurt to know they stayed because of the money, and not because they believed in her ability to get the cattle to market and the ranch back on its feet.

Yet who could blame them?

Hanging on by the skin of her teeth, some days she didn't even have faith in herself. All she had left was the stubborn fortitude bequeathed to her by her mother, and big dreams inspired by her father. Grabbing the cup still sitting on the porch rail, she took a big swallow of now tepid water, and slammed the mug back down. Guess that would darn well have to be enough, for until they buried her too, she wouldn't give up.

She glanced up and spotted a hazy ribbon of dust rising through the far line of trees. Someone was coming up the trail that led from the main road to the ranch. As the lone rider came into view, the heat of recognition warmed her cheeks. Low and behold, Nic Breedlove.

She had never thought to see him again. Why would he come all the way out here? Probably to deliver some sarcastic goodbye on his way out of the territory. She smoothed her hair into place. Then annoyed by the impulse, she quickly lowered her hand to her side.

Nic rode with the ease of a man who had known many hours in the saddle. He sat straight and proud, yet relaxed. The cocky angle of his broad-brimmed hat seemed to issue a challenge, almost as if he wore it as much to make a statement as for practical purposes. She smiled recalling the concern he'd shown on the train when he thought his headgear had gone missing. He'd been as cross as a sow grizzly with a lost cub.

At the house, Nic reined to a halt.

Her position on the porch equalized their height, and she returned his stare eye to eye.

"Afternoon."

His unexpected arrival took her off guard, and she grabbed the newel post for support.

"Good afternoon, yourself." Did her voice sound as much like a mouse squeak to Nic as it did to her?

"I've come for the job," Nic said.

Ochessa hesitated only a moment. "I don't need any more ranch hands."

"Not *a* job, *the* job." Nic. retrieved the bounty poster from inside his shirt, leaned forward, and held it up in front of her face.

Of course. Naturally he would be offering a gun for hire, not a strong back for bending.

Re-folding the paper, he tucked it away in his back pocket. Several similar fliers were poking out of his saddlebag. He must have collected all the ones she tacked up in town.

"It doesn't say anything about expenses."

"That's because I don't intend to pay any."

"That should narrow down the applicants considerably." His gaze settled on her lips. "Or are you planning to offer incentive of a more personal nature?"

"Listen, Breedlove. Don't get your hopes up—or anything else. Whoever I hire can live and eat at the ranch for free. And they can stay at Will's cabin if the search takes them back to Kansas."

He seemed disappointed. She didn't care, or at least she shouldn't care. What this man thought held no consequence for her. Being a drifter, he would most likely ride out of her life as quickly and unexpectedly as he'd galloped into it.

"Well..." Nic urged the mule one step closer.

"Well, what?"

"Do I get the job or not?"

"I'm thinking." She hedged her answer and studied his attire. Obviously fast with a gun, and not afraid to use one, his lean tough body proclaimed he could hold his own physically. But the way he sometimes dressed, would he be the type to want to get his boots muddy or his hands bloody.

"As you can see," he pointed out, startling her by seeming to follow her train of thought, "I have clothes less suited to dance halls and gaming parlors, and more suited to hard work."

He did appear hale and hardy and ready for action in those tight denim pants and that light blue chambray shirt. And like a true cowboy, and not some dandy, he wore his dark blue neckerchief loose and with just the right amount of roll. She folded her arms across her chest and stood taller. "What are your qualifications?"

"Really?" While he didn't roll his eyes, he did sigh in annoyance. "Well, for starters, I've tracked poachers through the rain forests of New Guinea, fought along with the rebels in Spain, and crawled halfway across the Arabian Desert trying to depose a Sultan so evil he ate the children of his enemies." He halted, took a breath as if intending to go on, then hesitated.

Words momentarily failed her, and she just stared at him. He must be joking. Did he really think she would believe such a pack of tall tales? Yet his face was as serious as the drought of '73. If he had been to all those places, and done all those things, he seemed to have a penchant for fighting on the side of the underdog. And why not, he was the type to enjoy spitting in the face of conventionality. Regardless, if he favored underdogs, he might just be the man for the job.

Nic's mouth flattened into a line of impatience. Then with a shrug, he turned that long-eared critter of his around and made to leave.

She grabbed the porch rail and leaned out over the wood. "You're hired." Even as she spoke, she knew it was either the best idea she'd ever had or the worst.

He reined in, glanced back at her, and flashed a smile that said he hadn't really expected her to say no. "Which room's mine?" He stared past her toward the house.

"First one on the left—in the bunkhouse."

Nic wheeled his mount around and faced her full on. "Not me." His mule made a strange disgruntled sound as if it too found the suggestion astounding. "I'm no farmhand, and I don't intend to rise with the chickens. I'd sooner sleep in the barn."

Good Lord, the man argued about everything.

"Suit yourself, Breedlove." She headed toward the door to the house. "I imagine you and the bull will get along famously. You both have similar dispositions."

Chapter Eight

As the train jerked into motion, Superintendent Jonathon Thacker forced himself to relax back against the seat—the same seat in which he'd spent the long hot night trying to sleep—the same seat he would occupy for two more days following this unscheduled stop.

Pocket watch in-hand, the conductor entered the train car and the atmosphere of boredom hanging in the air slipped out the open door behind him. A rotund man, he wedged and squeezed his way down the aisle, then halted beside the row in which Jonathan sat.

"Looks like we'll be a might late arriving in Denver, Mr. Thacker." As if their day and a half delay left any question to the contrary. "Still, we were fortunate, mighty fortunate. If the engineer hadn't spotted that washout as we rounded a curve, we'd have had a full-blown catastrophe on our hands. And being a mile from that way-station—why that turned out to be a blessing for sure."

"I must agree with you there. Any chance we might make up for lost time?" Jonathan's question had been motivated by an attempt at conversation rather than belief in such an eventuality.

"It's not entirely impossible." The conductor stowed his watch and rocked back and forth on his heels. "Course there's plenty of hills and dales betwixt here and there, so just between you and me and the coal car, it ain't likely."

With an unflappable attitude, he tipped his cap and labored off to speak with another passenger.

Retrieving a limp white handkerchief from his breast pocket, Jonathon wiped the sweat from his face, his stubble of a beard snagging on the soft cotton. Usually fastidious in his appearance, today he couldn't muster the incentive to shave. At least his worst fears had not been realized. He offered his gratitude on that account, as he refolded the square of cloth and returned it to his pocket.

Originally, when the train had screeched to an unexpected halt, he'd suspected the desperado locked in the mail car had somehow engineered an escape plan. Now-a-days, criminals had agendas, and backup plans, and motives more complicated than plain old greed and orneriness. You never knew what they had up their sleeves. He figured the man he'd trailed and caught in California was no exception. But a washout had caused the disruption, not criminal intent. The conductor reported a recent flood had taken out the railroad trestle, along with the lives of several people. Sometimes Mother Nature showed less mercy than an outlaw.

Thank goodness they were up and running again. As the landscape slipped by, he leaned forward, willing the train to pick up speed. He was anxious to return home. Eager was more the word. Duty rather than choice had sent him on this trip, and he wondered how things were going back home. News from the office indicated the dark horseman had been spotted in Colorado, and the leader of this outlaw gang had been recognized as one mean-hearted killer.

Jonathan eased back in the seat and folded his arms

across his chest, forcing himself to relax. But try as he might, his mind continued running full-bore, his carnival of thoughts leapfrogging along with the fence posts flashing past the window.

He was almost thankful the outlaws had come to his territory. It saved him the trouble of tracking them down. The two Wells Fargo Company men they murdered in Kansas were friends, one old, one new. They deserved justice, and he aimed to get it for them.

Although, truth be told, recently his enthusiasm had waned a bit. He'd worked for the Company for fifteen long years, with retirement just around the corner. He intended to live to enjoy it—with no new bullet holes. Wells Fargo had sold off the passenger transportation business, but the stage express line, and the detective agency were operational, and both departments offered more than ample opportunity for hazardous duty.

Good at what he did, he'd been shuffled around to troubleshoot dire-strait outposts all over the map. Well, he liked Colorado, and he wanted to stay there. He had a wife and two children and they liked it there too. He didn't see them often enough, but that would change when he started drawing a pension.

But first things first. Why hadn't the outlaws headed for Mexico? They had stolen three items in the Wells Fargo hold up—a large ruby, some high-ranking documents, and the lumber mill payroll. Why were they reportedly hanging around? Jonathan couldn't shake the feeling he was waiting for the other boot to drop. He had to admit, he found the conundrum intriguing.

With the sheriff laid up, and the deputy less than helpful, the job of tracking down these misfits fell to him. Retrieving the telegram from his pocket, he studied the missive he'd received, wondering just who was this fellow named Breedlove? Just another dog in the fight? Or a man who could help even the odds?

****

Reno studied the disgruntled faces of the men who stood between him and the door.

"I said we wait. You all knew the rules before you signed on. They'll be no changing them now."

"But it's been nigh on two weeks since we robbed that stage," Little Davy protested, "and I'm ready to make tracks."

"Yeah," another man piped up, "we got the payroll. Let's divvy it up."

"Least-wise, that little bastard back in Kansas got his due," someone sneered. "Thought he could steal from us and get away with it. Too bad we never found the ruby though."

Or, Reno thought, the documents, worth ten times more than the gem.

"You made him pay all right," Reno admitted. "But seeing as you killed him, the authorities will be itching to stretch our necks for two murders now, not just one. We lay low or risk a rope."

A momentary hush settled over the men, followed by false-hearted jeers of bravado professing they weren't afraid of no law-dogs, and they weren't worried about dying. But Reno knew better. Even the lowliest creature wanted to stay alive.

Survival remained the number one instinct in any species. That's what kept a man moving when he was so tired and hungry he couldn't see straight. And that's what made a man persist in hiding out when he was sick of his own stink, and the bad company he was forced to keep. They might be approaching the limit of this last stage. Soon these sidewinders would be ready to risk their freedom for their sanity.

"The ruby is nearby, it showed up at the shootin' match in town." Reno nodded toward Lanny Dalton.

Lanny was the only man in the group he trusted to leave the pack for reconnaissance. The young gun had done a good job of ferreting out information during his few covert trips to the city.

"Far as we know, it's the one we lost," the lanky young man said, as he stepped forward. "Turns out the gal bandying the gem around, was sister to the Kansas sodbuster what got in our way."

A buzz filled the air as the outlaws pushed and shoved this bit of news around the room a few times.

"Well how'd it get here?" Somebody called out.

"And what about Harlan?" another man chimed in, rendering the first question pretty much forgotten. "Why ain't we heard from him yet?"

"You can quit waiting on Harlan. He won't be coming back."

Reno knew someone had been tailing them since they crossed the Mississippi. After taking their revenge on that kid, and running roughshod through Monotony, the gang had moved on, leaving Harlan behind to track down and stop the man. His friends back East had warned him an old adversary was back in the country—it had to be him, older now and smarter, and they said the spitting image of his father.

But Harlan was long overdue, and by all reckoning dead because the man Lanny saw eating at the restaurant with that ruby toting gal, fit the description of the face from his past.

"What happened to Harlan?" Shorty persisted.

Might as well tell them the truth. Maybe it would stop them bellyaching about hiding out for a while. "He met his Maker back in Monotony." All chaos broke loose at this eye-opener. "So we continue to lay low." No one heard his last order over the ruckus.

You'd think these no accounts would be glad for a bit of breathing room, a respite from looking over their shoulder. No more wondering where their next meal was coming from or where they might throw down their bedroll for the night. Too late, Reno realized the latest revelation had the potential to be a dividing factor as well as a unifying one.

"I agree with Davy," Clive Brewster put in. "We settle up now and go our separate ways."

Things were getting out of hand in a hurry, before long he might just have a full-fledged rebellion on his hands.

"Simmer down," Reno yelled, again no one seemed to notice.

It angered him that they didn't think he could outsmart the authorities. He'd made a career out of doing just that—in the war and now as a civilian. But let them think what they would. These dumb gallows-birds thought this was just another job, something to tide them over until the next scheme, or until they took a bullet. For Reno, this was the final payoff. Soon he'd be living like a king, with a nice steady income. They didn't know the half of what was at stake here, and he intended to keep it that way.

As they blew off steam, he considered the rabble with whom he'd chosen to ride. They were feral hounds, dishonest as the day was long at midsummer. And while they were superficially loyal to whoever fed them, they were also liable to bite the hand delivering the meal. Still, his army of renegades provided good protection, and he needed them awhile longer.

"Anybody leaves now they give up their share of the take." That got their attention. "And they better spend the rest of their life watching their back, because I'll be right behind them." Except for Lanny, he could out gun them all. And even blind drunk he could outthink every one of these yahoos, and they knew it.

"Now get out." He took a menacing step forward, his hand resting on the butt of his revolver.

An uneasy hush permeated the cabin like a bad smell, and the men glanced sideways at one another. Overlooking disobedience wasn't Reno's strong suite. By silent mutual agreement, the outlaws held their tongues and shambled out the door.

Reno kicked it shut behind them.

Chapter Nine

Hiring himself out to Ochessa had been a bad idea.
No. It had been a terrible idea.

Teeth clenched, Nic trudged through the forest,
Sadie following behind. The smell of pine filled the air,
and Columbine flowers, the color of a summer sky,
nodded in the breeze. But thoughts of Ochessa clouded
his sensibilities, and Mother Nature's gifts didn't come
close to capturing his attention.

He stepped over a fallen log and scrubbed a gloved
hand across the nape of his neck—even the rasp of
worn leather didn't turn his thoughts in a new direction.
Could anything?

Over the past few days, he'd kept his eye on
Ochessa, fighting his baser instincts not to do more than
just look at her. She had reduced him to a mooning
adolescent—trapped in a full-fledged, hungry male
body. Now as he returned to the ranch, every grinding
footfall brought him closer to the woman who addled
his brain.

If he was smart, he'd be hightailing it in the
opposite direction.

Hoping to get a line on the desperados, he'd spent
the better part of the day prowling the far woods.
Rumor had it, the dark horsemen were holed up
somewhere in the foothills, well-hidden—yet
conveniently close. Other than a few game trails, he'd

found nothing suspicious.

In an effort to delay his return to the ranch, he slowed his pace. Sadie knew a shady stall and fresh hay weren't far off, and she gave him a hearty nudge from behind. She wanted to go faster.

"Dang it, mule. Don't you start giving me a hard time too."

As he continued to dawdle, Sadie huffed out her irritation. Then smart enough to know when to leave well enough alone, she nuzzled his neck.

Nic's feelings for Ochessa had come at him full-blown. He couldn't even say why he found her so captivating. True she was uncommonly pretty, but not beautiful in the classic sense, and he'd certainly known females far richer. Something about Chessy Cat's brave struggle to survive regardless of circumstance touched his heart. Yet tough as she pretended to be, she aroused his protective instincts. It was something he couldn't define. Whatever the phenomenon, it made his brain soft and other body parts hard. And seeing, yet not touching was driving him mad, or more precisely, making him mad.

Visions of what they would do together played over in his mind, each rendition more interesting than the last. His body and emotions were out of control, and he didn't like it one bit. It felt more disconcerting than delirium from Panama fever.

Approaching the barn from the north, he instinctively avoided the dip in the path which always managed to hold water no matter how dry the weather. The Rising Starr ranch almost felt like home. He'd become too familiar with the lay of the land, knew the placement of each boulder and sage bush, even the location of the closest prairie dog holes. Without looking, he knew the view to the east seemed to go on forever, and the white capped and rugged mountains towered in the west.

Skirting the tack house, he paused to study the corral. Crowded with ranch hands and bellowing cattle, the usual calm had become a downright beehive of activity.

Where was she?

As if drawn by a lifetime of familiarity, his gaze settled on Ochessa. Nearly sundown, he knew she'd been up since dawn, yet she continued to help with the branding and castrating, pulling her weight, never willing to call it a day before the last man.

Ochessa was a woman of extremes—extremely distracting, extremely desirable, and extremely hazardous to his solitary existence.

He observed the men and activity, but his line of sight drifted back to Ochessa, and without meaning to he memorized the soft curve of her cheek, and the proud arch of her neck.

During his short stay at the ranch, he'd seen many sides of her. She could ride a horse with the grace of a ballerina, obviously outshoot any man, and one night he'd spied her bottle-feeding an infuriatingly reluctant calf with the compassion of a protective angel. A wagon load of personalities fighting to survive in one tawny cat-like package.

It shouldn't matter. No reason to become involved with her darn ranch and bald-faced cows. Yet he remained—watching and waiting and wanting, surviving on expectation rather than reality. It was wrong, all wrong.

His own plans deserved top priority. Watching over Ochessa like some quixotic knight-in-leather armor, allowed her needs and concerns to become more important than his own, which complicated his opportunity for revenue and revenge.

****

Hiring Nic had been a bad idea. No. It had been a terrible idea.

Ochessa glanced up from the branding fire. Nic stood staring at her through the haze of smoke, his gaze sliding over her like thick warm syrup, the same feeling melted through the core of her body. Everywhere she turned she ran into him.

Releasing the hogtied calf, she straightened, removed her hat, and wiped her brow against the sleeve of her shirt. Lately, she feared to leave the sanctuary of her own house—afraid to come upon him unexpectedly—afraid to be alone with him.

Why was he still here anyway? He should be in Kansas gathering clues or something, not lingering underfoot—turning her thoughts from sound logic to muddled fantasy.

She swatted her hat against her thigh, dislodging the accumulated dust, then settled the battered felt back upon her head. By day or by night, she couldn't concentrate. Not while she knew he was as close as the barn. Not when she recalled their train ride and dinner, and the kissing and touching.

Ochessa glanced again in Nic's direction. He was gone. She breathed a sigh of relief. What was the matter with her anyway? Simple animal desire—that's all. Women felt needs just like men. At least she thought other women felt like this—wet with anticipation and carnal urges, throbbing with a hunger making her willing to risk just about everything to find satisfaction.

It would pass. It always had. But with Nic, surviving these feelings seemed to be taking a record breaking amount of time. Something was different. She'd never felt this way during her exploratory adventure with Dooley Wainright. That's when she learned love and sex were two different things, a hard lesson—she wouldn't be fooled again.

The experience hadn't involved true feelings beyond momentary pleasure, and thank the Lord hadn't involved any offspring. When Dooley up and married another girl, one he had gotten pregnant, Ochessa had been torn between anger at having been two-timed, and relief she hadn't been saddled with the cheating bum and his progeny.

At least the philandering Dooley had done the right thing. When the Mayor's son got a barmaid in the same condition, he denied even knowing the mother-to-be. Bereft and consumed by shame and guilt, the girl had killed herself. That had shown Ochessa all she needed to know about men. They were out for only one thing—pleasing themselves. And they offered no promises and granted no quarter.

It might be hard getting along without a man, but it sounded harder getting along with one. Although she had to admit, Nic Breedlove came close to making her doubt such a resolution—another misdeed to add to his list of offenses.

With a sigh she watched the last animal scramble to his feet, tear through the chutes, and head back toward his mother. Dog tired, she felt as if she'd been dragged behind a plow. Tugging off her leather work gloves, she massaged the small of her back. On occasion, the ranch she loved could take its toll. More often than not, it nearly stomped her into the very ground she was trying to save. But knowing the ranch hands were watching, she stood tall, and tried not to limp as she walked to the edge of the corral and climbed through the rails.

"Good job men. Lame Bear has this month's disbursements as well as the bonus I promised." The stud fees for Lucky Starr were already coming in handy.

The corral turned so silent you could hear the dust settle. Now what? Where were the usual yahoos and a good-natured shoving and scuffling as the men gathered around to collect their pay? After all, it was just a job to them. They didn't care if her struggle had become life or death. They didn't realize if worse came to worse, she would die with the ranch because her soul would surely die without it.

Hat in hand the foreman stepped up to speak to her. "The men wanted me to tell you they could wait another week or so for the bonus money if'n it would help."

Gratitude sprang to life and welled inside of her. Then the feeling waned as she wondered if Nic's presence had prompted their unexpected show of loyalty. Maybe they thought he was in charge of things now. Already he'd managed to win their acceptance. Even the grizzled old cowhands who had *seen it all* held him in high esteem. They invited Nic to their card games by night, and spoke about him and his exploits by day. She resented the awe she heard in their voices, resented Nic winning their respect strictly on the basis of being blatantly footloose and reportedly fearless.

"They've come a long way in accepting you as the boss," the foreman added, taking her by surprise. "Especially after the shootin' match," he said with a wink.

She gave a little laugh of amusement. Leave it to men to render judgment based on a show of skill with a deadly weapon. "Thank the men for their kind offer, but there's no need to wait."

The foreman informed the men, and the commotion she'd been anticipating finally broke loose.

She walked on, proud of the day's work she'd put in, man's work, but she had done it. She had shown them all. That knowledge made her back hurt a little less, and being so darn tired, maybe she would sleep well tonight. If she did, it would be the first time since setting eyes on Nic.

She headed toward Lucky's corral, to say good night and watch the evening shadows slip into place. But rounding the corner of the barn, she stopped short, and her heart felt as if it did the same.

Naked to the waist, and bent over the horse trough, his sculpted muscles standing out in sharp relief, Nic scooped handfuls of water over his head. A growl escaped him as he straightened to his full height, and slicked back the dripping mane of dark hair. Arms still raised, he met her gaze, as the excess water trickled happily across his bare chest.

Involuntarily she sucked in a deep breath. The distance between them felt charged with lightning, thunder pounding in her brain, leaving the rest of the world dead silent.

A look of surprise flickered across Nic's face. His

muscles flexed and bulged as he lowered his arms to his sides. "Good evening, *boss*." He emphasized the last word as if were a personal joke.

She swallowed hard, and fought to find her voice. "Time's a wasting, Breedlove. Why are you still hanging around the ranch? Shouldn't you be out earning your keep?"

"Well, we all have our own way of doing things, and my way is usually different from the norm."

"Why doesn't that surprise me?"

Retrieving his hat, he carefully dislodged a thistle from the battered brim then settled the coveted headgear upon his head. "What *would* surprise you, Ochessa?" He studied her with an expression that sizzled and danced through her like water on a hot griddle.

"Not seeing you every time I turn around would be a good start."

"You're not very good at lying."

She nudged a dried up cow pie with the toe of her boot. "Maybe not. But I am good at recognizing a load of bull when it comes my way."

He gave a deep chuckle, and reached for the shirt dangling from the water pump. "Sounds like you've been on both ends of the shovel."

"No more than anyone else, I guess."

He stood his ground, casually shucking into the article of clothing, his movements so sure, no wasted motion, no hesitation. Did he live his life the same? Taking what he wanted when and where he found it? She imagined him wanting her, taking her, and as his gaze slid down the front of her body, memories of their stolen passion again flared hot in the pit of her stomach.

His eyes brightened as if the same thoughts held him transfixed. Then his expression hardened, and the gleam in his eyes turned to flint. "I should have some information for you soon. I'll be out of your way come morning."

The fluttering in her belly turned to a panic. His leaving disturbed her more than running into him at every turn. Yet, it was what she wanted, wasn't it? Confusion had her at a loss as to how to respond or how to proceed. It felt as if she'd captured a wild creature, and now before ever knowing what made him so intriguing, so unique, she had to set him free.

His mouth softened into a mocking smile. "I'll be back in a day or two. I'm only going to Denver."

Apparently her face was an open book, and now she felt the fool.

"Don't hurry on my account. I was only worried Lucky might miss you."

****

After supper at the grub shack that night, Nic sought refuge in the corner of the barn he'd claimed as his own. He was tired, but couldn't sleep, and instead he paced the worn floorboards. Earlier, when he'd been washing up, it had been all he could do not to close the distance between himself and Ochessa. It had been all he could do not to sweet talk her into his bed, and take what he wanted so badly.

Eying him over the stall door, Sadie shook her head as if to help him clear such thoughts from his mind. And that's exactly what he should do.

"Got a minute to spare?"

Hand hovering over the butt of his revolver, Nic spun around.

Lame Bear stood just inside the walk-through door. Even Sadie hadn't heard the old man's approach. "If you hurt her, it will be the last mistake you make in this lifetime."

At least Lame Bear didn't mince words. His manner remained calm, the expression in his eyes almost sympathetic. He didn't seem angry, but the set of his jaw indicated he was dead serious.

In an effort to appear casual, Nic crossed his arms over his chest and leaned against a wooden upright. "Assuming you're speaking of Miss Ochessa. I have only good intentions where she is concerned."

Lame Bear's eyes narrowed, and he stepped forward. "Good intentions are an honorable thing, often forgotten in the heat of battle—or passion."

Silently they stared at one another, weighing each other's strength of purpose. Nic lowered his arms to his sides. "I'll keep your words in mind."

"It would be wise to do so. She acts tough, and in many ways her strength is equal to any man's. But she is still a woman in here." Lame Bear raised a fist to his chest, letting it come to rest over his heart. "Her father entrusted me with her happiness, and while I live, so shall it be."

"I understand."

Lame Bear gave a nod of satisfaction. "I hope that you do."

"She won't rest until the man who killed her brother is brought to justice." Nic's voice was matter of fact. "That might prove more of a danger to her than associating with me."

"Life holds many dangers, some we cannot avoid."

"That's true enough." Nic recalled the risks he'd

taken, and the near misses he'd survived. "Maybe the best we can hope for are good people at our side to share the journey."

"Paths cross for a reason," Lame Bear agreed, "but they can also divide without warning."

"There are never any guarantees, only promises. And I try hard to keep mine."

"I am glad to hear that." With a steely-eyed stare, Lame Bear gave a slight nod, and turned to leave. Although tempered with age, his bearing remained proud, his retreat as silent as had been his approach. The straw hardly rustled beneath his moccasin clad feet when he crossed the open space and disappeared out the door.

What would it take to earn the friendship of such a man? What would incur his wrath seemed pretty obvious.

As the twilight deepened, Nic stood inside Sadie's stall, brushing her shaggy coat, recanting what had just happened as if she hadn't been there and seen it all for herself. But as usual she had the good grace to twitch an ear in his direction, pretending to listen.

Once he finished brushing her, he gave his best gal a handful of grain and some fresh straw for bedding. Then he flopped down on the makeshift pallet across the way, and stared up at the rafters—the occasional swig of red-eye the only interruption to his silent soul-searching.

With the arrival of true darkness came the comfort of concealment. The stars winked on, and a shaft of moonlight speared in through the open door of the haymow. Nic glanced over at the bull.

"What is it about her, Lucky, that makes me want

to howl like a coyote and kick up my heels like a yearling in a green meadow?"

Lucky snorted and butted his head against the wall.

"Easy for you to say," Nic muttered, "you've got more willing females than you know what to do with—and no strings attached."

Of course Lucky also had a ring in his nose, by which a woman led him around. Not Nic. He wasn't about to perform like a trained bear. He answered to no one other than himself.

Suddenly a spark of misgiving smoldered in the far reaches of his mind. Even to his own ears his *go it alone* edict sounded like the rambling justification of a lonely fool. He was changing, and for the first time, he was uncertain regarding the direction of his life.

Draping one arm across his eyes, he rooted around in search of a more comfortable position. A good night's sleep was what he needed. Things would look better in the morning—most likely.

Chapter Ten

Ochessa stood in the yard and stared at the barn. No one had seen Nic ride out this morning, but he must be gone, it was nearly ten o'clock.

Heading toward the hulking red building, she tried not to think of the structure as the domain of the man who drove her to distraction. After all it was her property. Yet Nic had an uncanny way of fitting in, of seeming comfortable regardless of his surroundings, of taking charge without expectation or permission.

Was that an acquired trait? If so, it was one she'd yet to master. Maybe he'd just been born with too much charm, and the ability to politely make everyone else's' life seem pale in comparison to his own.

"Men," she scoffed, walking on. Life seemed a game to them, and to survive in their world, you had to play by their rules. But if you dared to play the game too well, as she had with Eustace, their almighty pride got bruised and they resented you. She needed a man strong enough to let her be herself. One who would accept her as an equal rather than always trying to be her better. A man like Nic Breedlove.

Nic was the kind of man soldiers followed into battle, even though the odds meant certain death. She hugged herself against the mid-morning chill, and quickened her pace. Nic was the kind of man no woman should love. One day he would ride out and never look back, never give a second thought as to what he might be leaving behind—she mustn't let it be her.

Yet, Saints preserve her, she couldn't stop thinking about him, and flirting with Nic equaled flirting with danger personified. Nic, a fleeting illusion at best, offered hot enjoyment for the moment, and cold regret forever. Still knowing this, she couldn't quell her attraction to him.

So what? Why shouldn't she enjoy the comfort a man could offer? Lately she'd been compelled to take on all manner of male responsibility. Why not some male attitude regarding the pleasures in life? She wouldn't expect honorable intentions or romance. Certainly not love. Any shared intimacy between them would simply appease the hunger, slake the thirst. And when Nic eventually sought someone new, or wandered off, she would be left mentally intact. No pain, no new wounds to heal beside the scars of grief already suffered.

It sounded like a good plan. Or she could continue to take cold baths, and ignore the handsome no account altogether. The last option was certainly the wisest.

Slipping through the barn door, she headed for the tool bin and the roll of chicken wire needed to repair the fence around her flower patch. As her eyes adjusted to the dimness she froze.

Nic hadn't left. For crying out loud, he wasn't even awake. Sprawled across the makeshift bed, his lanky fully-clothed body dwarfed the pallet. A spasm of yearning stuttered through her, and she imagined his eyes closed in ecstasy rather than sleep.

With a supreme effort, she studied the surrounding area rather than Nic's tempting body. His precious hat lay within easy reach, his saddle and packs piled along the wall on the other side of him.

She crept closer. He needed a shave, just like the night she'd come across him in Monotony. She remembered touching his cheek while he lay unconscious in the Pullman car. His scar appeared to be healing nicely. And how about the night they'd shared dinner in town. When she licked her lips, it elicited the taste of him, not the food. They'd only known one another for a matter of weeks, yet every shared minute remained intensely vivid in her mind, making their time together seem much longer.

Her gaze drifted the length of him then back to his face—so innocent in sleep. She watched the gentle rise and fall of his broad chest—a nicely muscled chest. A chest she had pressed her ear to after he'd been shot.

She needed to get out of here, pronto. Turning to leave, she spotted a sheaf of folded papers peeking from beneath the flap of one of Nic's panniers. Were they the legal documents Will had mentioned? She couldn't shake the feeling he knew more about her brother's death than he'd revealed so far.

Employing every skill Lame Bear had taught her, she advanced. Then dropping to her knees, she reached across Nic, snagged the edge of one missive between the tips of two fingers, and slid it free. As she tightened her grip, the paper crackled.

Nic lurched to wakefulness. With one arm wrapped her waist, he wrestled her sideways, his free arm now drawn back, his hand balled into a fist ready to let fly with a punch. The document forgotten, she threw up her arm to block the attack.

Recognition drove the dangerous expression from

Nic's face, and he lowered his arm. His upper body relaxed, but other parts of his anatomy came to attention, ready for action of another nature.

"Good morning, boss," he drawled, pressing his hips closer. "I planned to stop up at the big house before I left, but I must admit I prefer your way of saying goodbye to mine."

He angled his mouth across hers. Mind reeling, she swore she saw stars, but as surprise waned and indignation took its place, she twisted her head to one side, suffering a momentary pang of regret at the loss of warmth

"Let me go you dimwit."

His expression shifted from playful to dead serious. "I warned you before about stealing into a man's bed and not expecting consequences."

Imagining what those consequences might be, a whimper escaped her, and she fought the impulse to find out for sure.

Nic's gaze slid from her face to her chest. Glancing down, she gasped in surprise. The top two buttons on her blouse had ripped off, and with each panting breath, her scantily covered breasts bounced up and down under Nic's nose. He surveyed the cleavage revealed, his warm breath streaming across her neck, exciting flesh already on fire.

In a useless attempt to remedy her plight, she held her breath until the world around her spun at a crazy angle. She couldn't last. Angling her head back, she exhaled then tried to breathe normally, but the mesmerizing expression in Nic's eyes rendered her immobile. Like a deer cornered by a wolf, she resigned herself to his mercy—big mistake.

"The devil take me, I can't resist you a second time." Capturing her lips, he kissed her hard, then soft, then hard again.

This is the moment you've been waiting for, the voice in the back of her brain taunted. *Give in to the feeling. Just don't let him take more than you're willing to lose.*

****

Nic didn't just want more, he wanted it all, and as he shifted to one side he settled his hand at Ochessa's waist, cradling her closer. She melted at his touch then shuddered, never slackening the demanding exploration of her hands upon his body.

Breaching the leather skirt, he skimmed his fingers upward along the smooth curve of her naked thigh. He couldn't get at her fast enough. He wanted to leave his mark on her, let the world know she belonged to him, if only for a moment. And he wanted to satisfy the need in both of them. He could feel the longing in her and taste the hunger.

Ochessa buried her face in the crook of his neck, her tongue now playing over his ear. Like spontaneous combustion, desire flamed out of control, sending him running wild, not caring if he headed for the edge of a cliff at a full gallop.

But something about her enthusiasm seemed desperate, and that made him sad. It seemed as if she was afraid to take it slow, afraid to look him in the eye and enjoy the ride. She battled against him as if to punish him for making her feel so good. Or was she angry at herself? What difference did it make? He'd never before questioned why a woman came to his bed. Why should he care?

As their lips met in fevered kisses, Lame Bear's warning flashed through his mind, followed by sobering visions of every Indian torture known to man in North America. Again, he didn't care. He would suffer any forthcoming torment to relieve the current torture haranguing him right now. His body overruled his brain, leaving nothing to quell the frenzy ignited by the feel of Ochessa's warm and willing body beneath his hands.

Every instinct for survival warned him to stop while he could. If he tasted her fully, Ochessa would be a powerful addiction, an obsession from which he could not simply walk away. He would be domesticated, like Lucky, with a ring in his nose. This thought scared him more than Lame Bear's warning.

Coming to his senses he grabbed her upper arms and forced her away from his chest. She struggled to remain close, to sustain the heat radiating between them.

"Ochessa." He shook her, and her eyelids fluttered open. Then she glanced around as if trying to discern the reason for his abrupt change of heart.

Gently, he set her aside. As she lay upon his lonely pallet, her mouth seductively swollen, she seemed a beautiful phantasm conjured in a dream, and his good intensions wavered. Then fighting the urge to reach for her again, he gained his feet and stood staring down at her.

Panting and wild-eyed she sat up, hands splayed across the front of her body. The pagan expression of wanting still bloomed on her cheeks, reddening her lips to the color of ripe berries.

Lord above, he wished she would adjust her skirt

and cover those slim enticing legs—alabaster legs, hidden away from the sun like a rare treasure—a treasure more important to him than the reward for the ruby? Or the answer held by the documents?

"I'm sorry. I shouldn't have let this happen."

He reached down and offered her his hand. She slapped it aside, and lurched to her feet. Her tawny eyes brightened to a predatory glow, as confusion transform into anger. Instinctively he took a step back. This might be the first time in history where uncommon restraint incurred a woman's fury.

"Why did you stop? I wanted more." She sounded like a petulant child denied a promised sweet. But then he suspected she'd grown accustomed to having her own way around the ranch.

"You're my boss. It's not smart to mix business with pleasure."

"Pleasure. I've enjoyed more satisfaction breaking two year olds."

He gave a bark of laughter. Even in a verbal confrontation Chessy Cat always came out swinging.

Stepping forward he seized a thick handful of her unruly hair. "I like to take my time when I make love to a woman. You seemed in a great hurry." Her eyes widened at that bit of information. "And," he added, "being used like a stud bull and then sent back to work isn't gonna work for me."

Knocking his arm away, she tore her hair from his grasp. "You lowdown, arrogant... No problem about the work conflict. You're fired."

She turned to leave.

He gasped—but not at her words.

The heel of her boot crushed down on his hat,

ripping lose the band, and sorely wounding the brim.

Chapter Eleven

On her way out of the barn, Ochessa stiff-armed the door. The shock of pain went all the way up to her shoulder. Head high, her hands now clenched into fists, she stalked toward the house, and let loose with a menacing sound.

She'd never been so humiliated in her life. To have one's amorous advances rebuffed was a humbling experience. How could Nic be so cruel? She stumbled over a rock, and cursed. Was he watching? She wouldn't give him the satisfaction of looking back.

Why had Nic turned her down? She'd offered to let him sample the sweets without paying the pie man. Wasn't that what men liked, what men wanted? She pressed the back of her hand to one cheek. It felt hot as black rock at high noon.

And what about *her* behavior? She hadn't been able to keep her hands off of him. It had never occurred to her he wouldn't feel the same.

Her knees almost buckled at the memory of his touch upon her bare skin, his lusty groans inspiring sensations she'd never dreamed existed. A river of wanting had pounded through her, sweeping her away, and she sure had dived in headfirst. But then he'd stopped, and apologized as if he'd made a big mistake, an error in judgment. How infuriating. She hadn't expected commitment, or caring, or even kindness. On the other hand she hadn't expected coldhearted rejection. It hurt less to believe misguided noble intentions spurred his actions, yet the idea didn't seem in keeping with Nic's *all for one, and that one was him* attitude.

Glancing up, she noticed three ranch hands standing in the shade of a nearby cottonwood. As she marched past, they dared to let loose with a few good-natured hoots. She shot a glare in their direction, one with potential to kill a coyote at ten paces. Realizing their error, the expression on their faces withered like the fallen leaves.

"If lightning struck that tree, it would kill three men about to draw final pay for dawdling. Get back to work."

Like spooked cattle, they snapped to attention, and then fled in different directions.

Great. By nightfall everyone at the Rising Starr would think Nic had succeeded in having his way with the boss woman. He'd be the cock of the walk, and she'd look like a pushover for a hard body and a handsome face—and none of it would be true.

Striding on, she scowled all the harder, and shoved the tail of her tattered blouse into the waist band of her skirt.

He sure had a high opinion of himself. "Stud bull, my ass," she gritted. Although she had to admit what she'd felt beneath his denim trousers qualified him as some kind of stud. He'd wanted her all right. But he'd said he liked to take his time when he made love to a woman—a thought which simultaneously fostered curiosity and alarm. Going slow allowed too much time for thinking rather than doing. She didn't want that, didn't want to think about sharing the moment, only giving Nic what he wanted and taking what she needed. She knew it would be the only way to survive being with him.

Her lips flattened into a grim line. She supposed all the blame didn't fall on Nic. She'd acted the foolish female. Now she could be angry with herself as well, and maybe it was all for the better. She didn't dare risk growing attached to anyone. If things went wrong, another dose of heartache, on top of her concerns for the future, would be more than anyone could handle. Too bad she couldn't lock up her heart in the safety deposit box along with the ruby.

Besides, what did it matter now? Since she'd fired him, Nic would soon be gone for good. A pang of loneliness, struck deep. She would miss the promise of adventure in his eyes. She had to admit, when Nic held her in his arms, it had felt good—really good. His embrace, so strong and solid, offered protection and shelter, two things she didn't even know she had been craving.

Oh, to hell with Nic—to hell with all men.

Reaching the ranch house, she fled up the front steps, escaping into the cool dim interior. Slamming the door shut at her back, she leaned against the wood, her breathing slowed, and her heart rate followed suit. Now she felt safe, but from what? The world in general or Nic?

She headed to her bedroom to change her blouse. She shouldn't have fired Nic. Should have handled his rejection with a laugh, or at least an attempt at nonchalance.

Now she'd have to find another bounty hunter.

****

Urging Sadie into a loping gallop, Nic headed for Denver. Yet try as he might, he couldn't outrun his thoughts.

The faster he rode the more clearly he realized the seriousness of what he and Ochessa had almost done. Leaving her warm and willing arms had been difficult, to say the least, but calling a halt to their lusting had been the right thing to do. And that's what it felt like, lusting—not making love. It had been too rough, too animal-like to be labeled anything gentler. Not that lusting and baying like a hound didn't have its place.

Ears back, Sadie danced to one side. Nic slowed their pace. No use taking things out on his only friend. As if to make sure he understood her prior displeasure, the big mule kicked up her heels twice before settling into a purposeful walk.

"Okay, okay, no need to boil over. We'll take it slow from here on in."

That's the same thing he needed to do with Ochessa. Take it slow. Or better yet, stay away all together. A man lost his edge when he had a woman on his mind. And keeping the edge could mean the difference between life and death, especially going up against a man like Reno Benteen.

The leader of the dark horsemen, a cruel demon from Nic's past, should never have been given a reprieve from prison, and would not have save for President Hayes and the Compromise of '77. Stipulated there in, a handful of Rebel prisoners were to be granted pardon. Some of those men may have deserved mercy—not Reno. His atrocities were many, and he was an officer, not rank and file. For him to even be considered for exoneration smelled of skullduggery. Now, free to prowl, Reno wouldn't take kindly to anyone getting in his way, a proposition Nic relished, but one that spelled danger for Ochessa.

Ochessa... Pussycat eyes, with a come-hither tilt, popped into his mind, and he nearly took the wrong fork in the road.

"See there, Sadie," he proclaimed, directing the mule over a rough bit of terrain to get back on track. "The woman befuddles me. And befuddlement leads to saying and doing things better left unsaid and undone."

Even the fragrance of her skin turned cold clear logic to hot sweet madness, while unbidden thoughts of her followed him like a shadow—his desires dreamlike and always beyond reach.

Her rather straightforward albeit desperate approach to sex had come as a surprise. Frantically seizing what he would have freely given, she seemed a lost little girl, daring him to make her feel like a woman. Too bad the chance of again enjoying her company seemed so unlikely. Of course, he'd always relied on beating the odds.

****

Reaching Denver, Nic headed directly for the mercantile.

Whatever the future held, the immediate present demanded he procure a decent hat. His attempt at reviving the mangled John B had been less than a success. In the future, he doubted this currant poor specimen would even earn a backup position, but it would have to do for now.

"Good day." A wizened old man peered at him from behind the store counter. "What might I do for you today, sir?" He eyed Nic as if the reason was obvious.

"I need a new hat, one of Mr. Stetson's best."

"I'm sorry, I don't have that particular brand in stock. We have many other fine samples from which you may choose." The shopkeeper pointed toward a shelf piled high with hats of various color, material, and quality.

"Nope. It's gotta be a Stetson." Nic refused to lower his standard in headgear because of price, availability, or the cruel misstep of some female.

"I see. An excellent choice of course. On occasion they include some in the regular delivery, but generally I'm afraid that would be a special order."

"A Stetson *is* special, and worth the trouble."

Giving the man the necessary information, and to prevent the shopkeeper from raising the price upon delivery, Nic paid in advance. Too bad about having to wait.

He exited the shop, and leaving Sadie tied out front, he headed for Wells Fargo, & Company on foot. As he walked, Nic ran his hands along the curved edge of his hat, encouraging the brim back into its original shape. It had little effect, and he wondered if Ochessa hated men's hats in general or just his. Entering the office, he snatched it off his head, reluctant to allow any up-close and personal viewing.

"Has Mr. Thacker returned from California?"

"Yes, sir," the lad at the front desk replied, "just last night. He's in his office. I'll inform him you're here."

"Thank you, I'd appreciate it."

As the young man followed through, Nic kept an

eye on the front door and on the other men—most likely lawyers. Projecting an image of indifference, he leaned against the desk and idly toyed with his hat. Although he hadn't recently tempted the boundaries of authority, along with law-dogs, legal-beagles tended to make him uneasy.

"Mr. Thacker will see you now." The boy gestured toward the door. "Go right in."

Jonathan Thacker's office, a study in planned chaos, featured a wall of shelves spilling over with books on various subjects. Other tomes littered the top of a big oak desk. Another wall held wanted posters, tacked up at various angles in a seemingly random order. A large easel, off to the right, held a pad of paper covered with diagrams, maps, and other supposedly pertinent doodles.

The glass front display cabinet, labeled *Case Closed*, occupied a coveted space by the window and was the only well-organized square footage in the entire room. Paper folders, neatly compiled, were precisely labeled and dated. It seemed Thacker's mind could only reach a semblance of calm once a job had been completed, and the criminal he sought occupied a jail cell or a grave.

Tall and slim, with a full head of gray hair and a clean-shaven face, the man stood to greet Nic.

"Have a seat," he offered, as they shook hands.

"Thank you." Nic eased into a chair on the near side of the desk. Thacker returned to his.

"What can you tell me about the dark horsemen?" Nic asked, before Thacker could fire off a question of his own.

Thacker gave a wry smile as if aware Nic had beat

him to the punch. "They're evil on horseback, and each one would as soon kill a man as look at him. They don't trust anyone, not even each other, and they fear and answer to only one person—Reno Benteen."

Even after all these years, hearing the name spoken aloud put a knot in Nic's gut, and his hand itched to go for his gun. He'd been out of the country for nearly ten years, crossing swords with thugs and assassins in Turkey and Montenegro. But this villain always waited in the back of his mind. Fate now pushed the wretched good-for-nothing to the forefront.

"Folks still calling him Captain Benteen?"

The detective's gaze narrowed. He leaned forward and placed his forearms on the desk. "Yes. A remnant of faded glory from the war when he fought for the South. I take it you're acquainted with Benteen better than some folks."

"I'm even more familiar with the bloody nightmare the man leaves in his wake."

"You fought for the South then," Thacker ventured.

"Yes. You?"

"The North."

They stared at one another, and Nic became momentarily lost in a place only visited on rare occasion, and with great care. The wounds spawned by the devastation of war generally healed in a man's body, but they tended to fester a lifetime in a man's soul.

Thacker broke the silence. "Why the interest in Benteen? After all, it's been a long time, and you once fought on the same side."

"Uniform notwithstanding, we were never on the same side. And as you know, until recently, Reno was locked up and out of reach, and I was busy elsewhere." *Lost elsewhere*, was more accurate, but none of Thacker's business.

"Sounds like a personal vendetta rather than a professional commitment? It can hinder a man's current outlook if he's sidetracked by old hatreds."

Nic couldn't contest such logic, but there was no other way for it. Oddly enough, he would once have called Mr. Thacker his enemy. Could time and place now make them allies? "I hoped you and I could work together, but if the color of my old uniform is a problem for you, I can just as easily go it alone." This was a lie of course. If need be, he would face Reno and his men on his own, but it would be a long shot easier for him if he had the help and resources of this Wells Fargo detective.

"The war's over. It's what a man does now that counts with me."

That sounded reassuring.

"What's your involvement in all this?" Thacker's question was blunt and to the point.

Nic hesitated. He needed to trust this man, but trust usually had to be earned, or at least traded for and not handed out on demand.

"I met a young fellow near the Kansas border," Nic began, "and he mentioned your name."

"That would be Will Starr." Thacker's jaw tightened, and the muscle in his cheek twitched.

Nic saw he was on the right track. "I take it he worked for you?"

The Wells Fargo man studied Nic for a long piercing moment. Then as if reaching a hard-won conclusion he spoke more freely. "A bright young man, with a promising future, and now he has no future at all." These last words, sounded steeped in bitter juices, as if they had fermented in the man's craw a while.

"How'd it all come about?" Nic kept hoping to garner the missing pieces leading up to the abrupt ending of Will Starr's life. "Will trusted me enough to tell me to come see you. And I'm trying to honor that decision. It would be helpful if I knew the story leading up to where I came in."

Again Thacker held his silence.

"I know it wasn't simply the wrong place at the wrong time when he encountered Benteen."

"No, it wasn't a chance encounter. Will first ran into that nasty little group in Abilene."

"So that's where it all started, in Abilene?"

Thacker grimaced and shook his head, the remorse almost tangible in the small room. "His assignment started even before that. The home office in New York needed two men for an express shipment scheduled to leave from the east coast with a final destination in Sacramento, California. Since the trip required several stopovers, protecting the shipment was deemed a two man job.

"The company told the lad it would be good experience for him. What they really meant was being an apprentice they could pay Will half as much, and thereby cut costs on a cross-country trip.

"Will knew what they were up to, but he was excited as a young pup, and couldn't wait to get to New York City to start the first leg of such an adventure. At least they paired him up with a seasoned veteran, Michael O'Malley. For all the good it did. But even four men, with years of know-how, would have been hard pressed to come out on top when the stage got ambushed this side of Abilene."

"The dark horsemen?"

"Yes. With Reno in the lead. They shot O'Malley outright as if they knew who he was, and I suspect they didn't realize Will was also an agent, or they would have done the same to him right then and there.

"According to the driver, the outlaws forced open the strongbox, taking the third largest ruby ever mined, the lumber payroll in gold, and a packet of top priority documents destined for Denver, Colorado. Then before they hightailed it out of there, they unhitched and scattered the team leaving the survivors stranded.

"Will tried to help O'Malley, but it was hopeless, and when one of the horses wandered back to the stage, he caught it and lit out after the robbers. When he reached a midline train depot 'twix Abilene and Monotony, he sent assistance back to the stranded stage, and telegraphed me. He said he knew where the robbers were cold camped, and he thought he could get the stolen property back. I wired him to steer clear of them until reinforcements arrived, but I got no reply.

"My guess is Will didn't listen, and he must have been spotted raiding their camp. Somehow he made it to his cabin, with the bunch on his tail. We heard tell his sister found him."

Nic stared at the desktop, mulling over this new information.

"Perhaps, you could shed a little light on that particular part of the story, Mr. Breedlove."

Nic supposed it wouldn't hurt to fill in some of the blanks, omitting of course his participation in the back alley shoot-out which would implicate Ochessa, or the fact he'd been trailing the outlaws for days and was only a few miles behind them. The story was already convoluted enough. No use leading Thacker down any side roads.

"Why were you on the trail that day," Thacker prodded.

"I was heading for Denver, when I came across Will's cabin. The lad was beyond help, but based on the revolver in his hand, and the empty shell casings scattered around him on the floor where he lay, I'd say he put up one ferocious fight."

"Of course." Thacker nodded. "The best are always destined to give their all."

"Danger goes with the territory I imagine," Nic offered, trying to ease the older man's mind. "He knew the risks."

"Yes he knew. And regardless of orders, he did what he thought best and necessary under the circumstances. That's the stuff heroes are made of."

The word hero sent a chill down Nic's spine. For his money, hero and dead were all too often synonymous. That's why he avoided both four letter words with equal enthusiasm.

"Did he give you the ruby?"

"In a manner of speaking."

An almost wistful expression softened Thacker's angry appearance. "It was in a Chinese puzzle box right?"

"As a matter of fact it was."

"The darn kid was always toying with the thing. Said it would make a good place for hiding clues because nobody but him and his sister knew how to open it. Where's the cube now?"

"I don't have it any more. Nor the ruby it contained."

"Who does?"

"I'm not sure." He hedged the question, again unwilling to implicate Ochessa. "Someone stole it from me on the train between Monotony and Denver."

Thacker raised a brow as if he found this aspect of Nic's story rather unlikely. In retrospect Nic found it a bit hard to believe as well.

Thacker had been out of town during the shooting contest, but his agents must have gotten wind of Ochessa's entry collateral, and her win. They had to suspect she had the ruby.

"Exactly why are you here, Mr. Breedlove?" Thacker finally cut to the chase.

"How much for recovering the gem, the gold, and the papers you mentioned? And for bringing in Benteen?"

"For the agency nothing, it's simply our job. For an outsider ten percent of anything recovered." Thacker reached over and snatched a wanted poster off the wall. "$20,000 for Benteen. Dead or alive."

Ten percent plus twenty thousand. He'd never heard of a reward that large. Of course money didn't do a man much good if he didn't live to spend it.

"That's a pretty generous offer."

"There's reasons."

That sounded like somebody on the higher-up wanted the matter taken care of quickly. "Any leads on where the gang is holed up?" He didn't expect an answer, but it never hurt to ask.

Thacker hesitated only slightly. "We think Benteen and his men are hiding up in Brown's Park."

The man's candor came as a surprise. Either Thacker was desperate to collaborate, or the information was common knowledge. He'd bet on the latter and couldn't really imagine the former. "Brown's Park?"

"It's a regular *Hole in the Wall*, in the hills north west of Denver. Close by the ranch you've been frequenting."

So, Thacker had eyes watching the Rising Starr.

"I've seen one of those outlaws nosing around town on at least two occasions. Why haven't you arrested him?"

"That would be Lanny Morrison, the youngest of the gang. We tried trailing him back to the hideout, but he slipped past us. With the sheriff still laid up, we're obliged to work with Deputy Rawlins, and every time he takes the lead, he manages to obliterate the tracks or get lost. He's more a liability than an asset. Besides, Reno is the only one for whom I have an arrest warrant. Capturing the others away from camp and without evidence would be pointless and never hold up in court."

"Then how about just shooting them as they wander by?" Nic suggested.

"Effective, but not practical. Is that what happened in Monotony? I understand one of the dark riders met his end there."

"Really? Any suspects?"

Thacker's gaze intensified. "The list just got bigger. I'm calling in more men from the field, but it could take several days for them to get here. When they do, we'll ferret out their hideout and bring the lot of them in. Until then, you'd be wise not to try anything on your own."

"Why do you suppose they've remained in the area?" Nic registered Thacker's warning but didn't respond to it. "You'd think they would have headed for the border long before now."

"Again. There are reasons. Did Will happen to give you the documents along with the puzzle box?"

Here it came, the long awaited question, and asked so casually—almost too casually. As Thacker awaited an answer, his breathing quickened ever so slightly, and his gaze grew more intent.

Well what do you know? Finally, the real reason behind the murder and mayhem. It all had to do with the papers. The ones he had buried beneath a feed bin near Lucky's stall. There must be big names involved in this brouhaha, and big names equaled big money. But the documents were his ace in the hole, and for all he knew, Thacker could be involved, and maybe prove to be an even a worse enemy than Benteen.

"They're legal documents of the highest level," the Wells Fargo agent added, as if this incentive would make Nic come clean.

"So the Federal Government is involved?"

"Yes. For what that's worth," Thacker muttered. "Anymore, I don't know what's going on in this great country of ours. Following the fiasco of '76, I've had my doubts about some of the decisions coming out of the White House."

"What happened in '76?" Nic asked, happy to turn the conversation away from the documents and toward information bringing him up to date on the country of his birth.

"The election—the presidential election."

Thacker's annoyance was clearly evident in his voice. "Tilden won the popular vote fair and square."

"Then why isn't he president?"

"The votes in Florida, Louisiana, South Carolina, and Oregon were declared fraudulent due to voter intimidation. And when the electoral votes in those four states were thrown out, Hayes was declared president. Dang near started another civil war, only this time between Democrats and Republicans. And worse yet," he went on, with even greater exasperation, "the reconstruction of the South has been terminated.

Thacker sighed. "The rebuilding would have gone a fair piece in helping the economy and calming old hatreds. But not to worry, because by glory, we now have the Egg Roll on the Whitehouse lawn to look forward to every Easter. Sometimes I think the whole country's gone mad. I'm glad to be out west where at least on occasion common sense still prevails."

Like a timepiece that had run down, Mr. Thacker grew silent. He appeared tired and actually a little sheepish regarding his political outburst.

The older man poked at the wanted poster on his desk. "Reno is a dangerous man, and I imagine he's none too happy about how things are going."

"Why do I get the feeling the jewel and gold are just gravy on the biscuit, with the documents the main course?"

"Because you know Benteen is no two-bit stage robber. He's smart, and wouldn't have risked so much for so little. It's possible the men riding with him have no idea what the documents are worth, or that they even exist."

"So what are they worth?"

"None of your business or concern." Thacker gained his feet effectively putting an end to their talk.

Nic levered out of the chair. "I'll keep in touch."

"I'd appreciate it. Saves me the trouble of keeping you under surveillance."

Forgoing the ritual of shaking hands, they studied one another like two buck deer forced to share the same timber, and with a mutual nod, they parted warily, but peaceably.

Outside, still carrying rather than wearing his hat, Nic strode down the bustling street. Things were looking up—at least as far as the reward went.

Returning to the Mercantile, he shoved his hat in his saddle pack and untied Sadie from the hitching post, and not bothering to mount up, he ambled down the street to the livery. Sadie nosed him square in the back, this time apparently annoyed at him for making her wait in the hot sun.

"Hey, you're getting a might tetchy and persnickety in your old age," he threw at her. "Don't forget, I won you in a poker game, and could lose you just as easily."

With the darndest little whiny noise, the big mule eased up beside him and gently rubbed her muzzle against his arm. "That's better," he said, walking on.

Thoughts drifting, Nic decided the reward money for Reno, and ten percent of any recovered property, could set him up for life—if he took to living prudently. Of course he wouldn't. Besides what would he do if he *retired*? Lately, he spent way too much time thinking, rather than doing. He'd never been one to plan ahead—day-to-day worked just fine for him.

Nearing the blacksmith's shop, he ran his hand

along his belt, opposite his holster. He missed the weight of the Kukri, and the comfort of having it there at his side. It had been a part of his life since Tauchi, an old Nepalese man, had presented it to him as part of a rite-of-passage ceremony.

On that day, Nic had been welcomed as a member of their tribe. By their way of thinking no matter how old he became, he would always be a child of the universe with no particular place to live, yet every place in the world would be his home. He lowered his arm to his side. It sounded good on paper, but running unbranded turned out to be a dubious honor, and the recent ache of loneliness settled in his gut, heavy as a cold gray stone.

As he entered the stables, he heard the ringing of the smithy's hammer carried on the wind. He tied Sadie to a stall door, out of the sun, and promising grain to come upon his return, he made his way to the rear of the building to collect his property.

The smithy had done an admirable job replicating the knife, right down to the balance, weight, and fit. Like ripples in water, the steel had taken on a beautiful swirled pattern, the blade would be strong. Now he had two formidable weapons upon which to depend. But being well armed with your enemy out of reach, was like being all dressed up with no place to go.

He chatted a while with the amiable big man, praising his efforts. Then he paid in-full and went to fetch Sadie. Along the way he shook his head and laughed. He couldn't believe Ochessa had fired his ass. He'd quit many a job, but could honestly say he'd never been let go from one. A man took pride in a thing like that. And he didn't intend to allow such a blot to remain on his work history.

Chapter Twelve

Although only mid-afternoon, thanks to Nic, this seemed like the longest day of Ochessa's life. Eying the heap of bridles and halters piled high on the tack house worktable, she rolled up the sleeves on the blouse she'd exchanged for the torn one. A dozen more traces hung on the nearby wall.

Ever since she was a little girl, part of her responsibilities had included helping to clean and oil the leather used on the ranch—an important chore. The saddles, catch ropes, and leather accouterments were the sinew holding together man, beast, and a good day's work.

Opening a tin of mink oil, she set it aside. Then still riled over her encounter with Nic, she retrieved a bucket of water and slammed it down beside the leather straps. Water sloshed over the rim of the bucket, pooling on the tabletop and dripping onto the floor. She didn't even try to mop up the spill.

Her labors today were not because of tradition, nor for the desire to rekindle childhood memories. She needed to keep busy, needed a big dose of peace and quiet as she sorted things out in her mind. *As if that was possible.* When she thought about Nic, her emotions ran amuck with no logic or common sense involved. And when she thought about Will, and the future of the Rising Starr, pain and sorrow rode hand and hand with worry.

Grabbing a soft brush, she attacked the wagon traces, trying to scrub away uncertainty and self-doubt along with the dirt. Anger of a general nature seemed to roil inside of her. Why and at what? At everything, she supposed. At being left alone to take care of the ranch. At having to ask for help because she couldn't do everything herself. At wanting to be feminine, yet having to fight to succeed in a man's world. At wanting—to be loved.

She scrubbed harder, but the image of Nic hovering in her mind became all the more clear. Even gone for good and out of her life, the man disrupted her nice orderly world. And if she was truthful, she had to admit he kindled wishes deep within her, wishes as out of place as a goose in the hen house. Silly kind of things, like frilly dresses and church socials and even children. Thoughts of this sort left her unprotected and vulnerable. They diluted her energy, aligning her goals at cross-purposes. She had to keep her wits about her and not be sidetracked—or worse yet, led astray. Duty demanded she forge ahead, and she had fought too long and too hard to let anything or anyone jeopardize the continuation of the ranch. Or more precisely, the rebirth of the Rising Starr Farm.

Her new plans didn't involve struggling to raise animals only to see them end up on a dinner plate. Her vision involved making the world a sweeter more joyous place. The transition would involve a monumental rethinking of everything including land use and farm equipment. But she'd do it—one acre at a time if that's what it took.

Informing the men should be interesting, a meeting

she'd been putting off. Might as well let them get the herd to market first, a task she dreaded but couldn't avoid. The contracts had been signed while her mother still lived, and legally binding, Ochessa planned to honor them. The herd had to get to market and the men had to be paid. After the trail drive, she could do as she pleased.

Most of the wranglers would probably up and quit when they found out what she had in mind. She couldn't blame them. If they did, she'd find new help. Regardless, it would be her concept of the future over which she toiled, and not someone else's.

As the plans for her new life took shape in her mind, the tension in her lower back eased, and the cool dimness of the tack house soothed the pain throbbing in her temples. If only something could chill the desire simmering in her blood. She shouldn't want him. But his half-smile took her breath away, and his knowing expression turned Ochessa into a simpleton who couldn't figure her way out of the barn.

Nic Breedlove wore his independence like a badge, daring the rest of the world to join his posse. And when he was near, she didn't care he was a drifter, didn't care she might be weak enough to fall in love with him. At least she thought something foolishly close to love harried her soul. Only in her dreams did she dare to feel this way. Dreams—where it was safe to give your heart away. Dreams—where the man you trusted would be there the next morning, willing to swim the river for you.

Gritting her teeth she scoured the bridle harder, attacking the caked on dirt. This wasn't a dream. She had to stay strong.

With a slam-bang, the door to the tack room burst open. Ochessa jumped and spun around.

A man stood silhouetted in the opening, blinding shafts of sunlight spilled in around the faceless image. Startled, she clasped the dripping brush and leather to her chest. Cold liquid soaked through her blouse and ran down the front of her body. She glanced to the left. Propped up against the far wall, the rifle she'd brought along, seemed a world away.

The anonymous figure stepped forward and kicked the door shut at his back, and the glare of sunlight retreated. It was Nic, and he looked indignant.

"You can't fire me, because I quit."

The man had been gone for several hours. Was that the best rebuttal he could come up with? She opened her mouth to point out his lack of creativity, but a sputtering sound came out as her words collided with her mocking laughter.

He ran his hand through his hair. What had happened to his precious hat? Then the memory of stepping on it flashed through her mind.

"Sorry about your hat." That was a lie. And although unintentional, it had felt good.

His expression darkened, her comment apparently adding fuel to some fire already burning. Then his gaze gentled, and he unclenched his jaw, and an expression she shouldn't be responding to softened his mouth.

Neither of them said a word, and the weighty silence hung between them like a gathering storm. She set the dripping bridle and soapy brush on the table, and seeking to put a safer distance between them, she stumbled backward then realized the vastness between here and the moon would probably not be sufficient.

Earlier today when replacing her torn blouse, she'd given in to the noon-day heat and foregone a camisole. Now only a thin layer of wet calico stood between her naked breasts and Nic's scrutiny. Teased by the heat of his gaze, and encourage by the cold water, her nipples hardened, and she felt as if her bones had been rendered from her body. Too late she tried forcing her body to behave.

"I hope you're not expecting a letter of recommendation. To date I haven't been terribly satisfied with your performance."

He stepped closer. "Where I come from animals perform not men. And I didn't realize satisfying you was part of my job description."

If ever a man could satisfy her, Nic would be the one. "An employer always expects satisfaction. Too bad we'll never know if you were up to the task." Her words had come out more of a challenge than the reprimand she intended.

The crooked smile for which she'd been waiting, slipped into place. "We could still find out. I'm generally not the kind of man to leave a job half done."

"But I'm no longer your boss, and you're not the hired help."

"I'm still a man, and you're still a woman. Do you like being a woman Ochessa?"

What kind of question was that? Did he think because she managed a ranch and knew how to handle a gun she lacked feelings? Beneath the leather beat a soft heart, too soft, she reminded herself.

"Like it or not," he pressed, "you're very good at it—without even trying. Perhaps that's what makes you so dangerous."

He uttered the last few words as if speaking to himself, and she wondered how she could possibly pose a threat to a man like Nic.

Without warning he closed the distance between them, but recalling his earlier rejection, she refused to so easily capitulate. Sidestepping to elude his grasp, she skidded on the wet floor, and grabbed the front of his shirt as a last ditch effort to remain upright.

Strong arms jerked her up against his chest, and he roughly settled his mouth on hers. Before she could react, he shifted his hands to frame her face, holding her in place, his tongue teasing and tasting.

The desire she'd felt this morning regrouped in her stomach and burst into flames. The heat sweeping through Ochessa like a brush fire as she kissed him back.

Nic had come back for her, couldn't stay away. That sounded romantic, but in her heart she knew he only sought to satisfy the same needs she wrestled with. He wanted to scratch the itch, explore the unknown. Then he could move on with his life. She didn't care. She stroked his neck, and then worked at the buttons on his shirt.

He swept her hands aside. *Not again.* She refused to live through another episode of physical taunting only to be left hungry and wanting more. About to tell him so, she lost all train of thought when he cupped her breasts through the wet calico.

She reached out—again he stilled her actions. "Easy, Chessy Cat," he murmured, as if gentling a frightened mare.

Taking her by one hand, he crossed the room, tugging her along. At the far side, he turned her around putting her back to the wall. Urging her arms up over her head, he wrapped her fingers in the leather traces still hanging on the pegs.

Confused, she didn't move, then she grabbed the straps, and held on for dear life, thankful for something solid and secure in a world turned topsy-turvy. When Nic stood so near, she became off balance, about to tumble into an abyss both terrifying and mesmerizing.

His gaze captured hers, those seemingly all-knowing eyes holding answers to questions she dared not even ask. Then all semblance of proper thinking fled as he slipped free the buttons on her blouse. Peeling aside the damp fabric, he uttered a murmur of appreciation before lowering his head to savor first one breast and then the other. Tingling and aching, she thrust closer, offering him a full sampling. He straightened, pressed his hips against her, and grazed his thumbs across the swollen tips of her breasts. Inhaling a much needed breath, she drank in the smell of leather and the man-scent of Nic, and her excitement doubled.

"Hold on tight, Chessy Cat." His breath was a warm whisper against her skin as he nuzzled her neck. "It's bound to be a wild ride."

The words *Chessy Cat* stuck in her mind. He'd called her that twice now. Had he devised a playful name for her, something only he would call her, something making her special in his eyes? She liked that idea—and everything else he was doing to her.

Unbuttoning her skirt, he sent the heavy leather plummeting to the floor. She bravely stood before him, vulnerable and willing, clad only in her open blouse, her favorite pair of embroidered pantaloons, and her cowboy boots. The undergarments, mere whispers of fabric, were no defense against the coolness of the room, or the heat of Nic's fully clothed body.

He slid one hand between her cotton-clad thighs, the contact so soft she wasn't sure he was touching her at all, so soft she feared it was only wishful thinking. Then his attention turned deliberate, setting off a shock of delight. It was real, and it was wonderful. The desire to please him in kind quivered through Ochessa until wanting to touch him became an overwhelming and desperate need. She fought the leather straps around her wrists, but the more she tried to free herself the more tightly tangled she became.

His hands seemed to be everywhere at once, petting her, soothing her, gently breaching the walls of her emotional and physical defenses. Again he glided his fingers back and forth between her legs, slow and sure, over and over. The pull of fabric rough against her skin, heightened the pleasure, making her wet with need and wanting. Could he feel it, did he know he was driving her to sweet madness, to the point of no return?

"Give in to me. I won't leave you wanting this time."

As promised, he pleasured her, unselfishly—or did he just need to prove he could satisfy the boss lady. No, she wouldn't go there. She wanted to feel cherished and fragile, the center of the world, at least his world.

Unable to explore his body in return, all the feelings and sensations racing through her were magnified, and as her inhibitions began to fade, she closed her eyes. Giving Nic so much power could be dangerous—too late now. There was nothing left to do but hang on tight like he suggested, hang on and ride the whirlwind to the end.

****

Caressing Ochessa sent a strange new feeling coursing through Nic's body, and it came as a surprise. Wanting to please her, overtook pleasing himself. Perhaps because he knew what it cost her to put herself in his hands, both literally and figuratively.

Turning her head from side to side, she still fought the passion he felt intensifying within her, still fought against something he knew she wanted so badly.

"Easy now," he reassured, his lips only inches from hers as he tried to show Ochessa that loving could be a tender struggle, experienced without desperation. "There's no hurry, let me take you there."

He nipped at her neck and tugged at the fabric covering the part of her he desired to make his own. Her breathing turned ragged, her whimpering sighs assuring him what felt good, and what felt even better.

"Just a man and a woman, Chessy."

Slipping his hand inside the fragile cotton he glided his hand over her bare skin. She went rigid, but only for a moment. Then he dipped lower, through silky hair and warm folds of softness. He'd give a dozen new hats to shed his own clothes and bury the part of him begging for attention deep in her body. He wanted to move inside of her, wanted to watch her face as they joined and found release together. But he didn't, because he also wanted to prove she meant more to him than a quick roll in the hay. This was for her—only her. Next time...

Wrapping his left arm around her waist, he drew her body closer as his right hand continued to explore and claim the warm haven he sought. Again he regretted that only his fingers conquered the inner depths his hardened body longed to discover.

She moaned and writhed, and knowing he couldn't keep this up much longer and still maintain any semblance of noble intensions, he touched her with due diligence, deepening the stroke, caressing harder. "It's all right, just let go. You're so beautiful," he murmured, giving her pure pleasure with no strings attached.

Her breathing quickened. She cried out, and the sound of unbearable pleasure echoed around the small room. He felt the waves of delight slam through her body, and he bit back a groan as she gave herself over to the uninhibited emotion, as untamed as her tawny hair billowing around her head. When she stilled, he reluctantly slid his hands from her body.

Eyes closed, Ochessa sagged against the wall. In the aftermath of satisfaction her lips softened, and her cheeks glowed, and still holding fast to the leather straps, her fingers fiercely twisted in the traces, her knuckles showed white.

He tried, but couldn't loosen her grip—his knives were in his saddle bags. He grabbed a small blade from a nearby bucket of tools, slashed through the cords, then tossed the knife aside. As she crumpled toward the ground, he swept her into his arms, and set her on the edge of the worktable.

Savoring the fragrance of her skin, he couldn't resist again cupping those tempting breasts which fit his hands so perfectly. An after-shock rippled through her as she met his gaze.

Desire stabbed at his loins and roared in his head, and Nic decided going halfway to paradise didn't cut it—he wanted all of her, wanted to push her back on the table, wanted to spread her legs and make real love to her.

Don't do it, a voice warned as he reached for the top button on his denim pants. What they'd done so far could be construed as innocent pleasure, what he contemplated came with a commitment. One he couldn't make, and one he doubted she would accept. It would change their relationship forever. And forever was an awfully long time.

In truth, he shouldn't have done this much. If Lame Bear found out, there would be the devil to pay. But he hadn't compromised Ochessa, hadn't done anything other than satisfy her needs. And he had proven to himself that he could touch her, and feel her passion and still walk away—his heart unmoved, his soul unscathed, his freedom safely intact.

A loud noise reverberated through the room. It sounded like a battering ram hitting a castle door. Ochessa came to attention and glanced around as if unsure what she heard had been real. He spun around to face the portal, hand on the butt of his pistol, his wayward thoughts transformed into concern.

Sliding his pistol free, he inched toward the door, eased it open a crack, and peered out. No one was there, but the message delivered rang loud and clear. He drew the door farther inward so Ochessa could see too.

A large tomahawk protruded from the wood, the well-honed blade implanted deeply, just about level with his head. Two eagle feathers, dangled from the handle, and swayed in the breeze.

"Lame Bear," she whispered.

Nic holstered his gun, and shut the door. As he returned to her side, the heat from her body collided with his. It wouldn't take much to rekindle the previous fire raging between them.

A smile curved her lips, but sadness hovered in her eyes setting a sobering thought to clawing at the back of his mind. A tawny-eyed cougar could be most dangerous when it stopped hissing and growling. Searching her face, he tried to read her emotions.

"He still treats me like a little girl." Clutching the edges of her blouse together, she crossed her legs.

He scooped her skirt up off the floor, and handed it to her. "Believe me, you're anything but." Nic wanted to say more, but she had a knack for misinterpreting his words, and after this morning, he feared he might ruin what they had just shared, afraid to lose what little ground he may have gained.

She shivered. Retrieving a woolen work jacket from a nearby hook, he draped it around her. Her gaze drifted lower, snagging on the top button on his pants. He glanced down, and re-fastened it. Without Lame Bear's interruption, things may have gone even further.

"I suppose I could write you that letter of recommendation now." She glanced up at him. "With a caveat for women to avoid being alone with you in tack rooms."

"Ochessa…"

"Don't you dare say you're sorry like this morning, as if what you just did and how you made me feel was a big mistake."

He opened his mouth then closed it, never uttering a word.

"So, is this your way of saying good bye or what? Not that I'm complaining. Perhaps I should keep you around a little longer."

"First of all," he began, as he traced a downward path with one finger from her throat to between her breasts. "I'm a might put off that you think this is the only reason I came back?"

She gave him an accusing look. "Just a man and a woman."

Like well-aimed rocks, his own words came hurtling back to him. Guilt lassoed his conscience, and he fought against the rope as if it were looped around his neck. But he didn't regret sharing this interlude with her, and in truth getting into her pants hadn't been his sole reason for returning. He just wanted to see her again. Couldn't imagine riding out of her life forever never knowing how she was, where she was, if she was happy and safe. Dozens of reasons came to mind, none of which he could put into words.

"So what's your second reason, for coming back." she prodded.

Now what? It wouldn't do to let her know he actually liked her. Accept for taking care of his mule, he'd been a loner for a good long while. No one tied him down, no one else came first.

"Well," she pushed.

"You owe me the price of a hat. I'll expect to see that reflected in my next month's wages."

He crossed the room, and opened the door, and eyeing the tomahawk with renewed concern he slipped beyond it and out into the real world. Slamming the portal closed, he glanced around. No doubt Lame Bear hid somewhere nearby. Hopefully, the symbolic message concluded the extent of today's warning.

A grim smile fought its way across his mouth. Might as well admit it, he may have just said farewell to a big chunk of his precious freedom.

****

Ochessa quickly shed the old barn jacket. It smelled like a hard day's shoveling, but she'd been too embarrassed to relinquish its shelter in front of Nic. What must he think of her? She hadn't even tried to resist his attention. And mercy it felt good, beyond anything she'd ever imagined in her most lusty daydreams.

Careful to avoid splinters, she eased off the worktable and tugged her pantaloons into place. The seam wedged up against the still throbbing space between her legs, and a flash of remembered pleasure wavered through her. She twisted her fingers in the fabric, and a hot blush burned her cheeks.

Holy Hannah. Now he would really think he was in charge. But in charge of what? How she ran things around here? Or worse yet, of her? How could she ever look him in the eye again? She stepped into and fastened her skirt. Somehow she'd have to manage, because by unspoken agreement, it appeared he was back on the payroll—and part of her could hardly wait to see him again.

Reluctant to leave, she grabbed a brush, and went back to work. He hadn't been wearing his hat. Maybe if she kept destroying his precious headgear, she could keep him hanging around for years and years as he sought restitution.

Chapter Thirteen

A few hours later, Ochessa hung the last bridle on the tack room wall—the wall she would never look at in the same way again. She felt as if she had ridden a cyclone, and somehow lived to tell the tale. In truth, when lost to Nic's bold touch, she had never felt more alive.

Now she knew why her one and only previous encounter with *love* had been so disappointing. Dooley Wainright only wanted to satisfy himself, claiming her as a prize, and using her to feed his ego. He wanted sex and access to her land, nothing more. He'd shown less emotion than Lucky conveyed when he serviced the cows.

With nary a kiss or a thank you ma'am, Dooley had taken her virginity. And he'd left her lying unfulfilled and feeling empty. The following few times had been no better. She'd never told her mother about her foolish foray into carnal sin, and she had decided if that was all there was to sex, she would be better off without it.

But this had been a whole different rodeo. Nic had given her a taste of heaven, knowing instinctively what she craved, while taking nothing for himself. But he'd been wrong about one thing. They weren't simply a man and a woman. She had completely relinquished control, had ignored the rules, the ones she depended upon for survival. She liked to think it took someone special to coax her into taking such a chance.

With a sigh, she leaned against the table. Maybe romance wasn't reserved only for dreams.

The difference between Dooley's rough lovemaking, and Nic's seductive caresses, spanned the difference between learning to crawl and learning to fly. And even though Nic made what he'd done to her seem natural, society frowned upon a woman who found pleasure with a man when no promise had been given. Of course Nic excelled at convincing people whatever they desired seemed completely reasonable—especially if he happened to be selling what they needed. Just all part of his magic.

With little protest, she had forsaken her good sense along with her clothing, but now suspicion began to set in. What did Nic want from her? He'd already managed to get his job back. Did he still hope to get his hands on the ruby? He must want something. Men always did. Somehow she couldn't accept the idea he simply wanted her.

Ochessa stared at the door. Cold and hungry she'd been rambling around the dim seclusion of the tack house making up new chores when all were long done. Like a timid little mouse, fear and her inability to admit she cared for and wanted someone kept her hiding.

But she was a cat, not a mouse. At least Nic seemed to think so.

She crossed the room, determined to leave. But, hand on the doorknob, she hesitated. When it came to dealing with adult relationships she rode an untried horse over an unknown trail.

Bull… She was making this way too complicated. Nic Breedlove qualified as a *bad 'un*. Why would he treat her so special without some ulterior motive? She jerked open the door, suffering a momentary flash of embarrassment for having been caught locked away with Nic. Then gripping the tomahawk handle, she wrenched the weapon free, and stepped outside. With her other hand shielding her eyes, she scanned the horizon for any sign of the old man. Lame Bear was gone or well hidden.

In a final tribute to the day's end, the sun sent out one last burst of light before taking refuge behind the mountains. The shards of color melted into a canopy of pink and gold. Such a striking display usually calmed her senses, but not tonight.

Suddenly, she realized she had begun to enjoy the vulnerable reaction Nic evoked in her. It felt ironically emancipating, as if giving her permission to follow her heart, no recriminations—or self-imposed rules—or duty—or anything other than her own desire.

As hazy twilight captured the sky, suspending time between day and night, her thoughts seemed suspended as well, with no resolution in sight. Then the evening chill had her recalling Nic's warm embrace. She hungered for it again, and for answers to some pretty serious questions. Just exactly where did they stand with one another?

Running to the barn, she threw open the door. With a snort and a toss of his head, Lucky's wild-eyed gaze met hers.

Nic was gone.

*****

Declaring himself certifiably crazy, Nic trudged through the dense foliage. Sadie plodded sleepily along at his back, a reluctant participant in their *dark of the night excursion.*

It seemed he spent half his time figuring ways to be near Ochessa, and the other half analyzing reasons to run from her side. Of course, as long as Benteen and the outlaws were at large, he didn't have a choice, he had to stay nearby. But he didn't have to stay so close he could smell her and feel her heat.

Figuring Chessy Cat needed some wide-open space, he decided he couldn't remain at the ranch tonight. Plus he didn't cotton to the idea of sleeping with one eye open in case Lame Bear thought they still had a score to settle.

On the bright side, he'd gotten his job back. He'd never seen a woman more likely to need help, and less likely to ask for it. What a wild child, a filly destined to remain half-tamed. He knew if they were ever going to be together, Ochessa would need to come to him of her own free will. Otherwise, she'd never stay.

In the meantime, there were situations needing to be cleared up and settled. Ochessa had the ruby, Reno had the gold, and he had the documents. They were three people on a collision course, each bound and determined to keep what they had, and how things would play out was anybody's guess.

In a moment of weakness, he'd already convinced himself to share any reward money for Benteen with Ochessa. After all her brother had lost his life trying to do the right thing, he could at least see the kid hadn't died in vain. What Chessy did with the ruby was up to her. And what he did with the documents was up to him. The documents. Shoot, he'd left them back at the ranch, buried in the barn. Again he'd been sidetracked by a woman.

He paused and glanced back at Sadie. She made a less than attractive face, yawned, and gave a halfhearted bray which sounded like a laugh. Even his mule thought him a fool. Navigating around a large boulder, he forayed deeper into the woods.

Instinctively he followed the game-trail he'd previously discovered, but his thoughts strayed back to Ochessa. Would the excitement eventually fade? In time would he disappoint her? To pursue what seemed bound to fail, hardly seemed fair to either one of them. What if in the cold lonely hours of a long winter's night he craved something new? Or maybe this time he'd hunkered down and welcome the blizzard, be glad to have a good woman at his side to keep him warm until spring came. Again, both were good arguments—but unconvincing.

He forced his feet to keep moving, but the chain he envisioned around his heart now felt attached to an anchor. Act in haste, repent at leisure—discretion was the better part of valor—never be a volunteer—knick-knack pattywack give the dog a bone. He really was losing his mind, but he wasn't about to lose his independence, sadly the only commodity he had left.

The war had robbed him of his father, and his childhood. His mother and sister had died of cholera. And men like Reno Benteen had killed his belief in a merciful God. He couldn't give up his freedom. That was too much to ask, too much to answer to.

Sadie stopped, refusing to move. He glanced around, his rambling thoughts circling back to the present as he cupped a hand over her muzzle. "Stay quiet, girl."

When nothing materialized he exhaled the breath

he'd been holding. What had it been? Lame Bear, a dark rider, maybe a mountain lion or bear. She'd heard something, now apparently gone.

Making his way higher into the hills, he set up camp along a rocky ridge with a clear view of the ranch. The slope of trees at his back shielded him from becoming a silhouette against the sky, while offering wood for a fire.

As darkness ruled and the temperature dropped, he pulled on his long leather coat, fastening the buttons, top to bottom. The cold settled in, but with dry brush all around he decided to forego a fire.

After giving Sadie a good rubdown and half the water in his canteen, he staked her under a cottonwood tree with enough grass there to keep her happy until morning. Sitting beside her on a stump, he ate the cold beans and hardtack he'd purchased back in town.

Supper over, he stretched out on his bedroll near the mule, his head resting on his saddle. If any uninvited guests strayed by, human or animal, Sadie would alert him. Most animals were smart enough to stay out of her path, not necessarily so the humans.

Chewing on a dried grass stem, he studied the patterns in the stars. Someone once told him the stars were there in the daytime too, you just couldn't see them. He supposed it could be true, but just like his feelings for Ochessa, some things were too hard to reason out.

Now why'd he have to go and start thinking of that woman again?

It was gonna to be a long night.

Chapter Fourteen

Come the dawn, Eustace sat astride old Cactus Jack, enjoying the morning sun as it peeked over the prairie to warm his backside. Surveying the valley to the west, he wondered how long Miss Ochessa could keep the ranch going.

She should be watching the stream feeding her property, the one coming off the South Platte. The recent storms had piled up windfall, diverting the flow. Soon the best watering hole on her property would be a useless mud patch.

'Course her being a woman, what more could a body expect? Although, he had to admit, she'd surprised them all by winning the shooting contest. It still rankled. Everything about the Rising Starr Ranch riled his sensibilities, and set his stomach to grinding. And so it had been for a good long while.

Looking back, things had turned out a far cry different then he'd imagined they would. Oh, he was prosperous enough and had everything a man could need—but not everything a man could want. He didn't have children to carry on the family name, a name that should have been Starr. And he didn't have a woman with whom to bide his time—those expectations had all gone to ruin.

Time was, way back, he and Ochessa's father, Jedidiah, had been good friends, and not just because they were half-brothers, having the same father but different mothers. A father who never recognized or claimed him as his own. Then after they'd grown up, along came Ochessa's mother—Miss Olivia Langston—a one of a kind. She'd stolen the heart of every man in the county, and she'd been the only woman Eustace ever loved. But Jed had claimed her as his. And Olivia hadn't protested one iota.

For many a year, knowing she lived just across the valley—yet beyond his reach—had driven Eustace crazy. When Jedidiah died, and Olivia still didn't want him, his jealousy had turned to full-fledged animosity. Now he hated a dead man, and rued a dead woman.

The transformation of his feelings hadn't been a concerted effort, but like the rerouting of a creek bed after a gully-washer, it had been unstoppable. Death didn't absolve a man from his sins, or a woman of her fickle-hearted ways. He would never get over how he felt about being denied the Starr family name, or the woman who got away.

Jedidiah's son Will had been a good kid, but now he'd passed over to the great beyond too. Guess the Starr clan wasn't so high and mighty with most of them in the grave, leaving a pitiful girl and an old Indian to run the show. No. They weren't so high and mighty now.

Eustace leaned over, spat on the ground, and nudged his horse into a walk. Might as well head back to his own property. Miss Starr would be fortunate if none of her cattle got bogged down and crippled up in that quicksand of mud.

When his gelding balked, Eustace slid his rifle from its scabbard and glanced around. "You smell cougar, old boy?" Something must be making its way toward them.

Guiding his mount up alongside a rocky ridge, he urged the animal beneath a tree-veiled outcropping perfect for hiding both man and beast. He'd spent many an hour concealed there waiting for a whitetail to come within range. Although beef was obviously plentiful, he'd never lost his hankering for venison, besides it didn't make sense to eat his own profits. It also amused him to poach the game off Jedidiah Starr's property.

After a moment, a man on horseback appeared in the distance. "Well I'll be." It looked like one of them dark horsemen he'd been hearing about. His finger itched to shoot the black specter. Then he reconsidered. The outlaw might not be traveling solo.

The desperado seemed to be heading for the Rising Starr. He should circle around and warn them, or maybe just mind his own business. He'd become too sentimental in his old age. He didn't owe Ochessa a dad-blamed thing. Still, it vexed him to see these yahoos raiding and robbing like they owned the territory.

The dark figure drifted out of sight. Eustace clucked his horse into motion, but as he cleared the overhang, a hand snaked out and tore the rifle from his grasp. Taken by surprise, Eustace lurched in the saddle, and his horse reared back on its haunches.

"Holy hell, Lame Bear." He worked to gain control of his mount. "You ought'n to go around scarin' a fellow so."

Dad-blamed Indian could move through dry leaves quiet as a snake on snow.

"I thought maybe you were lost."

The implication that he trespassed on Rising Starr land did not go unnoticed.

"Just following a stray," he lied, gathering his wits about him like a well-worn coat.

The two men studied one another. Eustace glanced away first. Something about Lame Bear gave a man pause. He'd heard rumors the Indian had been some kind of a Sioux chief. But that must have been years ago. There were few free roaming tribes left, and nowhere for chiefs to lead them. Yet despite being old and gray, a special kind of fire lived in the eyes of the Indian, indicating he'd seen things other people hadn't—things both horrible and glorious—things that would have broken a lesser man.

"If I see the stray I will send him back your way," Lame Bear offered, returning the rifle.

"I'd be much obliged. I seen a stranger pass by heading south," he added, then wondered why.

"Yes," Lame Bear acknowledged. "I smelled him even before I smelled you."

With a grunt of amusement, Eustace turned his horse toward home.

****

Lame Bear had no trouble tracking the man of darkness. Like most white men, the intruder did not move as one with the land. He left a trail across the earth like a hungry hog turned loose in a vegetable patch. But even a hog could be dangerous if challenged, and even a hog had purpose. He wondered what intentions were at work here.

He jogged ahead, following a trail along the ridge. Reaching a small stand of aspen, he paused to study the place he thought the man would clear timber. He cherished this favorite vantage point to watch-over the land. Sometimes, as he studied the cattle, he recalled the buffalo once roaming the prairie. Herds so magnificent they took hours to pass by. Herds so vast they made the earth tremble as they filled the air with dust. Then even the sun dimmed at their greatness.

But that was long ago and, like the tree beside which he stood, he was getting old. And like his name, he was becoming lame again—his life had come full circle.

He silently scanned the countryside, and a sense of unease flickered through him. He saw nothing specific, but the voice living within him declared something amiss. The mud filled watering hole caught his attention too. He must warn Ochessa about it, but this did not cause his current unease.

The small group of cattle grazing in the last green meadow lifted their heads, and came to attention. At first they ambled about slowly. Maybe a lone coyote prowled nearby in search of food. Now they moved faster. The beating of his heart quickened as if keeping pace with the fear building in the animals.

Without preamble a man in black loomed up over the far rise, his dark coat billowing out around him. Shouting and swinging a lariat over his head, the howling specter frightened the cattle into a full-fledged stampede—and they were heading for the big watering hole. Panic stricken the terrified animals were sure to be injured in the deep mud.

Lame Bear began to run. How could he turn so many? More likely, in their fright, they would pay him no heed, crushing him like a river reed. Still he must try.

Thankfully, the land slopped downhill. But although his spirit stayed young, his body had grown old, and soon his breath came in gasps and his legs felt heavy. The sound of his lungs working double-time, echoed oddly around him. Then he realized a rider had come up beside him—the animal breathed hard too.

Thinking a second dark horseman bore down on him, Lame Bear ran as fast as he could, all the while tensing for the blow he expected at any moment.

"Get on board," a voice called.

Surprised, he glanced up into Nic's face and another time long ago came to mind. He was a young brave, running with his brothers as they practiced feats of daring for fun and for survival.

Nic slowed down. Never missing a stride, Lame Bear offered his left arm for Nic to grasp as he lunged upward. Gripping the back of the saddle with his right hand, he hoisted himself onto the back of the big mule.

Nic gave out a whoop and a holler, and together they charged down the hill toward the oncoming cattle. Lame Bear's ribs ached, and the muscles in his thighs felt stretched beyond mending, but he'd done it. Riding felt much better than running.

Spotting their approach, the dark-clothed interloper veered off and headed into the foothills. The frightened animals, however, continued on their disastrous path.

"Think we can turn them?" Lame Bear shouted at Nic.

"With a little luck. Take my pistol, and fire some shots in front of them.

Lame Bear grabbed the gun Nic handed off. Not knowing if Nic carried five shots or six, he only fired three times. It never hurt to have a few arrows left in the quiver.

The cattle in the lead seemed to take notice, and Mother Earth lent a hand too. The terrain grew rocky near the edge of the mud, becoming less agreeable for the animals to traverse. Today's unseasonably warm temperature also encouraged the cattle to slow their pace, their panic lessening in the rising heat. Nic wrangled the leaders westward toward the trees. Most of the herd followed suit, and although nervously milling about, the animals were under control.

Nic whoa'd the mule to a halt.

"Nice weapon." Lame Bear handed back the big Colt revolver.

"Nice shooting." Nic holstered the gun.

"It's hard to miss when you are aiming at the ground." Lame Bear slid from the back of the mule. He thought to speak when the sound of a calf bawling cut through the air.

Both men looked in the direction of the sound. One young animal had continued on in the wrong direction, and stuck in the mud up to its belly, the calf called for help. Nearby, the mother paced along the edge of the marshy pond, kept at bay by the obvious danger.

Lame Bear collected small branches and handfuls of trampled tall grass. Tossing them ahead, he approached the stranded critter. Remaining in the saddle, Nic maneuvered Sadie as close as he dare.

Lame Bear tried, but couldn't disengage the struggling calf from the sucking mud.

"Heads up," Nic called.

Glancing over, Lame Bear saw a loop of rope coming his way. He snagged it from the air and slipped it over the head of the forlorn critter. With the mule's help, they managed to drag the terrified animal to freedom. After a moment of stunned confusion, the calf gamboled over to its mother, and rubbed its head against her belly.

Lame Bear flopped down in the shade of the nearest tree, trying to catch his breath. Nic dismounted and joined him, a canteen and a small canvas poke in-hand.

They shared the water as if they'd ridden trail together for many years.

"Jerky?" Not waiting for an answer, Nic tossed the bag over.

"Thanks." Lame Bear sampled a piece before lobbing the bag back. "I'm glad we could save the calf. Too bad it will only end up on someone's dinner plate."

"Not Ochessa's I take it," Nic said, reloading his revolver.

"No," Lame Bear admitted. Grabbing a stick, he scraped the mud from his moccasins. "She hasn't eaten the flesh of any animal since the time she threw her fork back at her mother and me."

"Why is that?"

"It is just the path she follows."

Unaccustomed to sharing personal information with strangers, especially if that information pertained to Ochessa, Lame Bear didn't explain further. He guarded her privacy as fiercely as he guarded her property.

Nic holstered the Colt and stretched out under the tree. "Well lately, her path is crisscrossing with those dark horsemen. It makes me more than a might uneasy since they're the ones who killed her brother."

Lame Bear took a moment to consider this information.

"How do you know this?"

"I saw them riding away from Will's cabin the day he died."

It made sense. He had known all along the man who sat beside him was not responsible. Nic had been sent to help Ochessa.

"Evil rides with them."

"That's why I'm worried about her."

"Did you worry about her yesterday when the two of you were alone in the tack house?"

The younger man's eyes narrowed. "That's between Ochessa and me." The determined expression accompanying the words, declared Nic stood ready to defend his position.

Lame Bear appreciated Nic's show of respect for whatever had taken place behind closed doors, but it would not do to let him think his actions were without consequence. Lame Bear growled a response in Lakota Sioux and conjured an expression he used in the old days to keep defiant braves inline. Nic swallowed hard, but his gaze didn't waver.

Recently, Lame Bear knew Ochessa showed bouts of happiness. He thought winning the prize bull might be the reason. But she also seemed melancholy at times, and he worried the cause could be from listening to this man's bull. Still, a full-grown woman, she had earned the right to make her own decisions—and her own mistakes.

Lame Bear gained his feet. "I told you once before, do not hurt her."

The younger man scramble up beside him, standing

tall, arms loose but ready for action.

"I didn't. And I won't."

Nic's words rang true, and Lame Bear couldn't deny he liked this man. But Lame Bear also treasured freedom, and he saw the same need in Nic. Ochessa should have a man content to stand fast at her side, a man whose world ended at the property line. Would Ochessa be enough woman to alter this man's need to wander—would any woman?

"Sometimes," Lame Bear cautioned, "a little boy will kill a rabbit in jest, but the rabbit dies in earnest. Be careful how you play."

Chapter Fifteen

What a way to start the day. Ochessa raced across the valley, pushing her mare as fast as she dared. Eustace kept pace at her side. His warning about the cattle and the dark horsemen could be a spiteful trick, but she dare not take the chance.

Before heading out, she'd given Roy Thibodaux orders to locate the men working the south range. Pound for pound, the small Frenchman proved to be the toughest man in her employ. Still it would take Little Roy nearly an hour to reach the men and bring them back to the watering hole.

"Lame Bear's already out there," Eustace hollered over to her, as if such information would make her slow her pace. It made her wish to go all the faster. It would be just like Lame Bear to single handedly try saving the cattle and taking on the dark horsemen.

Since robbing the stage in Kansas, this deadly gang had become the local boogie man. From Leadville to Longmont folks were blaming the fugitives for everything from mine cave-ins, to missing livestock, to why the crops were failing and the hens wouldn't lay. She didn't believe in all the hoopla, but why were they still in the area. And why would they be interested in the Rising Starr? Only one reason came to mind, and she didn't like the answer.

Outdistancing Eustace she crested a hill and reined

in. What the heck. The cattle appeared safe enough. Maybe Eustace really had been up to no good, with causing trouble in mind. Then she spotted Lame Bear, and he wasn't alone. Although it didn't seem possible after her breakneck ride, her heartbeat quickened. Nic stood there too.

Glancing down, she tried to remember what she had on. She'd taken off in a flurry, not even bothering to bind her hair. Fingering the collar of her father's flannel shirt she relaxed. Although not fashionable, at least it was clean.

Not waiting for Eustace to catch up, she trotted the mare closer, drawing to a halt in front of Nic and Lame Bear. As they related what had happened, the two men stood companionably beneath a cottonwood. She barely heard the facts imparted as visions of what Nic and she shared yesterday flooded her senses. With heat flashing through her like a fever, she rued the fact her face probably appeared as crimson as it felt.

Eustace finally clamored over the hill, and rode up beside her. In unison, Nic and Lame Bear came to attention, moving closer as if she might need protecting.

"Howdy, Eustace," Nic said, "you know something about these doings?"

"Just happened to be in the area. Lame Bear can vouch for that."

Lame Bear grunted in affirmation.

"You run them all off?" Eustace glanced around.

"Only saw the one.

"Me too," Lame Bear confirmed.

"There were two more wandering around up in the hills. That's why I decided to circle back, and warn you up to the house." Eustace nodded at Ochessa.

His solicitous behavior took everyone by surprise, and apparently it showed in their expressions. "Well I don't like outsiders nosing about any better than the next man," he defended his good intentions.

Nothing brings two rivals closer together than a common enemy.

Ochessa studied the cattle grazing peacefully. If any were missing, it couldn't be more than a head or two. "Were they rustling stock, or just stampeding them?"

"The man did not cut any from the herd," Lame Bear assured.

"Then what could be the purpose for all this tomfoolery?"

They looked at one another, and the same idea struck each of them at the same instant. No one had been left behind to watch the ranch house, the barn, or the corrals.

Ochessa swung her mare around, and kicked her into action. The horse leaped forward sending up a spurt of dirt and rock. Nic ran for his mule, Lame Bear at his side. Eustace held back as if unsure whether to follow or not. Not, seemed to be the final decision.

****

Skidding to a halt in front of the house, Ochessa vaulted from the saddle and ran toward the steps. The door stood wide open. She'd left in a panic, but knew she'd closed the place up.

Reaching the porch at the same time, Nic grabbed her and held her back. "They might still be inside."

Before she could respond, he shoved her into Lame Bear's arms, drew his pistol, and eased through the doorway.

Ochessa vacillated between indignation at being told what to do, and wonderment at how good it felt to be wrapped in Nic's protective attitude. Standing silently in place, she perused the immediate area. There were no strange horses about, and as the dust settled in the yard, only quiet took its place.

What was taking Nic so long? Her need for action simmered hotter, and she began to fidget. Hadn't he been in there long enough? Overcome by impatience, she gave Lame Bear her best *don't try to stop me* look, and went inside. What she found left her in stunned silence.

The house had been ransacked. Heartsick, she hurried from room to room. Each one had been torn asunder. It looked as if a giant hand had plucked the house off its foundation, given it a good shake, and then set it back in place.

From the corner of her eye, she saw Nic shake his head in sympathy.

A good portion of her mother's dishes lay shattered on the kitchen floor. Her father's clay pipe had been smashed to bits. She picked up a faded photograph of her brother. The frame hung in pieces, the fragments of broken glass pricking at her fingers. She set the photograph on the mantel. It toppled over, and a lone tear slid down her cheek.

Nic raised one arm as if to comfort her. Then he hesitated, and lowered his arm to his side. He seemed to understand she dare not give in for one minute to the compassion he offered, lest she break down completely.

The tattered remnants of her family's history lay all around her. Sadly, no one else was left in the family to care accept her and…Sassafras.

"Where are you girl? Where are you Sass?"

The welcoming sounds of whining and scratching led her to the large brick-lined cupboard where she stored root crops. She yanked open the door. Sassafras sat huddled off to one side. Dropping to her knees, she reassured her best friend as the dog limped forward and into her arms. With a hesitant wag of her tail, Sass licked her face, and Ochessa examined her to be sure none of her injuries were too serious. Then her happiness at finding Sassafras alive turned to anger that the dog had been hurt at all.

Scrambling to her feet, she picked up the dog, and gently deposited her in the rocking chair by the wood stove. At the sound of approaching hoof beats, she hurried out onto the porch. The ranch hands from the south forty careened to a halt in the yard.

"Is everything okay, mademoiselle?" Little Roy asked.

No, she wanted to scream. "Yes," she said, instead.

"We saw your horse and Mister Nic's mule hitched out front," the little Frenchman explained, "so before heading to the watering hole, we thought it best to stop here in case you had new orders for us."

"You did the right thing. The initial emergency is over, and the cattle are fine. But after you catch your breath, and round up fresh mounts, I need you and the men to ride out to the far side of Deer Trail Ridge. The inlet to the waterhole is jammed with debris so take a wagon and rope and any other equipment you think necessary to clear it."

"Très bien, Miss Ochessa."

"See that you take weapons as well. And watch your backs. Someone's been causing trouble on the property."

The ranch hands began mumbling amongst themselves, concern clinging to their faces like trail dust.

"Tout de suite," the little Frenchman barked, ending the speculation, and spurring the men to action. "We have our orders."

Little Roy and the men headed to the corral to exchange mounts.

Ochessa remained on the porch. Lame Bear stepped to her side. "It is good you did not mention the dark horsemen by name. Although these outlaws are sad excuses for human beings, they have managed to take on mystical proportions."

"Obviously stampeding the herd was just a diversion. They didn't want the cattle."

"Off hand, I'd say they were looking for something a bit smaller." Ochessa knew exactly to what Nic eluded, but she held her tongue. "Something red in color," he prodded.

"But how would these outlaws even know I had the ruby?"

"One of the gang appeared to be sneaking around the fairgrounds during the shooting competition. And what you offered as your entrance fee is common knowledge. It appears they won't quit until they find the jewel."

She remained silent.

Arms crossed over his chest, Nic leaned against the doorframe of the house.

"It isn't here," she finally declared. "You don't think I'd let something that valuable just lie around the parlor."

"Where'd you stash it, Chessy Cat?"

Again with the Chessy Cat. What a silly nickname, or in this case, a Nic name. Yet, deep down, she liked it when he called her that. It made her feel special. When she was little, just to tease her, Will used to call her okra, saying she was slimy and gooey. When she cried and insisted she wasn't, he would smear mud or some other wretched substance on her face declaring now she was. Other than that, no one had ever come up with an endearing name for her.

So what? Nic probably had a cute name for his mule too.

"It's in Denver," she confessed. "At the bank, in a safe deposit box. Besides, it seems unlikely they would stay in the area and risk capture for one stone when they have the gold you said they also took in the robbery. I think they were looking for something else."

Her words seemed to have an odd effect upon him. Acting as if an unwelcome thought had ambushed him, his cocky expression thinned into wariness, and he had no appropriate defense or sarcastic retort handy.

"You seem at a loss for words," she taunted.

"Why don't we discuss this further at the pie social next Sunday?"

"What?" This sure hadn't been the response she'd expected. "I don't have time for pie baking. Besides I've not been asked."

"Well you have now. I'll pick you up at sundown. And we're going in that old carriage I share the barn with, not horseback, so wear a dress. See you then." Not waiting for a response, he sauntered over to that big mule he rode, collected the reins, and headed for the barn.

She stared after him, mouth open, but her sarcastic retort died before reaching her lips. Lame Bear issued one of his noncommittal sounds. She glanced at him, unable to tell if he were pleased, pissed, puzzled, or purely making fun of her.

She turned to face him, hands on her hips. "You just hush, now. It isn't funny."

But it was rather exciting.

****

Reno ground his right fist into the palm of his left. While two of his men had torn up the ranch house searching for the elusive missing gem, he'd spent his time looking for the missing documents. Where were those damn parchments? Who had them?

"Sorry we didn't find the missing ruby, boss." Lanny stood as far away from Reno as the little cabin would permit. "But we still got all that gold. Let's settle for that and be on our way."

"Yeah, sure. Go tell the boys we'll be leaving in a few days."

The men, having eaten their fill of restless, were gnawing on belligerent. They were hankering to split the take and the wind, and he couldn't buffalo them much longer into thinking they were remaining here because of one missing ruby.

Well who cared? Let them all leave. He'd stay on alone.

"Go on, get out of here," he ordered.

Not having to be told twice, Lanny hurried out the door, and Reno settled into what had taken on the illusion of his favorite chair. It seemed odd, but this ruin of a shack had transformed into a place where he felt safe, a condition not frequently present in his life.

Maybe Old Dobbs had been correct, this hideaway turned out to be a haven for a troubled mind and a wayward soul.

Old Dobbs... Reno settled back with the memory. He'd run across the man one winter back when they were river-boating the upper Mississippi. When plied with a few drinks, the old coot had turned cheerfully candid. Of course half his ramblings about the place where he'd grown up turned out to be nonsense, but the story of this cabin had been true enough.

With the old timer now being dead, having accidentally drowned in that big muddy river, he doubted anybody else knew about the place. Except that gal whose spread they had just left, she might know. Or her brother who they'd killed in Kansas. Odd the way these people seemed all tied up together—like this area was some kind of a confluence for these folks' beginnings and endings. And now Nic Breedlove had been thrown in the mix, an interesting turn of events. One could even say a pleasant surprise.

He laid his pistol on the table, unloaded it, and began swabbing out the barrel. The Army had impressed upon him the necessity of keeping his weapon clean, and although he no longer wore a uniform, he lived as if the war still raged on, skirmishing with the enemy, fighting to stay alive, making those he deemed had it coming pay but good.

A smile chiseled its way onto Reno's face. He'd seen Breedlove gambling in the saloon when he'd sneaked into Denver the other night. The man looked just like his father—only tougher. Reno had done hard time because of Breedlove. Now Breedlove's time had come.

And while Breedlove might have been winning that night, he wasn't so smart. Mostly he was just lucky. That's the way it had always been, and a man's luck, good or bad, always changed. Reno aimed to help Breedlove's good fortune hit rock bottom in the very near future.

Piece by piece, his smile of anticipation cracked and fell away. On that same evening, during his foray into town, he'd met with his *partner*. But he'd gained no new information, and not being in control of this operation left him unsettled. He didn't like the idea of putting his trust in other people, or answering to them. Especially people he was forced to associate with out of necessity rather than choice. But then war and politics made strange bedfellows—and so did blackmail.

Chapter Sixteen

Stepping twice on the hem of her dress, Ochessa stumbled from the table to the cook stove, and lovingly placed the object of her labor into the oven. It was the first pie she'd ever made. In fact, the first time she had cooked anything more complicated than biscuits and gravy. So far, so good.

She straightened and risked a sigh of contentment—the simple action quite a miracle considering her tight fitting corset. And her poor feet, they'd grown since she'd taken to wearing cowboy boots. Now the prissy little shoes she'd crammed them into made her mince steps as if she were walking on a creek-bed of moss covered stones.

Taking to a chair to ease her throbbing feet, she felt the possibility of dancing tonight grow more and more remote. Of course the thought of going to the Social with Nic seemed a bit farfetched in every aspect. The idea also made her happy, a feeling so long absent in her life, she nearly didn't recognize the emotion.

She reached for the little wooden box sitting on the table, and ran her finger over the carved flowers on the lid. Then she picked it up and clasped it to her chest. While setting the ranch house back in order, she'd found her Mother's recipe box, and following the directions to the letter, had made the apple pie. A pang of sadness ran roughshod over her happiness. Would her mother be proud?

She studied the room. The recent devastation of her world glared back at her. Losing so many personal items had her clinging to memories with even more resolve than before. Why did Fate seem determined to whittle away anything that gave her comfort? At least she still had Sassafras, for that she couldn't be more grateful.

"You doing all right, old girl?" The dog, stretched out in the corner, raised her head, gave a little yip in answer to the question, then settled back into her favorite sleeping position. She still limped a bit from the rough treatment, and smelled from the onions stored in the root-cellar, but she was doing just fine.

"Sorry they were so mean to you. Anybody who would hurt a dog is mean through and through."

Ochessa set the recipe box aside, and painfully gaining her feet, she lit two kerosene lamps. The glow drove away the loneliness ingrained in the walls, and gave the illusion of down-home comfort. Again her mother came to mind. There had been a time when the word domestic would have aptly described Olivia Langston Starr. But the day after Father died, Mother had donned a pair of pants and never looked back.

Treating the ranch as if it were her new love, her mother had put all her vigor and attention into running the place. It became her obsession. And at the end of the day, nothing had been left for anyone or anything else. Their meals became bare essentials, no more cakes on birthdays or fancy breads at Christmas. With a bit of a shock, Ochessa realized she teetered on becoming just as fixated on her own dream. The undivided passion her mother had felt for the ranch and the land beat strong in her heart too.

Of course, not possessing any domestic skills couldn't be blamed entirely on her mother's neglect. Even if her mother had attempted to school her in baking and sewing, she probably wouldn't have listened. One thing for sure, this afternoon the spirit of her mother had guided her hands baking that pie. At least she liked to think so.

Gathering the ingredients, she stored them in the pantry, and dusted the flour from her hands and the front of her dress. The frock, a treasured keepsake, now appeared outdated and way too flouncy. How did one function on a daily basis wearing such outlandish duds?

She peeked at the mantel clock in the sitting room. About the time the pie finished baking Nic should be arriving to escort her to the event. Would the town social turn out to be a childhood fantasy, or a load of adulthood foolishness?

Absentmindedly, she stoked the firebox with split wood, all the while picturing the glow of Chinese lanterns softening the world around them as she and Nic danced the night away, the last hoorah of honeysuckle fragrance hovering in the air.

At the idea of being that close to Nic, insecurity struck again, sending her hurrying to her bedroom. The reflection leaping out of the cracked mirror lacked reassurance. She smoothed away the wrinkles and creases in the dress then went back to trimming the abundance of lace and ribbon festooning nearly every seam. Partially detached, the remnants flap and flutter with every move she made. So far, it looked worse than ever. Oh who was she kidding. *You could put a straw bonnet on a long-ear, but it was still a mule.* That might be a good thing. Nic seemed to appreciate Sadie the way he catered to and took care of her.

She ran her fingers through her mop of hair. Maybe if her tresses were grand enough no one would notice her dress. At present, her hairstyle could be summed up as curly abandon. Cripes, being a girly-girl sure did take a lot of time—and apparently a good bit of practice. But Nic seemed to cotton to the idea, and it didn't cost her anything other than sore feet and a small ragged corner of her pride. Why not give it a try? Tripping the light fantastic for one night wouldn't change her necessarily, or fix the responsibilities she faced, but it might be fun.

Praying for guidance, she grabbed the comb and brush, wondering how some women managed to stack their tresses so high and mighty above their weak little minds. She should have paid more attention to the other women during her ventures to town. But she had no time for socializing, and her lack of interest in the latest styles hadn't gone unnoticed as she became the center of snide remarks rather than a party to them.

Shoving a clutch of ringlets into place, she stabbed an ivory comb into the uncooperative mass. That looked pretty good. Then she cocked her head to one side, and hazarded a coquettish smile. An architectural failure quickly followed, and the comb hit the floor with a sad little thud.

She bent to retrieve the useless ornament when the smell of something burning caught her attention. Oh, no. She headed for the kitchen at a limping run. Ribbons of smoke seeped through the seam in the old wood stove heralding disaster. She'd added too much kindling.

With a yelp of dismay, she wretched open the little door. A blast of heat, hotter than the floorboards of hell, radiated from the oven. Grabbing a towel, she waved aside the smoke, and wrapping her hands in the folds of cotton, she leaned closer to rescue the doomed pie. Like a tawny waterfall, her hair spilled forward, and a new smell, reminiscent of the corral on branding day, outweighed burnt pie aroma.

Her singed hair smoldered, and a sudden backdraft sent a flurry of embers in the direction of the semi-detached ribbons and lace. Flinging the pie onto the table, she swatted at the front of her clothing. Sizzling and smoking and ready to burst into flames, the sparks were already taking hold. Ouch. That one burned right through. Each time she slapped at the embers, they broke apart, doubling the peril and reducing her chances for salvaging the dress. If she didn't take care, the whole place could go up in flames.

Stumbling out of the house and into the front yard, she dropped to the ground, and using handfuls of dust and dirt, smothered the sparks and burgeoning flames. When she finished tumbling about, Ochessa eased up onto her hands and knees, and opened her eyes—two shiny black boots came into focus.

"Guess I must be a little early."

Nic…

She glanced up from ground level.

His expression of surprise turned to one of sympathy as he reached down and helped her to her feet. "You all right, darlin'?" With his free hand, he brushed the dust and debris from her backside.

"Yes, I'm fine." She jerked her arm from his grasp. "I was trying to bake a pie and …"

"And you set your hair on fire."

"My dress too." Mortified she couldn't say anything more.

"Poor Chessy Cat." Drawing her close, he held her tight. Like a devastated child, she offered no resistance, seeking the shelter of his embrace.

Finally Nic eased her away from his chest. Then without a word he ushered her up the steps of the house and into the kitchen. They stood facing one another, his gaze roaming aimlessly around the room, the act of focusing on her apparently too painful an ordeal.

Her dress was in ruins. The few parts not burned and smudged with char, now showed streaks of yard dirt. She gingerly patted her hair. A few bits crackled like prairie grass in August. Lord she must look a fright.

Nic eyed the still smoldering pie. "Apple?" he asked, finally meeting her gaze.

"Yes," she squeaked, staving off the hot tears pricking at the back of her eyes.

"The boys were sure you'd cook up one of those fancy lemon pies with the calf slobber on top. But I bet on Apple."

She couldn't help but smile at his meringue reference.

He reached out, rotating the blackened pie first one way then the other. "Look's done." He stifled laugh. "Want to try a piece?"

Setting his hat aside, he plunked down into one of the kitchen chairs. She couldn't take the pie to the Social, so they might as well eat it, or at least try. With great reservation, she retrieved two plates and forks, cut them each a hearty slice, and served the disaster with two glasses of cold milk. Joining him at the table, they hacked through the crust. The center turned out fairly edible.

What must Nic be thinking? Her one attempt at being feminine had failed miserably. Did he realize it constituted a huge departure from her regular life? He caught her watching him and grinned. Black chips of burnt pie crust stuck to his teeth. She grinned back, knowing full well her smile must appeared just as ridiculous. Then they both hooted with laughter until they were short of breath.

"This is nice," Nic said, around another mouthful of pie.

"What's nice?" Did he mean the hideous pastry, the place setting, the weather, what?

"Sitting here with you."

She'd been hoping for that answer. "Does it beat the Blue Palace?" Reaching for her glass of milk, she took a sip.

"Definitely. But not the tack room."

She sputtered and choked, as recollections of what he'd done to her in the cool darkness scurried hotly through her mind.

"When a cow laughs," he asked, "does milk come out its nose?"

The silly idea countered her thoughts of passion, and she couldn't help but laugh in earnest. She liked his off-center sense of humor.

As a comfortable silence surrounded them, his presence commanded all her attention.

His strong features were softened by some remembered innocence of childhood. And when his expression turned wayward, she wanted to throw caution out the window and find out what adventure he had in mind. But his looks didn't push her over the edge, it was the way he made her feel—special and unique and worthy of being loved.

"Still willing to insist there's nothing between us?" Nic challenged.

"No," she admitted. "But it's fragile as a newborn kitten. And I'm afraid without proper nurturing it might not survive in the real world."

He reached across the table and took one of her hands in his. "Whether new born or nearly over, life is a struggle, Ochessa. And a wise man named Lame Bear once told me that paths cross for a reason. Right now, I'm here for you."

A glow of happiness slipped over her like an old familiar shawl, one she thought lost forever, packed away with her hopes and dreams. Then she came to her senses.

"*Right now* encompasses a rather undetermined period of time."

"It's the best I can do."

That sounded honest enough, she had to give him points for that.

"Let me play in your corral," he tempted. "Let me be someone you can turn to for help. Sharing isn't a weakness, Chessy Cat. It's a gift between friends—or between lovers."

Her heart felt lodged in her throat. He'd called them lovers. They weren't yet, not truly. But he must think they would be in the near future. And calling her Chessy Cat still warmed her heart. It didn't matter where he'd come up with the notion, not when it felt like the only name she had ever known, transforming her into a different person—somebody meant just for

Nic.

His grip on her hand tightened ever so slightly, a shared moment to cherish—simple and heartfelt. But she mustn't forget Nic could be artful at stringing words together, and he rarely seemed at a loss for them. Whereas for her, translating deep feelings into clever phrases seemed nearly impossible. Which condition fared worse, she wondered. Not being taken seriously because you were always ready with a smart comeback, or struggling hard and never being heard at all?

"I want to believe you." She slipped her hand free from his grasp. "And right now, that's a big step for me." For something to do, she reached down and unlaced her high-top shoes. "Thank goodness I won't need these tonight," she added, steering their conversation in a new direction.

Kicking the footwear aside, she snagged her cowboy boots, pulled out the socks stored inside, and donned both. Still contemplating what they had just talked about, she pretended to be consumed by the menial task until she heard the violin music floating in through the open window. Nic rose to investigate, and turning back toward her, he smiled and extended his hand.

"Come take a look."

Gaining her feet, she crossed the room and stood before him to peer out the window. Heat from his body warmed her from behind, and the urge to sink back into that comfort teased through her.

"Looks like there's dancing tonight after all." He seemed pleased by the idea.

Apparently, the men had decided to have a get together of their own. They could have gone to town and raised a little hullabaloo there, but they appeared happy with a fandango of their own making.

Fiddler Joe McFadden stood under a big tree, demonstrating how he'd come by his name. A burly, rough-cut man of good faith and good humor, he cuddled the violin beneath his chin as if the instrument were made of fine china. As the first strains of music flowed, his gruff face took on an angelic expression, but after he got warmed up, and the tempo increased, his smile turned a bit devilish, and the music took on the raucous flavor of one of Joe's famous Highland flings.

One hand at the small of her back, Nic propelled her toward the door. She dug in her heels and refused to move.

"I can't go out looking like this."

When the burnt pie incident came to light, it would likely live in infamy, no point in the men also seeing her hair singed and smelling like branded cowhide.

With nary a laugh nor chiding remark, Nic retrieved his battered hat, and settled it on her head.

An unexpected honor—or an act of pity.

To compensate for it being too big, she stuffed the ends of her hair up into the misshaped crown.

Amusement shone in Nic's eyes, and a quirky smile softened the set of his mouth, and before she had time to dwell on his motivation, he fast-waltzed her out the door and onto the porch. They glided to a halt at the railing, and watched the ranch hands gathered around in the yard, stamping their feet and clapping their hands.

One man had tied an apron to a broom, and his comic dancing drew hoots of approval from the men. With humorous enthusiasm, they passed the Broom Girl around, along with large mugs of hard-cider filled from a barrel that had appeared out of nowhere. There were lanterns hung in trees and on fence posts, and as dusk settled in with a sigh, the magical glow softened the world around them just as nicely as any Chinese lanterns.

Nic urged her down the steps. They joined in the fun, but after a few moments, he leaned close and whispered in her ear. "Let's take a walk."

Moonlight replaced lamplight, and the merrymaking receded to a dull roar as they headed for a nearby stand of trees. At full brightness, the celestial glow filtered through the leaves and branches, embellishing the ground with lacey patterns spun by the stars. Feeling pretty in spite of her disastrous hair and dress, Ochessa indulged in the fantasy, enjoying the fairytale setting.

She wanted so badly to be loved and needed. And she wanted Nic to be the man to fulfill those emotions. What made him special she couldn't—maybe shouldn't—define. But like a half-remembered dream, an ethereal connection existed between the two of them and right now that seemed all that mattered.

When he halted and turned to stand before her, his gaze turned hungry, and he eased the hat from her head and lowered his mouth to hers. Accepting the full depth of his kiss, she braced her hands against his chest, gripping his shirt with both fists—she never wanted him to leave.

He pulled away first. "Ochessa," he whispered, in a husky voice. "I can't go on wanting you without knowing if you feel the same."

"I want you too. You know I do. But I'm scared,

and I don't even know what it is I'm scared of."

"How about change. Or the future or the raw need I feel in you. Sometimes I'm scared too—and lonely."

At his declaration part of her fears melted.

"You don't trust my intentions." He spoke the words that up until now had always sat like a dark harbinger in the recesses of her mind.

"No, I *do* trust you. Really I do." She was amazed at her own admission, but the decision felt right. "But I need time to sort out my life."

"Well time is about all I got." And I can bear the wait as long as I know what it is I'm waiting for."

If joy could be counted as a tangible commodity, she suddenly felt rich beyond compare.

Their gazes met and held until it seemed the writing on their souls told the same story, and what bound them emotionally could no longer be separated by Man or Destiny, but only by their failure to take a chance.

****

Reno Benteen sat alone in the gathering gloom. By his way of thinking a man could never be too rich or too lucky.

As the light dimmed, he felt his way across the small cabin, lit the kerosene lamp on the table, and returned to his chair. He glanced at the strong box containing the gold. There had been a time when it would have been enough. But he had better plans, bigger plans. He needed the documents, not the coins or even the still missing gem. He'd found a cash cow, and he intended to milk it for a good long while.

Too bad the cow came tethered with a rope or two. One had been cut when he paid-off his contact in New

York. But the local one still tripped him up, and he didn't like sharing.

Why did he need a partner anyway? He could execute the plan on his own, eliminate the go-between. He wasn't intimidated by the fancy-ass Captains of Industry who ran Denver. If not for the railroad swindles which had made them rich, they'd be no better off than him.

He pictured the high muckety-mucks he intended to fleece, and smiled. His bright new scam had been built upon their dirty old ones—time to pay the piper. And speaking of payment, Nic Breedlove's comeuppance was something to contemplate and savor—he was glad now Harlan had failed in Monotony. When he took Breedlove's life, it wouldn't be quick or clean. But right now, until his other scheme took hold, making such an overt move seemed unwise, which brought him back full circle to the papers he sought. He wondered if Breedlove knew where they were. Breedlove...

Reno jumped to his feet and paced the room, which suddenly seemed alarmingly small. When the war ended, he'd spent several weeks in a stinking Yankee prison—he still had nightmares about that place. The next thing he knew he'd been charged with war crimes, and thanks to Nic's testimony, found guilty. Federal prison turned out to be as bad as a Yankee compound. He couldn't get his time back, but he could shorten Breedlove's.

During the war he'd witnessed unimaginable cruelty handed out with coldhearted enthusiasm—he'd even been a part of it. The experience had spawned indifference, not compassion, proving he was willing to do whatever it took to survive.

Chapter Seventeen

As the herd disappeared over the horizon, a tear slipped down Ochessa's cheek. The animals were going off to the Denver stockyards—to slaughter. She'd sent them to their death. But what other choice did she have? The legal ramifications for breaching the signed contracts were impossible to counter, and she couldn't afford to buy the cattle herself and just turn them loose. Besides the men had worked hard all year toward this end, she owed it to them. And she owed it to her mother, her final request being *get the herd to market*, another example of her being as strong willed as the land.

At least this would be the last time. After paying the men's wages, the leftover would buy her a new livelihood, one that brought contentment to her soul and happiness to her heart. She felt bursting with the excitement of it all. Her plan would most likely garner a heap of ridicule, but being unconventional had always been her strong suit.

With a new lightheartedness, she turned her back to the road, and hands tucked in the pockets of her split skirt, she headed toward the barn. The Rising Starr belonged to her now, and she could hardly wait to begin.

Some folks would call her crazy, but she knew the decision had been the correct one. She couldn't keep pouring blood, sweat, and tears into an occupation that broke her heart. When the inspiration had struck, she'd felt reborn. Now she could make peace with the universe, and her place in it.

At the side corral, she lingered. Lucky bellowed, acting as if he missed the company of the other cattle.

"I know. But don't worry big guy. I kept your two favorite ladies, they're in the back pasture."

Reaching over the rail, she scratched Lucky behind his left ear. She'd never sell her hard won bull. The handsome son-of-a-gun had won a place in her heart. He would have a good life, no demands other than occasionally servicing the heifers of the local ranchers. Even Eustace might be interested in that possibility. And the extra money would be a boon until her new business began to show a profit.

"We'll be all right, old boy," she promised. He snorted as if in agreement, bobbed his head surprisingly gentle against her hand, then ambled off to stand in the sun. She wished they hadn't put a ring in his nose.

It would be a gamble, this new lifestyle, but one she had to take. The Rising Starr Ranch would continue to flourish, although definitely not as envisioned by her father or mother. The past was built on blind tradition. Win, lose, or draw, the future would be built on her dreams, her determination.

Standing in the middle of the silent yard, she inhaled deeply and surveyed the countryside. A feeling of gratitude and responsibility coursed through her. She didn't take lightly the stewardship entrusted to her, and even in the face of the recent loss of her mother and brother, she offered thanks for what she did have. The only thing missing—someone to share the ride.

Despite the pie baking fiasco, spending time with Nic had been wonderful—laughing, being carefree and feeling pretty. *Pretty*...It had been a long time since that word had popped into her mind. She stared down at her mud covered boots. Probably be a long time until it came around again.

Nic also made her feel fearless as if she could conquer the world, and do anything she set her mind to. He said he wanted her, was willing to wait for her to come to him, and that meant a great deal.

Heading back to the house, it dawned on her, except for Sassafras, she was totally alone at the ranch. The older men, not driving the heard, were scouting missing strays south of the ranch. They would most likely make camp out there, taking a few days for fishing and some well-earned rest.

Nic had gone to town hoping to light a fire under the Wells Fargo agent regarding the dark horsemen, and Lame Bear had taken off for the north fork of the South Platte. He'd gone to visit and help some friends repair their cabin before this coming winter.

Standing in the yard, feeling languid in the solitude, she jumped then smiled as Old Sass, in a burst of remembered youth, ran past her toward the woods. The dog pursued Frank the fox—the ranch's longtime tenant, and the dog's longtime honored enemy.

"Go get him girl." Even when fully recovered, a victory for the dog would be unlikely. Still, what a blessing to watch her try.

Rounding the barn, the idea of indulging in a hot bath teased through her mind. But she already felt drowsy, soaking would probably do-her-in for the rest of the day—and duty called. The final tallying of the books awaited her attention. Although a job learned long ago, she never enjoyed this responsibility, had in fact put it off for as long as possible. But she needed at least a guestament of the bottom line to see where her finances stood. The bath could be her reward later.

As she headed for the house, the quiet became disquiet, and a chill snaked down her spine. She glanced around, images of the dark horsemen hovering like wraiths in the back of her mind. She mustn't forget danger lurked nearby. Yet, feeling uneasy on her own property rubbed her the wrong way, and raised her hackles.

Still dawdling rather than returning to the house and the drudgery of bookwork, she decided to ride out and evaluate the condition of the timber and prairie grass on the west boundaries of her property. With the recent dry spell, between storms, a lightning flash could prove disastrous.

Ochessa grabbed her rifle and a canteen of water and saddled up her roan mare. While she was out there, she might as well look around Old Dobbs' mine and cabin. That thought evoked happy memories. She and Will had often gone adventuring there, going back would make her feel closer to him.

As children they'd spent hours exploring—until Father found out. Fearful of cave-ins, he had forbidden them to return to the area, and the solemn promise extracted from them way back then rang fresh in her mind. Now breaking her childhood pledge, she brushed aside the accompanying guilt, and urged the roan in that direction.

A pair of cottontails burst from a pile of dead leaves, and bolted across the trail. The mare tossed her head and sidestepped. It gave Ochessa the jitters too. What a bundle of nerves they all were. Since the arrival of the dark horsemen, people and animal alike seemed nervous. These outlaws needed to be rounded up as soon as possible—and made to pay.

Nic had finally admitted the outlaws were responsible for Will's death. She'd already put two and two together, but she appreciated the fact he'd come clean.

Coaxing her horse across a small stream, she halted to get her bearings. Steep going, this section of property rarely pulled watch duty. Even the most determined strays in the herd were smart enough not to forage up into this dark densely timbered section of the ranch. The bears and mountain lions liked it well enough though.

Soon the terrain became more familiar, and she knew the ridge overlooking the cabin stood just up ahead. She smiled at the thought of Old Dobbs...a scruffy but harmless miner who had told entertaining tales as he showed her and Will how to pan for gold in the runoff of the nearby stream. He'd disappeared one winter and never returned. She hadn't thought about him in years, and wondered what had happened to him. To the eyes of two young children, he'd seemed ancient, but probably hadn't been over forty years old.

Angling up the hill, she located the trail, discernable only to knowing eyes, and followed it to the top. Dismounting she left her horse ground-tied in a shady area with plenty of grass to keep the little mare happy and quiet. Then she set out on foot, instinct guiding the placement of her feet.

An unusual sound caught her attention, bringing

her up short. There it went again. Easing up behind a boulder she peeked around the edge, and was shocked to find a man dressed in black sitting under a large pine, his back wedged up against the tree. The outlaws had found the cabin. This is where they had been hiding.

Presumably a perimeter guard, his rifle now lay abandoned at his side, and his right arm cradled a jug more suitable for hard spirits than water. He appeared to be asleep or passed out. His snoring had been the sound she'd heard.

A magpie landed nearby. Driven by curiosity or hunger or both, the bird hopped closer to the man and pecked at a discarded bread crust. A whistle-pig gave a squeak and moved onto a flat rock to sun himself. The man neither stirred nor altered the rhythm of his somnolent breathing. He didn't look to be a threat.

Backing away, Ochessa turned and made a detour deeper into the trees. In about twenty yards she circled around, and picked up the sound of men talking. Seeking a better view below, she crawled to the edge of a ridge.

Nestled at the foot of the slope, and a bit worse for wear, the cabin and out buildings sat just as she remembered them. What a perfect set up. The shanties were nicely hidden from view. The nearby stream offered a ready source of water, while the branches of the surrounding trees dispersed and concealed smoke from the wood stove. The logistical advantages had gone unnoticed when she played here as a child, now they outweighed the adventurous qualities.

She glanced around. Approaching with a posse, regardless of direction, would be difficult—if not impossible.

Hunkered down, she noted the number of men in the gang and what weapons they carried. One man wearing a sour expression, lounged on the porch whittling, two men labored halfheartedly at chopping and stacking wood. Counting the perimeter guard, that made four men so far.

A huge clap of thunder rolled and tumbled across the valley. She studied the sky. To the south, one giant black cloud slid down off the back range and climbed over the foothills. It looked more like a noise-maker than a rain-maker.

A fifth man came out of the cabin door, he studied the sky too, then he stood tall—smoking a cigar as he surveyed his little pine tree domain. This must be the ring leader, Reno Benteen. With a shudder, she recalled the few details Nic had divulged about this man. And by Nic's deadly cold expression as he spoke, she figured there were plenty more horror stories Nic had yet to recant or recall.

Even from a distance, Reno appeared predatory. He wore his gun slung low and easy, the holster and belt appearing well used and not flashy. He fit the picture of a dangerous man, harboring dangerous ideas.

Careful not to set any rocks cascading downward, she crawled over to a shady area to contemplate the situation. It wouldn't be easy to smoke these varmints out, and it would take more than just Nic, Lame Bear, and herself. Nic had divulged the reason he'd come to Colorado was to track down the outlaws. That had come as a surprise. Then Nic swore she was the reason he wanted to stay. That was an even bigger surprise—a really good one.

Not willing to press her luck, she decided to head

back to her mare. Crouched low, she eased even farther back from the ridge. The sound of a round being chambered in a rifle, brought her up short, and put her guts in a knot. Standing tall, her heart pounding, she turned around. Guess the thunder had awakened the man snoring beneath the tree.

He stared at her down the barrel of his raised Winchester.

****

Ochessa heard movement beyond the storeroom door, and judging by the glow of light leaking in through the cracks she guessed it must finally be the next morning.

Out of pure frustration she gnawed on the rope binding her wrists. Then spitting aside a bristle of hemp she abandoned the attempt, and leaned back against a burlap sack filled with dried beans. She should have stayed home and worked on the books rather than reliving old times and gallivanting around the property

Rooting about, she stretched her legs, trying to coax some circulation into her numb backside. Her bones ached from spending the night on the cold dirt floor, and her patience was wearing as thin as the gruel they'd fed her last night.

Wondering what had transpired in her absence, she thought about Nic. Had he spoken with Jonathan Thacker? Had he divulged her secret about being in possession of the missing ruby? Admitting the location to Nic had put him in an awkward position if questioned, but while she felt regret for telling him the location, she felt no guilt for keeping the stone.

And what about Sassafras? The big bowl of food she'd left for her would have to tide her over. Or hopefully, she could catch a rabbit. The horses and Lucky were turned out to respective pastures, and could reach their water troughs—no worries there. But with Nic in town and Lame Bear still across the valley with his friends, no one would realize she'd gone missing. And when either one did figure out where to look for her, two men *storming the castle* would be hopeless—but they'd probably try. That thought brought a feeling of wonder to her heart as well as concern. She couldn't stand to lose either Lame Bear or Nic.

How many people had the outlaws killed? Probably an ever growing list to which she might easily be added. None of the men in camp had concealed their faces. That made her privy to what they looked like, and she doubted they intended to leave witnesses behind. Yet, right now, because of what they'd done to her brother, she detested more than feared them with a visceral hate she'd never felt before. How curious to discover hate and love at the same crossroads of her life.

Nic had known from the beginning these men were responsible for Will's death. Apparently some Quixotic notion prevented him from telling her sooner. A few weeks ago, his holding back would have irritated her. Now, at least she could accept his reason for doing so.

Being too curious had gotten her into big trouble. But more importantly it could put Nic and Lame Bear in danger. Cold and hungry, a sick feeling churned in her empty stomach. She hung her head and tears stung her eyes. Then anger warmed her blood, upping her need for action. No more patiently waiting. She had to find a way out of this mess, and that meant getting out of this dank dark storage room. With that in mind she kicked at the pantry door and hollered at the top of her lungs.

The door jerked open, and Reno glared down at her. Not a tall man, he had a sturdy and brawny frame, and leaning over he grabbed her by the arms, hauled her to her feet, and dragged her out into the other room.

"Stop all the noise," he ordered, shoving her into a chair.

"I have to use a tree, if you get my meaning."

"Christamighty," he swore. Then he grabbed a length of rope, tied it around her neck, and walked with her out the cabin door. "Hurry up," he barked, nodding toward the nearest clump of aspen, as he payed out line.

Hands still tied in front she stumbled forward as far as the rope would allow. No longer shining brightly, the sun hid behind leaden clouds which looked too heavy to be suspended in the sky. One or two billowy nimbus' sported a sickly green cast. Unlike yesterday, a real storm fumed above, a nor'easter by the looks of it. They'd been due for a gully-washer, this could be it.

After taking care of business, she breathed in the heavy air, trying to formulate a plan of escape. A vicious tug on the rope interrupted her thoughts on strategy. Coughing and clawing at the rope around her neck, she retraced her steps. *You could smell the rain in the air.*

The other outlaws, awake now, milled about. They stopped to stare at her, their heated gazes following her every move. Reaching the cabin door unscathed, she realized again this morning, only Reno stood between her and the rest of this pack of human wolves. "Thank you," she said, swallowing back the gall those two words kicked up in the back of her throat.

"Close your yap, and get back inside."

He followed on her heels, slammed the door closed, and roughly slid the rope free.

"I got a feeling you're gonna be more trouble than your worth."

She certainly hoped so.

Rubbing at the rope burn on her neck, she studied the room in the light of day. The dirty windows appeared to be nailed down, the door she'd come through the only exit. The fireplace had seen better days, the hearth crumbling, but the wood stove in the corner seemed functional with a small supply of wood in readiness.

Feet splayed and beefy fists planted on his hips, Reno stood before her. "Where are the documents?"

So they were back to that tired song. He'd asked her repeatedly about them last night. She didn't know their whereabouts, unless they were the papers she'd seen poking out of Nic's saddlebags in the barn. What to do, what to do? She had to keep disavowing any knowledge of their existence. It might be the only thing keeping her alive.

****

Biting back a curse, Reno kicked an empty coal bucket across the floor. The woman remained silent, anger blazing in her eyes, her mouth set in stubborn opposition. What had the crazy bitch been thinking, riding up here poking around? She had more cohunes than most men he knew. And while she might be easy on the eyes, she was painful on the ears, and worse yet, she was a liability he hadn't counted on and didn't need. Sooner or later her people were bound to come looking for her.

"We know you have the ruby. You must have the papers too."

"Had the ruby. It's been a tough year. I sold it to pay off my creditors."

"And you sold the papers too I suppose."

"I don't know anything about your papers."

"You're lying."

He held his tongue, watching as her expression transformed from angry to hateful. Dammit. Enough was enough. Never having been partial to long winded negotiations he backhanded her across the face, sending her spinning up against the wall. Blood oozed from her cracked lip, and she appeared bleary eyed for a moment, but she didn't lose her footing. She stood there fuming, and he swore if her hands had been free she would have come at him swinging.

Deep down, Reno figured this kind of treatment probably wouldn't make her talk. So far she'd acted stubborn enough to die before giving in. He flung himself into a chair and studied her. Maybe she'd come around if she thought holding back meant someone else's peril, someone important to her. Unfortunately, seeing as they'd already killed her brother, only Breedlove and the Indian were left to choose between. He didn't much favor either option.

"Maybe you'd feel more talkative with that gunslinger or the old Indian here to take the punishment for your lying.

"Lanny," he hollered, "get in here."

The door creaked open, and a menacing clap of thunder poured in around the younger man as he entered the cabin. Lanny walked with more swagger than usual, and like the rest of the men, his gaze latched onto the girl, heated up, and stayed put.

"You need something, Boss?" he asked, not shifting the direction of his gaze.

"Bring me the Indian," Reno ordered.

That got Lanny's attention as well as the girl's.

"The Indian. You mean her Indian?

"That's the one."

"I don't know boss. That's a pretty tall order."

"He's an old man. You can handle him. But I want him at least mostly alive."

Lanny stood staring at the floor as if it had suddenly acquired hypnotic properties.

"Can I take Curly with me?"

Reno thought over the request. He didn't blame Lanny for wanting someone to watch his back, but he didn't want them clamoring around the territory drawing attention to themselves.

"All right. But don't make a ruckus, and be damn sure nobody follows you back here."

Lanny turned to leave. The woman hurried forward—blocking his exit.

"Stay away from Lame Bear." Lanny grabbed her, an expression of consternation crossing his face. He looked like a man caught between a rock and a soft place—a soft place that felt good in his arms.

The wind shrieked across the opening of the chimney. The mournful howl rushed down the brickwork and burst into the cabin like an evil harbinger.

"He'll do as he's ordered," Reno barked over the noise.

Renewed thunder crashed around the cabin, the impending storm shaking the walls of the flimsy shack.

Lanny flinched as the second clap of thunder let loose on the heels of the first. Then he set the girl aside.

"It'll be hard goin' when this storm breaks."

"Yeah, I know that," Reno agreed. "Wait until morning."

It aggravated him all the more that even the elements seemed against him. On the other hand they'd waited this long. No use screwing everything up by getting careless.

A look of relief eased the worried expression from Lanny as he hurried from the cabin.

Ochessa whirl around to face Reno. "Lame Bear is Lakota Sioux. He'll have those two for breakfast."

He wanted to slap the smug smile off her face.

"Could be," he agreed, not completely disregarding the validity of her words. "But Lanny and Curly cut their teeth on range wars and rustling, so don't discount their success too readily."

And if they failed, it would simplify dividing the take.

Chapter Eighteen

Finished eating his breakfast at the Old Buffalo Exchange, Nic braced himself for another day in Denver. Being idle made him as restless as a thoroughbred at the post. He needed action. Not even his Stetson, newly arrived, eased his impatient spirit.

Along with this week's pots, pans, and sundries, the hat had been included, coming in earlier than expected. The shopkeeper declared the hat's unscheduled appearance a miracle. Nic left miracles and praying for them to other folks.

Then he remembered the reason for purchasing the new hat—a whirlwind of a woman named Ochessa. Leaving her at the ranch didn't set well with him, especially since his trip to town had turned into a two day affair. Guess she'd be okay with all the ranch hands around, but he'd sure rather be back at the Rising Starr than cooling his heels here.

Mulling over thoughts of the recent time they'd spent together, he recalled the flavor of burnt pie tempered by sweet kisses, and a smile chased away his frown. He was probably worrying for nothing, yet deep down, nothing quelled the feeling that somewhere in his world something had gone terribly wrong. He'd had that feeling once or twice before and it never paid to ignore it.

Figuring the Wells Fargo office should be open by

now, Nic took to the streets, and adjusting the fit of his hat, he considered the cloud formation in the west. He'd bet the inclement weather was already letting loose up in the hills behind the ranch—and it looked to be heading this way.

Reaching the office, he took up position and stood glaring at the closed door to Thacker's inner sanctum, as if doing so would make it open sooner. Finally when it did, a man dressed somewhere between countrified and city-slicker made a quick exit, a folder of information clutched in his hand.

"Come in Mr. Breedlove," Thacker beckoned. "Sorry you were obliged to stay over last night due to my absence. Trouble in El Paso County kept me there until this morning."

"No doubt you're busy. I appreciate you taking time to see me again." Nic's tone remained polite, even though thoughts of good manners were the furthest thing from his mind. "There's been trouble at the Rising Starr Ranch." He took the seat the agent offered.

"What kind of trouble?" Thacker dropped into the chair on the opposite side of the desk.

"The dark horsemen."

Thacker's eyes flickered ever so slightly, but no other emotion found a path to his face. "Tell me more." He leaned forward, his elbows resting on the arms of the chair, his hands clasped in front.

"A few days ago the cattle were spooked with mischievous intent, and the ranch house was ransacked."

"Lots of folks have been plagued by misfortune only to blame it on the dark horsemen. What makes you think it's the gang from Kansas?"

"Cut the bull. We've witnesses," Nic challenged.

If anyone knew what went on out there, the man sitting across from him did. What game did he play at?

"Are you ready to tell me the whereabouts of the missing ruby?" Thacker asked, ignoring Nic's insinuation. "The one Miss Starr laid claim to at the shooting competition?"

Maybe he could make a trade for the information.

"Or perhaps, you're ready to hand over the documents we discussed at our prior meeting."

Well, how quickly they'd slipped from trading information to a bit of arm twisting. Nic mentally kicked himself for underestimating Mr. Thacker. When it came to his job, the man showed marked determination. Could he be ruthless enough to use the Rising Starr as bait to flush out the desperados? Or use Reno to frighten Ochessa and himself into revealing all they knew? He supposed this man felt justified in using whatever means necessary, but putting Ochessa and other people at the ranch in danger crossed the line.

"You knew Reno and his gang had menaced the ranch. You had no right to let them do your dirty work of intimidation."

"I had every right, Mr. Breedlove. Your allegiance is obviously self-serving and so is mine. Don't take it personal. Now if you please, let's start with the whereabouts of the missing ruby?"

He couldn't divulge that information. Which left him with only the papers as a bargaining chip, and both Thacker and Reno wanted them.

"You'll have to ask Miss Starr where the alleged ruby might be. And if she does happen to have it, she should get the finder's fee and a reward for keeping it safe. As far as the papers, they're gone. Reno must have found them." Let's see what reaction this little white lie kindled.

Thacker's gaze narrowed, and he clenched one fist and leaned back in his chair. Then recovering his composure, a sarcastic smile pulled at his mouth. "I don't believe you, Mr. Breedlove. If Reno had them, I'd know."

Again, it looked like the papers were the key to this whole maneuver. "Maybe if I knew why you wanted them so badly, I'd be more certain of their location."

"Maybe if you weren't in this up to your neck, I'd be more inclined to tell you."

Nic considered the remark. Now they knew where they stood, they both held information neither felt compelled to relinquish. "I have a proposition for you," he ventured.

"I'm listening."

"Come back to the Rising Starr with me and we can put an end to this once and for all. I'll help you track down that miserable dog of a human—and his gang—and maybe those documents will turn up."

"Again, you sound like this is a personal vendetta, Mr. Breedlove. I've never known an outsider so anxious to tangle with known cutthroats and thieves.

"Why I want in, is my business."

"I'll consider your offer."

"Well consider fast. At some point Reno will cut his losses and run. And based on history, the trail he leaves behind won't be a pretty sight."

Thacker appeared to consider this information before speaking. "Are the men at the Rising Starr willing to posse up?"

"I doubt it. They don't see it as their fight."

"That's been the problem all along. Everybody wants Reno and his gang gone, but nobody wants to help make that happen. Not even the Deputy. I've asked for assistance from the home office, but haven't gotten a reply. Meantime, I have to take care of Wells Fargo business clear across Colorado, and that spreads my resources mighty thin. Right now, several of my men are in Cañon City to meet a gold shipment coming up from Santa Fe." Thacker rubbed at the crease between his eyes, before asking, "Are you sure none of the wranglers will help?"

"Most of the ranch hands will be tying one on in town once Ochessa decides it's time to get the herd to Denver. But you could count on Lame Bear and me."

"I'll come by tomorrow and maybe we can come up with a plan. That's the best I can do right now."

Figuring Thacker's offer to be take it or leave it, Nic acquiesced. "I'll hold you to that, and see you then. Meantime, I'll think about where those documents might be."

"You do that."

Not willing to give Thacker an opportunity to renege on their agreement, Nic gained his feet, settled his Stetson in place, and fixing Thacker with a look he hoped conveyed his determination, Nic took his leave.

Reaching a side street he paused and tried to organize his thoughts. Had he considered all the available options? He wanted to ride up into the foothills right now, track down, and have it out with the low-life's running roughshod over the territory. Conversely when you were about to kick-open a hornet's nest of trouble, doing so with the best laid plan possible and with the greatest number of willing *soldiers* made the most sense.

Reviewing the situation over in his mind, he mounted Sadie and moseyed across town. A herd of cattle being driven into the holding pens on the outskirts of Denver interrupted his progress. Attempting to go around, he angled off to the right, then halted in surprise. Several of the cowpokes moving the animals appeared familiar. This was Ochessa's herd. She'd decided to move them earlier than he thought. Urging his mule around a couple of bystanders watching the activity, he edged closer to the stockyards.

"Little Roy," he called, as the man rode by.

The Frenchman glanced up, then smiled and headed his way.

"Comment allez-vous, Monsieur Breedlove?" He reined to a halt beside Sadie.

"How long have you been gone from the ranch?" Nic asked, his concern bypassing pleasantries.

"We left yesterday noon, making camp last night just east of town as we waited for the pens to be available. A good thing too, *mon amie*. We will miss the storm forming in the foothills. The weather will not be pleasant up there today, or down here later," he added, eying the sky. "But now that we are in Denver, the cattle will be loaded in the railcars, and the weather she will not matter to them or to us."

"Is Miss Starr with you?" Right now, Nic couldn't care less about the weather report or the strategy of loading and shipping beef cattle.

"Oh no, monsieur, she remains at the ranch."

"Is Lame Bear with her?"

"That I do not know. I did not see him since two

days now."

"Is there anybody left at the ranch?

Little Roy shook his head. "The ones too old to make the trip are rounding up strays. Then they will come to town to spend some of their bonus money. We intend to do the same very soon." The gold tooth on the left side of his smile sparkled even in the dim atmosphere.

"Stay safe, monsieur." With a nod goodbye, Little Roy urged his horse to join the men herding cattle.

The little Frenchman's weather prediction quickly came true. And although the rain spattered down with a lack of enthusiasm, the tightness in Nic's chest came over him full force.

Chapter Nineteen

By mid-afternoon thunder and wind rattled the shack like a wooden cage, and Ochessa felt like a bird trapped within the trembling walls.

She rubbed her wrists. Reno had untied her hands to accommodate his order for her to make a pot of coffee and fry up a side of bacon, this may be her best chance to get away. She must succeed so she could alert Lame Bear. If they still tried to hunt him down tomorrow, at least he would be forewarned.

While frying up the bacon she spied coal dust behind the stove, and recalled the coal bucket Reno had kicked. In the winter Old Dobbs had often used this alternate heat source, and she remembered where the coal chute was located.

The next time the lightning flashed and thunder boomed, she shrieked and cupped her hands over her ears. "I can't stand the noise a moment longer."

Wild-eyed she gave her best portrayal of a hysterical female, and by the expression on Reno's face she did a pretty good job. Howling as loud as the wind, she cowered in a corner, screeching with each new clap of thunder.

"Shut the hell up," Reno barked. "You're more annoying than the storm."

She sat down in a chair, rocking back and forth like an addlebrained child.

"Don't tell me a tough little cowgirl like you is afraid of a little rain storm," he mocked.

"There's nothing I hate worse than thunder and lightning," she keened. "Except small dark spaces."

Reno glanced at the cupboard where she had spent the night, and a mean smile settled with familiarity upon his mouth. She followed his line of sight.

"No. Please don't put back in there." Jumping to her feet she tried to reach the door to the cabin knowing full well she couldn't make it in time.

Reno grabbed her from behind, and clasped one arm firmly around her waist. Dragging her across the room, he opened the door to the storage cupboard, and flung her none too gently inside. She landed in a heap and pretended to cry.

"Maybe you'll recall where the ruby and documents are after a few more hours in the dark. You should never divulge your weakness to the enemy."

The door slammed shut, and she smiled.

"You should never take your enemy at their word."

He'd forgotten to re-tie her wrists and crawling on her hands and knees she made her way across the little room.

In the blinding darkness she gingerly ran her hands along the wall, coming into contact with a variety of objects she doubted she would touch in the light of day. Finally locating the small hinged door, she unhooked the latch and swung the panel upward. A brigade of mice tumbled out, scurrying across her lap as they fled toward the burlap bags of stale beans and rice. Taken by surprise, she reared back and snatched her hands away. The metal panel slammed shut. Dang-blast. What a sissy-pants. Had Reno heard the commotion?

When all remained quiet, she opened the metal flap again, and laying hands on an old barrel stave, propped the door open. Scraping out the leaves and other debris accumulated near the bottom, she stuck her head up the chute for a look-see. This side of the cabin was built into a berm, and the chute was long, traversing through the dirt to a flat area at the top.

Luckily the old metal trap door at the top appeared rusted out and canted to one side. Although the storm clouds turned the midday sky dark as dusk, another bolt of lightning flashed across the heavens, illuminating her narrow path to freedom. It seemed much smaller than she remembered—of course, she had been a child then and smaller too.

Before she could change her mind she extended her arms up into the opening and wedged herself into the passageway of no return. Square shaped and lined with wood, the years had not been kind to the structure. Tree roots poked through splits in the pine slabs, and rain mixed with coal dust trickled down the chute spattering onto her head and face making her gag. She clawed at the wet sides, grabbing at invading tree root, dragging her body upward until her hips were wedged firmly in the opening. She couldn't move.

She sucked in her belly making herself as thin as possible, and swallowed back a cry of real panic. What if Reno found her like this? What if he never came for hours and hours?

Gritting her teeth she twisted back and forth, wiggling and squirming only to gain a few inches. But it was enough. She found purchase with one foot, broke free, and started making better headway up the canal. Finally reaching the top, Ochessa burst through the opening, flopped sideways onto the ground, and gasped for air like a new born babe seeking its first breath.

If only she could rest a bit, but fear of discovery spurred her on. She scrambled to her feet and ran. Rain mixed with sleet pelted down in earnest, and taking refuge under a stand of fir trees she glanced around. No outlaws were in view—or her little mare. The far corral held only horses she didn't recognize. Hopefully Trixie had headed back to the ranch. If she hadn't made it home, Ochessa vowed to come back for her.

Soaked to the skin and shivering, she knew she had to keep moving. Unbuttoning and stripping off her flannel shirt, she draped it over her head and shoulders for a bit more protection, then grappled her way down out of the foothills.

In her heart she wanted to run, but the return trip would take a while so she forced herself to a moderate pace. Even at that, she soon felt winded as an old plow horse and chilled to the marrow.

How could it only be a few days since she had broiled in the heat and dust of the branding corral? Colorado weather had a wicked penchant for trickery, and today fickle-hearted Mother Nature displayed the full range of her talents.

Halting this time beneath a large cottonwood, Ochessa forced herself to breathe deeply and slowly. Her heart thudded in her chest, and uncontrollable shivers beset her, making her teeth chatter. Yet again, she mustn't linger. What if her escape had already been discovered? Spotting a straight and sturdy fallen branch, she snagged it off the ground, and using it as a walking staff, pressed on.

Freezing on the outside, her anger boiled on the

inside keeping her moving forward. When shear guts and determination finally wore out, she staggered on barely conscious of her surroundings. *Had to get home, had to warn the others.* With each step and ragged breath, she recited the litany on nearly frozen lips.

The rain stopped, but the wind took its place and like a giant unseen hand, the force propelled her down the hillside, threatening to throw her to the ground. And although the wind pushed her closer to her destination, it bore the chill of death. Her body shook and jerked so violently she could barely breathe. Her muscles ached and threatened to go into spasms, and with her dwindling strength, clear thinking became a challenge. She barely recognized Deer Trail Ridge up ahead. *Hadn't she progressed farther than that?*

Dismay shadowed her steps now and each one felt mired in wet sand. What if she couldn't make it back? Her chest hurt and her ears rang, and she clenched a fist at her stomach trying to ease the nausea churning inside.

The shirt covering her head and shoulders was frozen stiff weighing her down, and the mud coating her boots turned to unwieldy chunks of ice. Pummeled by the wind, she slid to one side then regained her balance. She dare not fall—she might never get up.

Halting beneath the next tree, she bent forward, hands on her knees, gasping for each breath, as she gather her energy for the final leg home. About to set out once more, the sound of wood cracking grabbed her attention. Too late, she saw the cottonwood limb come crashing down from above.

****

Head down against the wind-driven rain, Nic felt a

flash of pity for his new hat, but he supposed it had to get broken in sooner or later.

The storm lessened slightly as he reached Rising Starr property, and glancing around, he trotted Sadie past the corral and tack room. On the near side of the barn he halted, stepped down from the saddle, and led Sadie around toward the house. Totally deserted the place darn near felt haunted. Ignoring the spooky feeling he kept walking.

"Ochessa?" he called out. The sound of his voice only succeeded in disturbing a red-tailed hawk perched under the eaves of the house. He ran up the steps and went inside and searched each room. Nothing seemed amiss, but the emptiness struck him to the core. Even the dog had disappeared.

Maybe she just went for a ride. Or could she be in town—had they crossed paths unknowingly? Neither option seemed very likely, especially in this downpour. Besides, Chessy Cat seemed like a homebody. It didn't make sense, and it didn't feel right. He should check and see if her horse was here.

Crossing to the other side of the stable, Sadie tagging along behind him, his worse fear became real. There by the backdoor trying to get out of the wind, stood Ochessa's mare, wet to the hide, saddle on, reins dangling.

"Easy, girl," he crooned, taking hold of the bridle.

Shoving the big door open to accommodate him and the horse, he led the animal inside to a stall. Sadie followed like a concerned mother hen. Quickly removing the saddle, blanket, and bridle, he ran a clean dry cloth over the mare, and tossed her a little hay.

"Sorry there's no time for a proper rubdown." He

left, and locked the stall door. "You're mistress is obviously in trouble."

Not knowing where Ochessa might be, Nic decided to make a systematic perimeter search by reconnoitering in ever widening circles. He allowed Sadie a few mouthfuls of hay, and then coaxed her out of the barn.

About to take to the saddle, a flicker of movement caught his attention, halting his actions. A ghostly image took form and broke through the far curtain of rain as Lame Bear came walking out of the woods— Ochessa in his arms. Sassafras whimpering and trotting at his side.

Chapter Twenty

Nic sprinted up the steps to the porch, and held opened the door to the house. Lame Bear followed, and they both rushed inside to the parlor.

The old Indian laid Ochessa on the couch.

"What happened to her?"

"I do not know. Coming back from across the valley, I heard the dog barking and found her by chance beneath a tree. I think a fallen limb struck her head. Start a fire and bring in more wood."

Nic obliged and returned with the wood and started a fire while Lame Bear stripped off Ochessa's wet clothing and covered her with a quilt. Searching the bedrooms, and gathering all the blankets and feather bedding available, they piled them in a mound in front of the hearth and carefully snuggled Ochessa in the middle of the warm cocoon.

Lame Bear knelt at her side, rubbing her wrists and patting her cheek. Nic watched, feeling helpless. Ochessa appeared white as the snow on the mountains. To keep busy he put a kettle of water on to heat, and then went to stable Sadie and get more wood. He figured they'd be going through it pretty fast. Upon his return he noted Ochessa remained unconscious and still deathly pale.

"What in God's name was she doing out in this storm?" Nic muttered, disheartened by her condition.

"Her horse came back without her, so I think she must have ridden off on her own accord."

"It looked like she came down from the foothills," Lame Bear confirmed. "Nothing up there but trouble."

"Trouble that needs taking care of."

Lame Bear grunted in agreement. "First, we gotta take care of Ochessa then we go hunting."

"She's not coming around. Maybe I better ride to Denver and fetch the doctor."

"Won't do no good. Leadville had a mine cave in three days ago. I hear the doctor is still up there trying to help."

As Nic waited each tick of the mantel clock sounded like the banging of a sledge hammer. He bargained with God to save Ochessa no matter the cost, but still she didn't wake up. With a shock, he realized how much he loved his Chessy Cat.

"She's still cold as the heart of winter." I must think on this, and talk to the Spirits."

Lame Bear rose from Ochessa's side and crossed the room. At the door he paused and turned to study the young woman Nic knew Lame Bear loved like a daughter. In his heart, Nic felt the same pain and uncertainty written on the older man's face.

"The wheel has turned," Lame Bear said. "Now you are the man destined to save her. We will meet again in the morning. Tonight we must each do whatever is necessary to bring her back to us."

****

Leaving his cryptic message still hovering in the air, Lame Bear left the house and trudged deeper into the woods. The rain had stopped, but the wind howled with a mournful cry as if it too suffered a great agony.

Locating the small clearing, his sacred space, he entered the circle, and lifting his face toward the sky he prayed.

Would Ochessa come back to them from the realm in which she wandered? The land through which she traveled was not a bad place, and there in lay the problem. It could be a good place, filled with old friends and family and reasons to stay. Why would she wish to return to a world where happiness always seemed bound with sorrow and uncertainty? Nic was the answer. Only a love greater than self would bring her back.

Lame Bear danced the circle, and burned his sweet grass. The aroma took him to another time and place, evoking years of memories as fragile as the smoke rising from the bundle of herbs. He danced on and on until his body ached, and his breath came in gasps. He danced on and on until his inner strength slipped away and his soul felt thin as an aspen leaf.

Finally knowing he had done all he could, he crawled beneath a nearby outcropping and sat down to wait. The point of a rock dug into his back, and tonight the ground felt unusually hard. Old age had many disadvantages. A vision of his life passed before him as he knew Ochessa's life winged its way before her mind's eye. His own story seemed tattered now, and not as interesting as it had once been. Then he slipped deeper into another realm recalling his younger days when he fought a bear single-handedly and won.

The bear had fought hard too, leaving him crippled. The medicine man declared the bear had crossed his path by mistake, and had not been ready to die. Therefore, the creature still roamed the land with one foot in the next world and one injured foot in the spirit of the man who had taken his life.

When Lame Bear realized what a mighty animal he had taken, and when he showed reverence for the bear with prayer and fasting, only then did the bear enter completely into the next world. Ochessa now journeyed through two realms as well. She must have her own reason to fight her way back to them. A reason to abandon the peace and everlasting goodness of the great beyond.

Lame Bear stretched out his leg, his right hand unconsciously seeking to ease the sore muscles of his thigh. While healing from the bear attack, Lame Bear had stayed close to camp, learning many things by listening to the teachings of his elders. Eventually, as the medicine man had foreseen, his body became whole again. His limp vanished, but even after he became chief, the name Lame Bear was his forever.

"You must fight, Ochessa," his spirit called to hers. "My season is past, but your time is yet ahead of you."

His breathing slowed as more memories became clear. Every summer, like the magnificent creature whose name he bore, Lame Bear had led his tribe to safe hunting grounds. He had shared his wisdom with the younger braves of his tribe, knowing someday they might grow stronger than him and try to take his place.

Looking back he had worried without reason. The young braves had died of disease and bullets, or had been put on the reservation. Now the only young brave he knew was Nic Breedlove. Nic must be strong enough to take over where he could not tread.

Lame Bear fell into a deep sleep. He was alone, an old bear limping again.

****

Nic threw more wood on the fire. He swore if the room became one degree hotter the whole ranch house would spontaneously combust. He wiped the sweat from his face with a towel and lowered himself to the floor at Ochessa's side. Dragging yet another blanket over her unresponsive form, he called her name and chaffed her wrists. Wrists that bore the marks of having been tied up with coarse rope. Exactly what had happened to her?

Had she found the outlaws? Anger momentarily outshone concern, and Nic's imagination took flight. She had a bruised lip, marks on her neck, and a bump on her head. If she had found them, he prayed that's all they'd done to her.

Why didn't she wake up? He'd seen men suffer from raging fevers, and knew what to do for them. But this was just the opposite. Ochessa seemed an ice princess, pale and still as if carved of lifeless wax. How great in contrast to the spitfire woman he had come to love. How great in contrast to the hot passion he suspected burned within her, the same passion often reflected in those golden eyes.

Easing beneath the covers, he turned Ochessa on her side and lay down at her back, drawing her closer, fitting their bodies together like pieces of a puzzle. Cradling her naked body in his arms, he rocked her back and forth.

"Chessy Cat, come back to me. Just take one step in my direction. You can do it. You've fought too long and hard for your life out here to give up now. Reach for my hand, I'm here."

The hours passed, yet she remained unresponsive and freezing to the touch. What else could he do? Never in his life had he burned with such love for a woman, and it wasn't because of the sweltering heat of the room. Still, an ethereal barrier seemed to lay between them. Something inhibiting the transfer of his life force to hers. Shrugging out of his clothing, he gathered her against the length of his now naked body, and willed his life energy into her. "I love you," he whispered, and meant it with all his heart. Then his eyelids drooped, and without meaning to he drifted off to sleep

****

Ochessa wandered in the dark and the cold. Her body seemed to weigh a thousand pounds, and she felt as if she was encased in frost. She was back in Timpkin's pond, her ice skates and heavy wet clothing dragging her down into the blackness. She couldn't breathe. Will would save her. No. Will was dead. They were all dead. Was she dead too?

She tried to break free, but she felt so tired. It was easier to give in, give up, turn her life over to the Fates. It would be over soon if she just let go.

"I love you." The words seemed to echo around her. Who had spoken them?

Like flint and steel, the words struck a small spark lodged in the tinder of her heart. "Fight harder," another voice called to her from farther away adding fuel to the tiny ember.

Someone rocked her back and forth. Was it her mother? It felt good, it felt safe. But Mother was gone too.

She began to shiver—couldn't stop. So cold, so terribly cold, jaws clamped tight making her teeth hurt, limbs so numb they cried in pain at any attempt to move them. With desperation she held the hand that gripped hers. Then with profound effort she drew the hand closer, pressed it to her lips. It was a strong hand.

She wanted to scream, "Yes, please save me, I'm not ready to go." But the sound materialized in her mind only, and nothing came out of her mouth. With a second effort, a mewling noise like that of a puny child's issued from between her lips. It had been enough. The arms around her tightened and drew her closer.

"Ochessa," a voice whispered at her back. The warm breath around the words touched her neck and cheek—infusing her with hope.

Like a swimmer returning from a deep and dangerous dive, she surfaced, breaking free of the other side. Turning into the comforting embrace, she clung to the warmth offered there.

Tender kisses brushed her hair, falling upon her cheek like splashes of warm summer rain. The touching anchored her a little more in the world where life awaited. A world where there were all things, pain, and pleasure, and the promise of tomorrow. Her dream became real—and what had seemed real felt like a dream.

Her mind cleared momentarily, and she recognized the face of the man whose arms held her tight.

****

"Nic—"

"Thank God, you're awake."

He drew back in order to study her face. Still too pale, but not deathly so—that was an improvement. The bump on her head had gone down too, and her eyes, although sleepy, were clear.

A wagonload of questions rattled across his mind,

but he cut off all save one before they reached his mouth. "Are you hurt?"

She took a moment, as if inventorying her body, a frown upon her brow. "No. Not really." Her expression relaxed, but her voice came out breathy and far away, as if the world she'd gone to visit still claimed her. "Just battered and bruised. And my head hurts. That's all," she mumbled. "I've had worse…" Her rambling words trailed off into a whisper. "I found them," she added, eyes closed. "I found the hideout."

He waited for her to say more, but no words came. "Ochessa?"

She gave a tiny shiver, then her body went limp. She was slipping away back to where she'd wandered.

"No," he shouted. "You stay here. Stay awake. Do you hear me?"

He thought she murmured, but couldn't be sure. He had to keep talking. Had to keep her awake, or at least keep her fighting to stay on this side of forever. With head injuries, he knew if a person slept too deep, for too long, they didn't always wake up.

"Listen to my voice, Chessy Cat. I'll tell you a story about a cougar of a cowgirl with bourbon colored eyes, and taffy colored hair—and oh that hair. Wild and willful, just like she is."

****

He glanced out the window, the sky remained true dark, but the fire had burned low. He must have been talking for hours. His throat sure felt like he had.

Ochessa no longer shivered, yet she remained overly cool to the touch. He gained his feet, threw more wood on the fire, and stoked the coals. Then he snagged the pint bottle of whiskey near the hearth. They'd hoped to get a drop or two of red eye down Ochessa to bring her around, but even getting water in her had been unsuccessful. Besides he needed to keep her awake, not make her more woozy with hard liquor.

He could sure use a snort though. Uncorking the bottle, he took generous swig. It burned his raw throat, but he didn't care, the whiskey helped to simmer him down. Ever since Lame Bear had carried Ochessa's unmoving body into the house, he'd been crazy with worry, at times it felt as if he could hardly take a breath. The drink helped. He inhaled long and slow, then blew it out slow as well, along with some of his fear.

When the fire roared once more, he stood close warming his backside. Then he wended his way back beneath layer after layer of quilts and blankets, finally reaching Ochessa's side.

"How about you talking for a while, Chessy?" he suggested, closing his eyes. "How did you grow up, what made you, you? It's only fair. You've heard all about my adventures."

"Childhood..."

As if hard won, the word came out a whisper, but he'd heard it plain as day.

"Yes, childhood. Tell me all about yours." Tired, his thoughts drifting, he wondered if her childhood had been wonderful. His had not been. "Was it glorious, Ochessa?"

"Yours," she mumbled. "Tell me yours."

"I didn't really have a childhood." He meant it jokingly, but the truth of the words struck deep. He took another belt of whiskey, then corked and set the bottle aside.

Chessy's body sagged, and her breathing sounded

wheezy. She was headed the wrong way again.

"All right, all right," he complied, giving her a little shake. If she weren't so weak and cold, he'd get her up on her feet and walk her about.

"Where were you born?" she murmured.

Nic tried not to think about home, but for her, he faced down the rarely visited memories. He gathered his thoughts, and maybe it was the effect of red eye on an empty stomach, or maybe because no one had ever asked before, either way his childhood visions transformed into words and came pouring out. "I was born in Tennessee, it's green and cool there in the springtime. And I had one younger sister, a sprite of a girl, full of mischief and song. She loved animals and could talk the squirrels right down from the trees." For the first time, he smiled at the memory of his little sister, and a torn piece of his heart mended.

"My mother, full of kindness and hope, made us feel wealthy even when times were tough and we had nothing. Father was a bricklayer, a grueling yet honorable trade, but not always in demand. Then when the state seceded, in '61, Grayson Breedlove went to fight for the Confederacy.

"You still with me, Ochessa?"

"Yes. Don't stop."

The strength of her voice, much improved, gave him encouragement. But her words also dragged him from the past to the present, and he was glad. He didn't want to remember, didn't want to see things he'd fought so hard to forget. But he couldn't let her drift off to the edge again either.

"I was twelve years old when my father went off to war. Momma got a job taking in washing and mending, and I worked in the brickyard. After a couple of years, I got laid off at the yard, and we barely had enough money to feed two mouths let alone three. I tracked down my father using the letters he wrote, lied about my age, and joined his regiment. That's when I first ran across Reno Benteen."

The impact of those words hit him like a right cross to the chin, but he kept talking.

"Reno, or rather Captain Benteen, was whipping a man mercilessly for a minor offense. My father stepped in to stop the butchery. In one unforgettable moment I saw brutality and inhumanity reflected in the face of an evil man, and I saw decency and compassion shining in the face of a good one. From then on, Grayson Breedlove was doomed.

"Reno never forgave the loss of face he suffered in front of his men. In the next big skirmish, my father was killed, shot in the back. Several men saw Reno do it, but no one would back me up. I was fourteen by then, but still no match for the ruthless Benteen. I kept out of the man's way and plotted my revenge, and Reno continued to wreak havoc, using the war as a cover for raping women and shooting injured prisoners, because they were too much trouble to keep alive.

"When the South fell, and Reno was captured and charged with war crimes, I testified against him. I would have rather seen the man dead, but then prison must be a slow death, and that worked for me too. I never dreamed a reprieve would be possible."

"I'm sorry about your father." Ochessa spoke softly, barely above a whisper. "Your mother and sister. Are they still back East?"

"They're gone too. Both died of cholera, a faceless

enemy in both war and peacetime."

Nic snagged two small pieces of wood from the nearby pile, and lobbed them over the fireplace screen and into the fire. Then he told her about Sadie, and how he'd come to own her.

****

Nic awoke with a start. The fire had burned low again—they must have been asleep for hours. He glanced out the window. False dawn hazed the sky. They had at least an hour until sunrise.

Reluctantly, he slid out from beneath the mound of warm blankets, encouraged the fire back to life, and then with the morning chill nipping at his nether regions, he crawled back in beside Ochessa.

She opened her eyes, and glanced around as if seeing the room for the first time. "Where's Trixie?" She rose up on her forearms as if intending to gain her feet.

"Your mare is safe," he reassured, marveling at the fact her first fully rational thought was for her mount, rather than how she'd gotten home or ended up on the floor naked beside him.

"And Lame Bear?"

"Safe as well. He found you, and brought you home. Everything's going to be okay."

She relaxed at his side, her gaze drifting downward from his face to his bare chest. Then her lips parted, and her eyes widened, but she didn't pull away. Instead she curled against him, and a heady rush of need, more potent than last night's whiskey, shot through Nic.

****

Thankful to be alive, thankful for another chance, she sought the warmth. Now the heat came from inside too as Nic's hand slid down her back to the curvier part of her anatomy. She touched him as well, and the ember of love she held just for him found new life. Nic's breathing quickened, as if he too were caught in the wave of exhilaration.

Easing onto her back, Ochessa urged him to follow, and pinned beneath his weight she found comfort, a shield of protection against all the bad she'd been through. Her arms holding him tight, she opened her mind, her soul, her body to him.

He took what she offered, no hesitation—quickly, deeply, a joining long awaited. In the woods, she thought she might die, now she had never felt more alive. The heat of passion replaced remembered cold and pain, and she realized the reason she had not been ready to leave this world was because of the possibility of this kind of love.

New found desire rushed unstoppable, a stream unrestricted, careening over smooth river rock to a place unknown, yet deeply sought after. A spasm shot through her to where they met as one, and she arched upward, craving what he offered.

Taking and giving, time seemed endless. Then going over the top, her mind tumbled into a chasm of delight, and her body gladly followed. Nic breathed out the name only he called her, and claimed her as his own.

They lay perfectly still, recovering their senses. Then together, they rolled to one side. The intimate connection was lost, but she kept her eyes closed, blocking out the world, but not her thoughts. Now that they had both gotten what they wanted, would he be drifting on? Oh please, don't let this be the beginning of the end.

"I thought I'd lost you forever," he admitted, drawing a coverlet over them. "And just when I was growing accustomed to those pussycat eyes."

"You've only become accustomed to my eyes. How disappointing." Keeping hers closed, she wriggled against him.

He slid one hand between her thighs, creating an aftershock deep inside her. "I'd be more than happy to become accustomed to your other attributes. But I imagine some parts will always be a wonderment."

That sounded promising. Maybe he'd be around for a while after all.

She laughed and opened her eyes, nearly blinded by the sun streaming in the window. Ye gad. It had to be well beyond first light.

"I have to find Lame Bear." Again, she struggled to rise. "They're coming for him."

"You need food, Ochessa, and rest. You're going nowhere until you eat. Lame Bear will be here shortly. We're all safe—for now."

Chapter Twenty-One

Lame Bear entered the main house. The rain had stopped, and the sun was shining. That had to be a good omen.

"Now my heart sings," he said, as he sat at the kitchen table across from Ochessa. "I saw you healthy and smiling in my dream last night, but wanted to be sure."

"I'm fine. Better than fine."

Lame Bear did not miss the dreamy glances Ochessa aimed at Nic. Their relationship held new meaning.

"Thank you for bringing me down from the hills, Lame Bear. You saved my life. Both of you saved my life."

"Keeping you warm didn't turn out to be too cumbersome a chore." Nic spoke without thinking.

Lame Bear let the remark slide. "Keeping her safe from here on out may prove the harder task."

"Amen to that." Nic adjusted the damper on the cook stove, and finished rustling up the eggs, beans, and biscuits. As they ate, he described his meeting yesterday at the Wells Fargo office, and Thacker's promise to help.

Ochessa relayed information about the hideout, how many outlaws there were, and what weapons they had. And she warned both Lame Bear and Nic of

Reno's idea to kidnap one of them to use as leverage in hopes of making her reveal the whereabouts of the documents.

"Even if he no longer has me, he may follow through with his plan."

Lame Bear found it curious the leader of the Black Devils sought these papers as if they were made of gold. They must not be treaties. Those documents had no worth, they only carried lies betraying his people, sending them to live and die in poverty. But who could say what a white man thought important.

After they finished eating, Nic volunteered to tend the livestock, and Ochessa promised to shade-up for the rest of the day. Lame Bear reassured both of them he would stay close to the ranch—but he didn't. Instead, he retraced the path Ochessa had taken the day before. If any of the dark horsemen were foolish enough to leave their lair he would be waiting.

****

Lanny led the bay gelding from the corral, and waited for Curly to saddle up. "Old or not I ain't partial to fightin' no Indian—or a gun slinger."

"Me neither," Curly agreed. "With the girl gone, I don't see the point. Reno's full of big ideas, but it's us takes the chances carrying them out."

"We did all right with the stage robbery."

"Maybe." "But I think there's something else going on. He's gone loco about something, and this waiting is getting on my nerves. I'm ready to divvy out the gold, and be on my way. I'm tired of livin' in this stink hole thinkin' about all the things I could be buying and enjoying."

"Give it a little more time," Lanny suggested.

"With that woman escaping, Reno's mad as a bull seeing red. It wouldn't do to cross him today."

"She's sure better lookin' than her brother." Curly gave a cackle and made an obscene gesture with his hips.

Lanny felt bad about the woman's brother dying. The young man looked about his own age. Would the men with whom he kept company be just as calloused should he die? Although the youngest in the bunch, thanks to his Maw he was also the best schooled. Best with a gun, too—at one time it seemed to count for a lot. But he knew now there would always be somebody faster, and the excitement of being tough and living hard had worn thin over the past year.

Lately, he'd been thinking about making amends. He didn't want the bad things he'd done in his life to be his legacy. He also realized seeking redemption could also be his best chance at getting himself killed.

"Let's ride," Curly ordered, shattering Lanny's daydreaming. "We're getting a late start as it is."

Shaking off his reverie, he stepped up into the saddle. But as they let out, his thoughts returned to the girl. She truly was pretty, and brave to boot. He couldn't help feeling compassion for her. On occasion, when Reno sent him out to reconnoiter in town, he'd gone by way of her ranch, and he'd seen her playing with her dog or sweeping her front porch. Simple things reminding him of home.

When all this was over, would it be possible to go back to the way things were before he crossed the line? Maybe he could find a girl of his own, one who wanted him for who he was, and not for how much he could be worth some day on a wanted poster. A girl and a patch of land to call his own. It didn't seem too much to ask.

****

Lame Bear sat quietly in the shadows of the tall trees, thoughts of Ochessa having been kidnapped marring his contentment.

He should have watched over her more closely. But with Nic strutting around like a young buck, he wanted to give her room to discover the possibilities of her heart. Not such a good excuse, but it made him feel better than admitting she had gotten into bad trouble because he had gotten old, unable to take care of his tribe. He would not let danger touch her again—an optimistic promise when one watched over a headstrong young woman.

Hunkered down in the underbrush, he checked the string on his bow and tested the sharpness of each arrow point.

He had to admit, Dobb's old cabin, up in Lost Canyon, would be a logical place for the outlaws to hole up. Lame Bear knew the land between Clear Creek and Bear Creek as a man comes to know the curves and hollows of a lover's body. Over the years he had wandered and explored the terrain with nearly the same interest and enthusiasm.

He smiled. It had been a long time since he had a real lover. Thoughts of his wife took shape in his mind. Washta... She had been a good woman, and beautiful, as proclaimed by her name, but gone too soon. What would she have thought of the things he had lived to see? Things like pants, tough as leather, but made of blue cloth and rivets. Or glass in windows to keep out the bugs, yet let in the light. And music, captured to be played over and over. Open-minded and fanciful of thought, Washta would have enjoyed these new wonders. He favored the old ways. Too bad they hadn't grown old together discussing such things.

Shifting position to ease the pain in his leg, he closed his eyes. He looked forward to seeing his wife again in the next world—but maybe not too soon. She would understand—she had always been good at waiting.

****

His chores done, Nic sat on the porch smoking a cheroot, contemplating his past, the present, and the future. Quite the overwhelming passel of thoughts for this early in the day.

Still worn out from the previous night, he refused to feel guilty about enjoying a sit down. Life seldom offered comfort, and when it did, he rarely denied himself the pleasure. By his way of thinking, a man fought his way into the world, and he fought his way out, and in between, with any luck, he rested a spell and enjoyed what came his way—no strings, no sad songs.

Quite the lighthearted philosophy, and while there weren't any strings, a definite connection existed between him and Ochessa. A bond he didn't want to break.

Making love last night had been all he'd imagined, and then some—an experience he hoped to repeat soon and often. Did she feel the same? At breakfast, she'd sent him a sizzling glance or two, but she appeared tired and needed rest. Had he taken advantage of her last night? After holding her in his arms for hours on end, when she seemed interested, he hadn't been able to turn back.

Sassafras padded up the porch steps, and flopped

down in a puddle of sun.

"Thanks for your part in finding her, old girl." The dog yawned, and leisurely stretched as if to say *all in a day's work.*

Despite the sunshine, a chill washed over Nic. He'd come close to losing Ochessa. At times life could be so fragile, its continuation a matter of luck and timing. If not for an old hound and an old Indian, Ochessa may not have survived the elements.

Finished with his cheroot, he crushed the ash between thumb and forefinger making sure it was out, then he tossed the butt over the porch rail. He should probably go make sure Ochessa was feeling all right and resting as promised.

Before he could gain his feet, a shadow fell across the wooden porch planks. Ochessa stood by the door— barelegged, barefooted, and wearing nothing but a huge flannel shirt that he hoped had belonged to her father. She sure made one captivating picture, and he wondered what she had on beneath the shirt.

"Well hey there," he ventured. "Feeling better after resting a spell?"

She edged closer, smiling like she knew a secret. "Better. But not as good as I felt last night."

His pulse quickened, and he rose to stand before her. Capturing her hands, he held them, happy to feel how warm they were. Her smile broadened, as she stepped backward, drawing him into the house.

Reaching the kitchen, she halted and wrapped her arms around his neck, kissing him softly then urgently. He had the feeling he was being taken advantage of— that worked for him, six ways to Sunday.

Hands around her waist, he lifted Ochessa onto the

edge of the table, and stood between her straddled thighs. Her breath caught in her throat when he unbuttoned the flannel shirt and eased the material off her shoulders.

Beneath the soft fabric, she sat bare-ass naked, and beautiful beyond words. With his gaze never leaving her face, he cupped her breasts, and roughed the peaks with his thumbs. Eyes closed, head back, she sighed and moaned softly. Nic pressed closer, kissing her slender neck, matching her need, his body responding at a reckless pace. If he wasn't careful this might be over before he could get his Levi's open.

Recognizing his urgency, Ochessa worked at the buttons on his pants, wasting no time in liberating him. "I need all of you." The words tumbled from her lips as she grabbed for him and scooted closer to the edge of the table.

Hands on her backside, he jerked her hips forward, answering her request.

****

She cried out, and he hesitated, as if he feared he'd hurt her. "Don't stop," she pleaded, wrapping her legs around him.

She couldn't get enough of Nic. He made her feel wild and free as if she raced across the prairie on her fastest horse. Her fingernails bit into his back, but he didn't seem to notice, and the escalating frenzy of desire overtook her body unstoppable, and overwhelming.

Ochessa no longer felt the cuts and scrapes and sore muscles, only the hunger urging her to the joyful finale, leading her to the delirium she wished would never end.

"Yes, oh yes, oh yes," she shouted.

Their bodies worked in rough harmony, driving one another beyond all reason. As an uninhabited crescendo ripped through her, Nic groaned, the sound muffled against the curve of her neck as he spilled himself into her. Breathing hard, they stayed locked together in mind and body—a moment in time reserved for lovers. Then he eased back enough to kiss her. She reeled with aftereffects, returning his kisses, holding tight a little longer to the part of him she now claimed as hers.

Nic carefully untangled her legs from around his waist and slipped free, leaving her gasping as their shared universe split in two. He slid the flannel shirt up over her, and she pretended the warmth came from his embrace as she watched him button up and tuck-in his own shirt.

"Here I thought your apple pie would be the most memorable thing to happen in this kitchen," he joked. "What could top this?"

"If you stick around you might find out." As soon as the words left her mouth, she regretted her show of uncertainty. Only begging him to stay outright would have been more obvious. Gingerly, she slid off the table.

"I told you before I'm here for the long haul, Ochessa. When you went missing, it felt like a piece of me was dying. That's never happened to me before. I've made it a practice not to need anyone—same as you. Don't you think it's time for both of us to change our ways?"

She wanted to say yes. Wanted to trust the heat of emotion in his eyes, and the love she felt in her heart.

And this time she did.

"In that case, I guess you better move your gear from the barn to the house."

Waiting for his response, her heart pounded harder as if they were making love again.

"Thank you," he said, quietly. "I'll do that."

The smile on his face seemed genuine, not sarcastic or victorious. Still it wouldn't do for him to start feeling too cocky.

"Lucky complained about your snoring." She tried to make light of the offer, but her remark came too late, and they both knew it.

****

A silhouette on the far ridge caught Lame Bear's attention. Then there were two, and although small, the images stood out sharp and black against the mid-day sky. He held his place. No use chasing the buffalo if they were coming your way.

The featureless unknown figures, faded in and out among the trees. A half-hour later, they became detailed creatures with faces and guns. The men were talking. Their voices low yet easily audible. They might be good outlaws, but they were poor hunters. The younger of the two had a shock of flax colored hair. He looked none too anxious to be here, but he wore his gun like he knew how to use it. The older man was thin and dried up, like sinew. Cruelty lived in his aura, and the scowl on his face appeared well-established.

Certain of his enemy's intended route, Lame Bear angled closer to a nearby rise, and took up position behind a large clump of sage. To attack the stronghold of the outlaws alone would not be wise, but taking care of these two lone coyotes would help narrow the odds later.

Oblivious to the danger awaiting them, they rode directly in front of him. Lame Bear rose to his knees. His first arrow hit the holster worn by the young one, pinning the leather tightly together, rendering the gun unattainable.

The second arrow went straight to the heart of the older man. Gun drawn, the mean expression on his face faded to surprise. No sound did he make as he tumbled sideways, out of his saddle and onto the ground.

Startled and confused, the younger one yanked back on the reins sending his horse careening first left, then right. Leaping from the small rise, Lame Bear employed his war club, knocking the man from his horse. He hit the ground with a bone jarring thud, and Lame Bear gave him another light tap on the head, just to be sure.

Retrieving both horses, he calmed their fears and tied them to a nearby tree. Disarming the unconscious man, he secured his wrist with a leather thong. Next he dragged the dead man closer to the horses. Hoisting the inert form face down across the saddle proved difficult, but again defeating the hindrance of old age, Lame Bear gritted his teeth and got the job done. Tying the outlaw's hands and feet together under the horse's belly, he set the animal free and gave it a healthy swat on the rump, sending it back the way it had come.

He guessed even a white man of low intelligence would understand this message.

****

Jonathan Thacker had spent the night knowing that, with or without backup, he needed to do something about the outlaws today. He would start with his

248

promised visit to Rising Starr ranch—after his goodwill call.

"Good day, ma'am. Doc Meeker back yet?" Hat in hand, he smiled at the woman who opened the door to the doctor's house.

"No. He's still up to Leadville." The doc's new housekeeper looked him up and down. "Hard to say when he might return. Something I can do for you?"

"I'd like to speak with his patient, the sheriff. Just for a few minutes, if you think he could tolerate the excitement."

"And who might you be?" Broom at the ready, the woman appeared as if she wouldn't hesitate using it on him if she didn't like his answer.

"I'm Wells Fargo detective, Jonathan Thacker. The sheriff and I go back a long ways."

The housekeeper, a small woman with big brown eyes, considered the request. "A little company might do him good," she concluded. "Doc said the shoulder's healing nicely, and since his fever is down he seems more alert. But don't stay too long. And see if you can get him to take the medicine at the bedside."

"Much obliged, and glad to hear he's doing better." Jonathan eased on through the door she held open.

"Just follow the hall to the back of the house."

"Thanks, I know the way."

Sheriff Winslow sat propped up in one of two beds pushed against the far wall of the dispensary.

"How's it goin', Sheriff?"

"Howdy, Thacker." The man in the bed sat up a little straighter. "Good to see a friendly face—or anybody who ain't totin' medicine or a thermometer."

"Figure out yet who did this to you?" Thacker took

the chair beside the bed.

"No sir, and it's wearing on my nerves. Don't know why I should be a target, or who pulled the trigger."

"They hit you twice I hear. Once in the chest and once in the shoulder. It's a miracle you're alive."

"More like romantic dumb luck. Robert Browning saved my life."

"Robert Browning, the poet?"

"Yep. That's the one. I sent away for a small leather bound volume as a present for Katy over at the hotel. You know I've been sweet on her for a good long while. Anyway, I was on my way to give it to her that same night. Had the darn thing right here in my breast pocket." He patted his chest. "It stopped one of them bullets, or I'd be dead for sure."

Thacker tried hard not to laugh but couldn't help himself.

"Swear you won't tell nobody," the lawman demanded. "It would plumb ruin my don't-mess with-the-sheriff image if folks knew I read verse on occasion."

"You're secret's safe with me. But I'm still worried as to why this happened."

"You and me both, partner. Can't wait to get out of here and do some investigating on my own. Doc saved the bullets for me. Maybe they'll tell us something."

"How about Deputy Rawlins. He come up with anything yet?"

"Rawlins—that man's useless as tits on a bull. He got elected by hook and by crook, and I've just been hopin' for a good enough reason to fire his ass."

"Shooting the sheriff might qualify."

"Don't think that hasn't crossed my mind. There's something funny going on with Rawlins. Clandestine meetings, telegrams a comin' and goin'. I been watching him since before all this happened. But for all his lazy beer drinking ways, he's a clever little weasel. The messages he sends make no sense, and they're not incriminating."

"Several important legal documents got stolen in the Kansas stage holdup, along with the gem and the gold," Thacker divulged. "Any indication Rawlins might be involved with such a commodity."

"Could be. He needs watchin' that's for sure. Wish I could be of more help. I'll be up and about in another day or two," he boasted. But as he reached for a glass of water on the bedside table his hand shook, and pain transformed his expression from confident to grim.

Jonathan rose from the chair, and handed him the cup. "Here, you old badger."

When the sheriff finished his drink of water Jonathan handed him a small glass of vile looking brown liquid. "And take your medicine while you're at it."

"That's nasty stuff," the sheriff complained. "A coyote wouldn't touch it, and they ain't too particular." Holding his breath, he downed half of the treatment, then dumped the remainder into a vase of flowers perched on the little table.

"Can't be all that bad. Those blossoms look surprisingly healthy."

"Those are fresh this morning. I already killed off the prior batch. Come back in a day or two and then see who looks best. Me or the posies."

"I'll do that." Thacker chuckled, settling his hat on

his head.

"I'm counting on it. Hey, before you go. Do me a favor."

"Sure. What do you need?"

"My revolver's in that cupboard over there. I'd feel better having it within reach."

Jonathan met the request, and the sheriff checked the load and then tucked the big Colt under the covers.

Maybe it would be prudent to have a little chat with Deputy Rawlins before he headed out to the Rising Starr.

Chapter Twenty-Two

At the sound of a horse approaching, Reno stepped away from the rickety cabin and stood waiting in the muddy yard. The other men gathered around as well, anticipating the return of Curly and Lanny and a new hostage. When Curly arrived alone, and dead to boot, things started getting out of control.

Reno grabbed the horse's bridle. "Settle down," he hollered. Then he glanced around wondering if Lanny, or whoever killed Curly, would be next to show up in hot pursuit?

Untying Curly, they dragged him off his horse, and spied the broken shaft of an arrow protruding from his chest. The girl had been right. The old Indian still had the fight in him. Things were going from bad to worse. Now what? He didn't have the documents, and the men looked about ready to bolt and run.

"It's already late afternoon," he pointed out. "Won't anything be happening until morning."

Reno figured Curly was just a warning. If this was a full-fledged attack they'd a come on in after him. But one thing was for sure, he wouldn't be going to Denver tonight. Maybe his contact would realize he needed help. He hated to bet his life on it, and he might be doing just that.

"What about Lanny?" somebody asked. "Shouldn't we go a lookin' for him while we can still see?"

"No," Reno barked. "We stay together, and if necessary we make a stand here. Lanny's on his own, and so is anybody else who leaves camp. Is that clear?"

The men exchanged nervous glances, but mumbled in the affirmative.

"You two men take care of Curly's body. The rest of you start stockpiling the weapons up by the cabin, and bring some water too in case they try to burn us out. When you're done with that, pick straws for first watch on the eastern perimeter. That's the only direction easily assessable. They'd be crazy to try comin' from the hillside.

"Well get a move on," he growled, spurring them into action.

****

Nic lost no time bringing his packs up from the barn—God forbid she should change her mind. Then he made love to Ochessa again. This time in their bed, and this time slowly like he'd always promise he would.

With evening not far off, he fed her an early supper. Then he brought in more wood, and extracted a promise from Ochessa that she would stay put from now on through the night. He figured she agreed only to placate him, but he'd take whatever he could get.

As he stood on the porch, thinking he should go meet up with Lame Bear, Jonathon Thacker rode into the yard. Things were looking up. Maybe they could take care of the outlaws right now, while Ochessa remained sleeping and oblivious to their plans. He'd put a big slug of whiskey in her chamomile tea, and by her expression she knew but drained the cup anyway. If they put off going until she was awake, she'd insist on leading the charge—giving them each one more thing to be concerned about.

"Glad to see you, Thacker." Descending the steps, Nic headed toward the man and away from the house.

Cradling one arm to his side, the Wells Fargo agent awkwardly stepped down from his horse.

"What happened to you?"

"Had a run in with Deputy Rawlins. I accused him of all the things the sheriff and I reckoned he's guilty of. He panicked and went for his gun."

"Dead or in jail?"

"Jail. Only because I need the man alive. I got the first shot off, but he managed to just barely wing me as he went down. There's lots more names and information to be wrung out of that scoundrel. He seemed surprised when I mentioned Reno and the documents."

"You feel up to taking care of that nasty piece of work and his boys right now?"

"Works for me. Do you know where they are?"

Nic explained what Ochessa had been through, and where the outlaws were holed up.

"Tarnation. That gal's lucky to be alive."

"I'd like to keep her that way. But she's headstrong, and I can't blame her for wanting to protect her property, and maybe get a little revenge in the bargain. She won't listen to reason, or stay down long."

Leading his horse, Thacker turned and followed Nic to the barn as he went to saddle up. "Any chance we can find her Indian friend? I sent most of my men to Cheyenne Wells. Some yahoos tried to hold up the train station there, during which they managed to set half the county on fire. With the Indian it'd be three of us

255

against those sons of darkness. Better odds than two."

"I've an idea where he may be." Nic placed a pad and saddle on Sadie. "He's a good man," he added, feeling Thacker out as to his attitude toward Indians. Some folks had inflammatory histories with the Native people. He didn't plan on tolerating any attitude from this or any man, especially where Lame Bear was concerned.

"I've heard he is. And if I hadn't, I'd take your word for it."

The comment caught Nic off guard. For Thacker to take his word about anything seemed a bit of a leap, but no use looking a gift mule in the mouth. He gathered up some odds, ends, and necessaries—anything useful for what they intended to do. As he stuffed everything into a pack, and they mounted up, he considered leaving a note for Ochessa. Then he discarded the idea. The longer it took her to figure out where he was the better.

They rounded the barn, and he glanced back at the house. Sassafras sat guard at the front door, and he knew Ochessa had a pistol and rifle close at hand. Hopefully this would all be over soon enough.

****

Circumventing a jumble of boulders, Nic carefully made his way up a steep incline. Then entering a familiar clearing, he spotted Lame Bear sitting beneath an aspen tree, his back resting against the trunk, a curl of smoke drifted from the long-stemmed pipe he held. A few paces away, a man rested on his side, awake and trussed up like a Christmas goose.

"How is Ochessa?" Lame Bear rose to greet them.

"She's doing fine," Nic reassured. "And if she stays put and takes it easy for a while, she'll soon be right as rain."

"You might as well ask the wind not to blow, but I am glad to hear she is doing well."

"This here is Jonathan Thacker from Wells Fargo. Jonathan, this is Lame Bear." The two men acknowledged one another. Nic pointed toward the man lying on the ground. "Who's that?" Dismounting he led his mule closer.

"He came down from the foothills. I believe he is one of the men Ochessa said would come to try and capture you or me."

"Was he out here wandering around alone?" Thacker asked.

"No. The one who came with him is no longer a problem."

Nic glanced around. "Where is he?"

"I sent him on his horse, back the way he came. He won't be talking though."

Nic got the idea.

"I been waiting to see if any more came looking for this one. You come alone?" Lame Bear asked the Wells Fargo Agent.

"He's alone. It's just the three of us."

"Then that will have to be enough. If we delay too long the others may go their separate ways, and leave for parts unknown."

"In light of your successful day's work, I'm thinking the same," Nic agreed. "Reno's leading desperados not soldiers. If things get too tough they'll bolt and run. This might be our last chance to catch them all together."

"What shall we do with him?" Lame Bear questioned.

Nic studied the kid. He seemed young to be involved in so much trouble. "I suppose we'd best take him along. You can ride his horse, he can walk. At least that way we'll know where he is. If we leave him, he might escape. Or get eaten by a bear or cougar." He watched as their prisoner's eyes widened in horror. "Can't say as I'd want that on my conscience."

Lame Bear glared at the lad. "You are too soft hearted." He untied the leather strap from around the young man's feet. "Mountain lions gotta eat too."

****

Side by side, Nic, Lame Bear, and Detective Thacker lay in the dirt at the edge of the ravine.

"Appears they anticipated our arrival," Thacker spoke, as they silently studied the men, and the clutch of dilapidated shacks down below.

Even in the fading light Nic could make out the pyramid of rifles leaning against one another military style. And several containers stood at the ready filled with water.

"That looks like all of them," Nic put in. "I wonder how their provisions are holding out."

"We could ask the kid," Lame Bear suggested, looking over at their prisoner, now gagged and tied to a tree.

"Why would he tell us the truth," Nic asked.

"Because today while I waited, I told him what would happen if he didn't."

Nic stared at Lame Bear. That had to have been one interesting conversation.

"Most of it was true."

Nic and Lame Bear crawled over to their prisoner as Thacker kept an eye on the outlaws. Nic held his revolver at the ready as Lame Bear removed the bandana from across the young outlaw's mouth.

"Keep your voice down," Nic warned, "or your first word will be you last. What's your name?"

"Lanny," the kid croaked, eying Lame Bear. "Is that ranch owner gal all right?" His pale complexion gained a bit of color, and his eyes took on a near lovelorn expression.

Seems Chessy Cat had ambushed another heart. Lanny must have seen her while Reno held her at the hideout. "Not your concern. What about supplies? You must be running out by now. And how many men in your gang?"

"We're down to beans and hardtack," Lanny admitted. "And not counting me and Curly there's five plus Reno. Where is Curly anyway?" Lanny glanced around hopefully.

"He's dead. And chances are you'll end up the same unless you help us.

Lanny opened his mouth to speak, then seemed to change his mind. He hung his head avoiding Nic's eyes.

"Is Reno still looking for the documents? Is that why all of you are still holed up here?"

Lanny met Nic's gaze, his expression now one of puzzlement. "I don't know nothin' about no documents. Ain't none of us can figure why Reno don't want to move on."

So, Reno had his own agenda, and it didn't include the men he rode with. He double crossed his own gang while using them for protection. They might turn against their leader if they knew the truth.

"You got any more questions for the young cub?" Lame Bear asked.

"Not a question, just an offer. You play it straight with us, Lanny, and you might live to tell you grandchildren about this night. You don't and it ends here. Think about it."

Lame Bear retied the bandana around Lanny's mouth, then followed Nic to the edge of the wash separating them from the cabin. "It's only six against three," Lame Bear said. "I faced worse, with less to gain on the trade blanket."

"You still in?" Nic asked Thacker. "Busted wing and all?"

"I'm in. Only need one hand to shoot with."

Nic glanced up at the sky. The light was fading fast. "We could wait until morning, but now we're here, we might as well get on with it. And I don't want to leave Ochessa alone at the ranch any longer than necessary. "

Lame Bear nodded in agreement. "I say we go in after sundown. Rumor has it Indians don't attack at night. It will be more of a surprise."

Still unsure of Lame Bear's humor Nic glanced at the man. He seemed dead serious, but a spark of mischief brightened his eyes.

"Wish I had my tomahawk instead of my war club."

A vivid image of the hawk embedded in the tack room door flashed through Nic's brain. Nic guessed this was either the best time or the worst time for what he said next. "When this is over, I plan to ask Ochessa to marry me. That okay with you, Lame Bear?"

If he couldn't win the trust and respect of Ochessa's guardian and friend, he knew his relationship with her would be doomed. Nic held his ground as

Lame Bear's pensive stare seemed to reach his very soul.

The lack of response resurrected an idea Nic had been toying with for a while. Not a decision to be made lightly, and he hoped he wouldn't regret it later. Rummaging around in the pack at his side he withdrew a leather bundle.

"Here—" he handed the object to the other man. "This is real special to me. It represents a friendship with a man who taught me many things about the world and about myself. I want you to have it—as a promise I will always take good care of Ochessa. And I hope one day you and I will be friends, and you will also teach me many things."

Lame Bear unwrapped the Kukri, and admired the knife from every angle. "It is a formidable weapon. Strong and dependable. You are the same I think. I accept your gift, and give you my blessing to ask for Ochessa in marriage. It will still be her decision." He fell silent, his face stern and unreadable.

Nic felt relief and trepidation all in the same heartbeat. Did Lame Bear think she would refuse?

"I'm betting she will say yes," the old man added, allaying his doubts. "Now we better make camp or make war."

"Right. We need a diversion. Something to draw their attention in one direction as we attack from another."

Lame Bear grabbed Nic's arm, indicating he should be silent. "Somebody's coming.

Nic didn't hear anything, but he'd learned to take Lame Bear at his word. Leaving Lanny tied to the tree, the three men crept off to wait near a large thatch of juniper. Had the lad lied to them despite Lame Bear's threats? Were there more outlaws in the area, closing in on them this very moment—maybe even circling around to shoot them in the back?

They heard a person on horseback wending his way through the fallen timber. When the man halted and swung down out of the saddle Lame Bear, Nic, and Thacker sprung at him. Taken by surprise the interloper quickly gave in.

"For pity sake you crazy Indian. It's me Eustace."

Lame Bear released his arm from around the man's throat.

Nic took a moment to study the intruder he'd been thrashing, then all four men crawled to neutral corners as they worked at catching their breath.

Nic spoke first. "What in Hades are you doing here?"

"It's okay," Lame Bear explained. "When it comes to outsiders he's with us."

"What makes you so sure?" Nic wasn't convinced Ochessa's neighbor had anybody's best interest in mind other than his own.

"I'm her uncle you damn fool," Eustace huffed, acting as if the painful admission should be obvious. "Her father and me was brothers. Well half-brothers. Same Pa different Ma. When I saw the three of you heading up here, I followed. Horse took a rock halfway up, so's I had to stop and pick it out, slowed me down a might."

Nic remained silent, trying to get a handle on what he'd just heard.

"What's this all about," Eustace asked. "Why are those scoundrels still holed up in these parts?"

All eyes turned toward Thacker, who seemed to take this as his que to finally explain in detail what in blue blazes was really going on. "Apparently Deputy Rawlins and Reno go way back," he began. "And they have a friend in Washington D.C.. They all rode together during the war, and seeing as the three of them were cut from the same dishonest bolt of cloth, they kept in touch. After Reno was released, this Easterner learned about a bundle of legal documents being transported on the same stage as the ruby and gold—the perfect take. "

"I'm surprised there were two men in the entire Confederate Army could stand to be around the ruthless lowlife," Nic put in.

"Evil seeks out evil," Thacker said.

"But what do the documents have to do with Denver?" Nic finally hoped get a straight answer as to why they were so valuable.

"They're evidence for the prosecution in a state supreme court case being put together. Has to do with a land swindle took place here about three years ago, when the railroad first laid track up Clear Creek Canyon.

"Originally the path was to cut along Bear Creek, but the engineering studies proved that route unacceptable, and they scrapped the plan. Then the alternate proposal through Clear Creek Canyon took shape. But the changes to the proposal were kept quiet pending the results of yet another engineering study. Unbeknownst to Palmer and Loveland and former Governor Evans, a few unscrupulous investors found out about the rerouting prior to it being made public knowledge. They lied to the settlers in Clear Creek, telling them their land would be useless because the railroad line would bypass them.

"Still skittish after the panic of '73 the poor sodbusters and miners sold out for pennies on the dollar. And if they balked at the idea, they were bullied and threatened until they changed their way of thinking. One stalwart family even died in a *mysterious* fire. Then these shysters turned around and sold the land to the railroad for a fortune."

"How do Reno and Deputy Rawlins fit in," Eustace asked.

"I'm guessing blackmail," Nic said.

"You got it," Thacker confirmed. "Without the papers the government can't prosecute or make restitution. With the papers, Reno and his friends can threaten to expose the men responsible, making for a lifetime of easy income."

"So where are the documents now?" Eustace wanted to know.

Thacker stared at Nic.

"They're safe back at the ranch. I didn't know what they represented, or if handing them over might put Ochessa in danger. Then when you started asking about them, I didn't know who to trust. Even you, Thacker."

"It's just as well you kept them safe," the agent relented. "No telling where Reno and Rawlins may have cached the papers once they got their hands on them. Although, now that the jig is up, those papers won't be of any use to him."

Mulling this information over, Nic studied each man, trying to calculate their combined chance of success. Lame Bear and Eustace were hardly in their prime, and Thacker, looked to be in pain on occasion.

They were also at a disadvantage regarding terrain. "We need something to smoke Reno and his boys out of that cabin. Winning by attrition, even with dwindling supplies, could take days, with the possibility of the men escaping one by one. I don't have the inclination for that."

"Would a cannon help?"

Now surprise hung in the air rather than silence as everyone turned toward Eustace.

"Sure couldn't hurt," Thacker said. "Where is it?"

"Up in the mine entrance just behind that stand of firs."

"You mean the one Old Dobbs used to have?" Lame Bear asked.

"The very same. Dobbs used it for claim jumpers, or so he said. Mostly he just shot rocks and empty tin cans out of it for fun. It ain't big, but it makes a powerful sound."

"You think it still works?" Nic asked.

"One way to find out," Eustace challenged.

The four men rose in unison. They gathered all the rope they had between them and headed for the mine. The cannon sat just inside the entryway, a moth eaten wool blanket draped over the barrel. Rimmed with iron, the wooden wheels barely held the brittle-looking spokes in place.

Nic knocked on the barrel with a stick. When nothing hissed, buzzed, or came flying out, he poked the stick inside a time or two then dared to thrust his arm through the opening. He didn't detect any cracks in the metal, and it felt free and clear of recent nests or critters. They had only to move it into position.

Employing discarded boards, they scraped aside

the refuse and dirt blocking the forward path of the field gun. Tying four ropes onto the frame, Eustace and Thacker held the two in the front, and Nic and Lame Bear manned the ones in the rear. Once they started down the slight incline, gravity would be both their friend and foe. They'd need some means of regulating the speed of the cannon. Out of control, it could plunge over the edge into the gulch, or land at the front door to the cabin, which although not what they wanted, might prove interesting in itself.

Grappling and straining with all their might they worked to hold back the unwieldy piece of artillery. Halfway to their goal, Eustace lost his footing in a patch of wet leaves and slipped to the ground. The cannon swung to the side, the iron reinforced wheel heading straight for his extended right leg. If it didn't sever the limb, at the very least it would crush the bone.

"Heads up," Nic hollered, "bear to the left."

He dug in his heels, hoping to prevent the forward momentum. It slowed but didn't stop. Thacker lunged sideways in an effort to divert the oncoming wheel. Lame Bear wrapped his rope around the only available tree—a small sapling.

The cannon ground to a halt. Eustace scratched and scrambled, unable to find purchase in the wet terrain. Nic ran forward and hauled Eustace out of the way. The man suffered a twisted ankle and a wrenched knee, but otherwise he seemed unhurt.

The sound of a branch breaking quickly changed the focus of their attention. The sapling holding back the artillery piece splintered, and the cannon rolled into action. Eustace's abandoned rope snaked around Nic's ankle, catching and dragging him along as the cannon plunged downhill.

Lame Bear leaped forward, Kukri in hand, and in one well aimed swipe, he severed the rope, freeing Nic. The cannon rumble on, gaining speed and momentum. A large fallen log, lying directly across the trajectory, appeared to be their only hope. Metal hit wood with a sickening thud. The cannon teetered on the uneven ground about ten feet from the edge of the gulch. Then it settled into place, and everybody breathed a sigh of relief.

Lame Bear gave Nic a hand-up off the ground.

"Thanks." Any doubts Nic had about gifting Lame Bear with the Kukri were gone.

"Works pretty good." The older man tied the knife to his cloth belt. "It deserves a painted rawhide scabbard. I will make one come winter.

Surveying their situation, they found the cannon positioned surprisingly close to where they were hoping to set it in the first place, so they decided to leave well enough alone.

"What we gonna use for powder?" Eustace asked.

They'd hoped to find some in the mine, but no luck.

"We could empty out our bullets," Thacker suggested, "but that will take a long time and most of our limited ammunition."

Nic retrieved a small cloth bag of black powder he'd seen fit to bring along from the ranch. "No worries. He held it up for them to see. "Now we just need a good fuse, and good luck."

Again using his Kukri, Lame Bear cut a large piece off of Lanny's shirt then he wrapped and tied the fabric around the end of a stout stick to make a ram rod.

"How much powder you reckon we should use," Nic asked.

"I don't think we'll get a second chance at this," Thacker pointed out. "I say use it all."

In went the powder. Then they gammed in some dry grass to plug the opening. Finally they poured in a variety of rocks, a bagful of dried beans and a bag full of cut nails found in the mine, and just for fun, a few Concho medallions off of Eustace's saddle. Using a long twist of dry hemp Nic fed the string down the touch hole.

They were ready.

"What's the plan?" Eustace wanted to know.

Nic held his silence and glanced at Thacker, the only man among them with any legal authority. The rest of them were present to fulfill personal quests and vendettas. But to Nic's surprise the Wells Fargo agent deferred to his opinion. "Got any ideas, Breedlove."

"Well," he began, "depending on what response we get from the explosion, I say you and Eustace man the upper level. Watch which way the outlaws run, see if you can pin them down or take them out with rifle fire. Meanwhile, Lame Bear and I will be at the bottom of the gulch, ready to go for the cabin and Reno. He won't run like the others. He'll make a stand to live or die, guns blazing."

"If I didn't have this busted wing I'd challenge you for the right to take on Reno." Disappointment was evident in Thacker's voice. "But the two of you are the only ones not injured, and you're our best chance of catching him. Reno mustn't be allowed to escape."

"You have my word, he won't get away." Nic thought of all the innocent lives Reno had taken, and it felt as if legions of restless souls seeking justice watched his back tonight.

"Then I guess your strategy sounds solid to me. How about the rest of you?" Thacker put the idea up for debate. Lame Bear and Ochessa's uncle nodded in agreement. "Then it's decided. Eustace and I will remain here, and be ready to move in any direction. We'll give the two of you a few minutes to get down the ravine and closer to the cabin before we touch off this pile of powder and high hopes. What about the kid?"

"We'll take him along. He might have some knowledge that will come in handy." Nic settled his Stetson securely into place, and glanced at the determined faces of the men around him. "Let's show these black-hearted vermin how it's done."

Chapter Twenty-Three

Ochessa hugged a pine on the far side of the outlaw's corral. Yes she'd promised to stay at the ranch, but all she could think about was Nic and Lame Bear and the no-account responsible for the death of her brother. And even if anger outpaced good sense, this time she would meet Reno on her terms.

Besides, nobody would expect a man to just lie around waiting for someone else to fight his battles. No, of course not, they would expect a man to haul his sorry ass out of bed, and drag himself out to meet the devil head-on. Well, she'd earned the right to do the same. Nic had earned the right too. She remembered his soothing voice, and a good deal of the stories he'd told, especially the sad ones about his childhood. Now they shared a new closeness beyond the magic of making love. They could talk to one another about the past, and hopefully about ideas and dreams and building a future together.

The shot of redeye in her tea hadn't been enough to muddle her senses, and it had been easy to follow Sadie's and the other rider's fresh trail leading away from the ranch and to the area where imprints from boots, horses hooves, and Lame Bear's moccasins all met up. The little group, now united, appeared to have headed to the hill overlooking the cabin. Not her. This time, she opted to go straight for the cabin itself. It would be hard to find for most people, but she remembered little used path.

Reaching the thick woods around the cabin she paused, and loosened the top few buttons on her jacket. It seemed awfully quiet. Why weren't the outlaws milling about? And what if her presence caused more harm than good. Her being here could confound Nic's plan—assuming he had one. She'd come to avenge Will's death, but not at the expense of the living. The dead were safe where they were. Nic and Lame Bear might not be.

She studied the ridgeline at the top of the ravine, catching a glimmer of metal and shadowed movement. Friend or foe? At the corral she eased through the rails to mingle with the horses. No one would think to look for her there, and it gave her good cover and a better view of the main cabin.

****

As true darkness canopied the night, Nic half-slid and half-loped down the ravine. Lame Bear, admirably silent in his approach, followed close behind. Lanny, his hands tied, and a rope around his neck, tripped along in the rear.

The position of the cannon ensured the makeshift load would strike between the horse corral and the largest structure. It would be like getting hit with 100 rounds of grape-shot. Would the blast be enough to panic both the men and the animals, creating enough chaos to carry out their plan?

The three reached flat terrain, the outline of the old cabin in sight. Muted light bled through the cracks in the walls, escaping into the night, but no sounds could be heard. Nic adjusted his grip on the Colt revolver, and wondered what was taking so long? Had the powder been wet or the fuse no good?

The next thing he knew, a terrific explosion shook the earth beneath his feet, and he swore it raised his Stetson right up off his head. Guess they used enough powder. The terrified horses in the dilapidated corral bucked and kicked crashing into one another. They knocked down the top two rails on one side, and jumping the third rail the majority ran off into the darkness.

Sparks from the twists of grass included as fodder, hit the kindling and wood pile setting it to smoking. He hoped Thacker and Eustace hadn't been standing too close when Old Barker Bill went off.

The door to the cabin flew opened, and four men ran out shooting wildly in every direction. "Stay inside you fools." The angry words went unheeded as the outlaws bolted. The door slammed shut at their backs.

"That's Reno's voice," Lanny offered.

Without a backward glance, the outlaws hightailed it to the north, fleeing in the same direction as the horses. In truth they were headed right into the rifle sites of Eustace and Thacker as indicated by the shots soon ringing out from that direction.

"You're surrounded, Reno," Nic called out. "Give it up, and come out with your hands where we can see them." Would Benteen buy his bluff? "We have the documents, and know all about your scam. Oh, and by the way, Rawlins is in jail, singing like a well-trained canary

****

Reno cursed as he peered through a knothole.

Apparently his other men, positioned by the

outhouse, had taken off too. Lily-livered snakes, running like scared little girls. Well so be it. With Deputy Rawlins out of the picture, he only had to worry about himself and that suited him just fine.

One thing for sure, he'd give up the ghost before he'd let a turncoat ex-Rebel get the best of him. Too bad about the documents though. Still, he had the gold. He opened the strongbox and started transferring the bags to a saddle pack. If he could make it to Mexico he'd be home free.

Listening to the quiet, he figured the worst must be over as far as a frontal attack. Now it all came down to man on man.

****

With a groan Ochessa crawled off to the side of the corral, and spit the dust from her mouth. What had just happened? One minute the night had been still as death, and the next all she saw were hooves and tails. Nic and Lame Bear must have found Old Dobbs' canon. Her grimace of pain eased into a smile. Wished she'd seen that from the other end.

Inhaling a calming breath, she quickly regretted the action as a spasm of pain speared through her right side. When the explosion went off, the nearest horse slammed into her, now her ribs hurt, and her head began to ache again. Panting shallow and quick, she tried to get the pain under control.

A few of the horses remained nearby, and she could hear the muffled voices of men running through the surrounding woods. She needed a safer place of concealment. Arms wrapped tight around her chest, she gritted her teeth, and rolled under the bottom rail and farther into the underbrush.

Lying on her back, panting up at the night sky, she took a moment to get her bearings. Deciding nothing felt broken, she struggled to sit up then buttoned her jacket tight from top to bottom. With her ribs supported, she breathed easier, and holding onto a nearby tree, she dragged herself to her feet.

Should she try to reach Nic and Lame Bear? But where exactly were they? Maybe she could at least let them know her position. Supporting her midsection with her arms, she tried giving the owl call Lame Bear had taught her. The first try came out a croak, sounding more like a frog. The second hit the mark.

****

Lame Bear nudged Nic with his elbow. "Ochessa is here. Near the corral."

"She can't be. She promised."

"Take my word for it, she's there."

"Well what do we do now? We can't fire toward the cabin at the risk of a ricochet hitting her."

"Let me go down there and try to reason with Reno," Lanny said. "If nothing else maybe I can flush him out so you have a chance at him."

Nic studied the lad. He seemed sincere, but what if he lied?

"I didn't have nothin' to do with that kid being killed in Kansas." Lanny shook his head. "It was wrong, and it's been worryin' my conscience ever since. And I sure don't want nothing to happen to that gal who owns the ranch. Please, let me do this."

Ochessa's presence changed the complexion of things. "I don't know." Nic wasn't sure he was ready to risk the safety of the love of his life on the guilty conscience of a smitten young gunfighter?

Lanny gave a quick glance at Lame Bear. "After Curly got killed, Reno never even bothered to come looking for me. I owe him something for sure, but it ain't my loyalty."

Nic studied Lame Bear's face. They had to do something before Ochessa took matters into her own hands. Lame Bear nodded his consent.

"Okay." Nic cut the thong binding Lanny's wrists, and removed the rope from around his neck. "But if you double cross us. you'll die where you stand." He handed the lad his spare loaded pistol. No man should face Reno unarmed.

They eased closer to the cabin. Lame Bear returned the owl call to alert Ochessa of their position. Lanny squared his shoulders, and step into the little clearing in front of the shacks.

****

Ochessa could just make out the image of a man picking his way toward the front door of the cabin. She couldn't see him clearly. Could it be Nic? Panic soured her stomach, and she debated on whether or not to call out again. It could just as easily be one of the outlaws returning.

Sidestepping closer, she halted at the edge of the cabin just as the man raised a fist to knock on the door. He had a gun in his right hand, his face turned away as if looking back at someone. She still couldn't tell who he it might be.

The door squeaked opened a crack, and the light from inside spilled out. She recognized Lanny, the young outlaw Reno had ordered to find Lame Bear. Confused she held her tongue.

"Let me in."

"Well I'll be, you're alive." Reno made no attempt to admit the kid.

"No thanks to you," Lanny replied. "Give it up, Reno. This place is surrounded."

"So why ain't they shooting at you? Oh, I get it. You're whoring for the other side now."

"I'm sure as heck not here to do your bidding anymore." Lanny's words were courageous, but his voice trembled.

"Then you're not here at all."

A shot rang out. Lanny stood stock still for a moment, one hand on his chest. Then he lurched sideways and staggered along the building toward Ochessa. Pistol still in hand, he fell at her feet.

The cabin door slammed shut. She knelt beside the young man.

"I'm sorry for all I done wrong, but mostly for what's happened to you," he whispered. Then he closed his eyes, and breathed no more.

Tears burned in her eyes. The vision of her brother dying seemed to overlay the image of the young man before her, both so young, both dead. Out of control she stalked over to the cabin door. She hadn't heard Reno throw the bolt, and in a fit of rage she kicked the door as hard as she could. To her surprise it flew wide open.

Reno rounded on her, a canvas bag in each hand. He dropped them and went for his holster, but he came up empty. Her gaze followed his to the table several steps away. After shooting Lanny, he must have set his pistol aside, his concern for stowing the gold taking over.

"I knew you couldn't stay away, cowgirl. Revenge is an unrelenting master. But you've got things all wrong. I didn't kill your brother." He went squint-eyed as if measuring the distance between himself and his revolver.

"Whether you pulled the trigger or not you're the reason he's dead. You're the one who assembled this brigade of devils, and you're the one who ordered him shot. He outsmarted you, and aimed to see you pay for all the terror you rained down on innocent folks. And now I'm going to finish what Will started."

"I ain't goin' to jail," Reno declared.

"No," she agreed, "you're going to die."

Reno's eyes flickered, and he lowered his arms ever so slightly.

"Keep your hands where I can see them." The gun she held never wavered, and the desire to kill this man raced through her veins hotter than the whiskey Nic had put in her tea. Itching to pull the trigger, she recalled the words Nic had spoken to her on the train the first time they were together. *It's harder to pull the trigger when you can see a man's eyes.*

Not in this case she thought. Reno was murder on horseback, pure evil, unrestrained by conscience or compassion. He had just shot one of his own men with no evidence of remorse. A young kid who might have had a chance to change his ways and live a decent life. Yet, as angry and fired up as she felt, she realized taking a life was not something to be done lightly nor would it soon be forgotten.

It didn't matter. She owed Will.

A jeering smirk transformed Reno's expression as if he could smell her hesitation. He leaped sideways toward the pistol on the table.

Ochessa fired at the man for whom she felt nothing

but hate.

****

Nic fired at the same time, and the sound of the two shots echoed as one.

Before he could draw a final breath Reno slumped to the floor.

As Ochessa stood staring down at the dead outlaw, Nic eased up beside her and slid the revolver from her hand.

She turned to face him. Anger at his interference evident on her face, she grabbed her pistol out of his hand and jammed it into the holster she wore.

"Were you afraid I wouldn't shoot him," she accused, eyeing the final bit of smoke drifting skyward from the barrel of his gun.

"No. I was sure that you would."

"Then why did you fire as well?"

"Now only God will know which bullet sent Reno to the hell he so richly deserved. That might not mean anything to you today or even tomorrow. But someday it will."

She studied his face as if trying to understand the implications of his statement.

"When left with no alternative I've killed men before. It's hard on the soul and brutal on one's philosophy."

Still she remained silent and contemplative.

"I'm not trying to steal your victory, Ochessa. I'm offering to share the burden when the reality of it sets in. And when this night becomes a part of our past I don't want it in any way, shape, or form to interfere with the future I intend to spend with you."

Understanding finally softened her expression. She

stepped closer into his waiting arms and laid her head against his shoulder. "Don't ever leave me."

"I won't," Nic promised, knowing he meant it without reservation or trepidation.

Epilogue

Officially Ochessa and Nic should still be on their honeymoon. Instead, last week, the two of them along with Lame Bear had ridden to Monotony to bring Will home.

Nic had consigned his blacksmith friend to construct a coffin lined with metal to transport Will, and now Ochessa knelt in the soil transplanting rosemary and forget-me-nots onto his final resting place. It gave her peace of mind to know he would be safe at home when the snow began to fly this winter.

Gaining her feet, she stepped to the side, and reached for the watering can. The heel of her cowboy boot caught in her skirt, nearly sending her tumbling to the ground. Nic caught her elbow, preventing her from falling. She still refused to wear a corset or fancy shoes, but on occasion she actually enjoyed wearing a dress. Something really could be said for feeling feminine and alluring. But right from the start, she'd made it perfectly clear, no way would she ever be dressed like a tart while riding a horse.

"Careful, Mrs. Breedlove. I hate to admit it, but I think you were safer toting a forty five and chasing outlaws than you are wearing petticoats and a long skirt."

"I'm doing better. I haven't fallen down in over a week. And don't start in with me about my attire, or I shall stomp your Stetson flat, and hide the other half-dozen I bought you as a wedding present."

Nic's expression turned serious. "I see there's still only one way to deal with a woman who would threaten a man's headgear with such an unspeakable fate."

As he reached for her, Ochessa squealed, hiked up her skirts, and ran through the buffalo grass toward the house. She slipped, cursed, gained her footing and forged onward.

"Save me, Lame Bear," she pleaded as she streaked past.

"Not my job anymore. I'm officially retired."

Nic, only one step behind her, easily closed the gap between them. He encircled her waist, and as they careened to a halt he kissed her long and deep.

"Oh sir," she feigned in protest, "We couldn't, we mustn't, not here."

Over the nearby fence, Lucky and his two favorite cows, studied them with startled expressions. Nose in the air, Sadie ran circles in the corral.

"I think we're embarrassing our few remaining livestock," Nic observed as Ochessa toyed with the buttons on his shirt.

"How dreadful. We wouldn't want them to bolt and run, telling tales and spreading rumors."

He took one of her hands, and they ambled over to the shade and shelter of their favorite cottonwood tree. Ochessa slipped her arms around Nic's neck and kissed his cheek. But just as things were getting interesting, Lame Bear moseyed over and gave her braid a tug.

"Company's coming." He pointed to a cloud of dust forming along the road leading to the ranch.

Nic eased her away from his chest, and she felt his

muscles grow taut at the possibility of trouble heading their way. Ochessa kept silent. Then unable to contain her excitement a minute longer, she clapped her hands in glee and bouncing up and down like a delighted child.

"I know who it is," she teased.

"What's this all about, Chessy Cat?" Nic and Lame Bear relaxed their stances.

"You'll just have to wait and see."

"Does this have something to do with the fact that you never replaced the cattle you sold at market? And I noticed you had the south forty ploughed under last week.

"Could be."

At Nic's hurt expression, she relented and gave him a clue. "Ever hear tell of John Chapman?"

"John who?"

"Johnny Appleseed. I read about him when I was a little girl, and what he did seemed so amazing and wonderful. We're going to do the same thing—sort of, only right here."

Still puzzled, Nic watched as a caravan of wagons came into view. Axles groaning, burlap covers masking the contents, the fully laden conveyances lumbered forward—circling the property like a wagon train under siege. As one of the transports rolled to a halt near the corral, Nic stepped up and threw back the cover. His mouth dropped open, and Sadie let loose with a remarkably loud heehaw of approval.

Ochessa hurried to his side. "They're fruit trees—apple and cherry. And some of the other wagons carry alfalfa seeds. From now on the Rising Starr Ranch is officially the Starr/Breedlove Farm."

Several of the ranch hands had remained in her employ, thankfully Little Roy being one of them. They came out now to help unload their future.

"No more cattle?" Nic asked.

"Only Lucky and his girls."

"No more roundups and branding and riding the range?"

"Nope. Just pickin' fruit and making the world a happier place."

Lame Bear took his place beside the two. "Looks like it's back to eating venison for you and me Nic. It will be like the old days. I will teach you to hunt with a bow."

"I'd like that," Nic replied, clapping Lame Bear on the back.

Filled with joy and wonder as she pictured how it would be, Ochessa reached for and held Nic's hand. "We'll grow alfalfa on the south forty where we can irrigate the fields. That way we'll always have feed and forage for our livestock, and we can bale and sell what we don't need.

"And the fruit trees will go in the protected valley. Why, before long, we'll have tons of apples and cherries for sale. I could bake you a pie every week if you want."

Lame Bear hooted with laughter.

Nic made a choking sound.

A word about the author...

Gini Rifkin writes adventurous romance—past, present, and into the future—sometimes with a bit of magic or fantasy, but always with a happy ending. When not reading or writing, she cares for a wonderful menagerie of abandoned farm animals on her little patch of land in Colorado. Her writing keeps her hungry to learn new things, and she considers family and friends her most treasured of gifts.

http://ginirifkin.blogspot.com
www.gini@ginirifkin.com

Thank you for purchasing
this publication of The Wild Rose Press, Inc.

For questions or more information
contact us at
info@thewildrosepress.com.

The Wild Rose Press, Inc.
www.thewildrosepress.com

To visit with authors of
The Wild Rose Press, Inc.
join our yahoo loop at
http://groups.yahoo.com/group/thewildrosepress/

www.ingramcontent.com/pod-product-compliance
Lightning Source LLC
Chambersburg PA
CBHW070836280626
47161CB00015B/685